To David
Best w...
— [signature]

OFFSIDE:
A MYSTERY

BY WILLIAM P. BARRETT

Booktrope Editions
Seattle, WA 2014

Cover design by Greg Simanson

This is a work of fiction. Aside from historical figures and events, names, characters, places, brands, media and incidents are either the product of the author's imagination or are used fictitiously. Any resemblance to similarly named places or to persons living or deceased is unintentional.

PRINT ISBN 978-1-62015-443-4

EPUB ISBN 978-1-62015-452-6

Library of Congress Control Number: 2014913390

*To Nancy and Alessandra, and to Ida, who was the first
to read the manuscript twice.*

"It is not an offence in itself to be in an offside position."

—Laws of the Game

CHAPTER 1

"MAN ON!"

"MAN ON!"

"MAN ON!"

Okay, they weren't men. Not even boys. They were girls. Twelve-year-old girls. But in soccer that was always the shout when an opponent got an advantage.

The screamer was Coach Diego Diaz. He yelled at his defensive fullback because the other team's offensive striker was streaking up the far sideline on attack and starting to veer in toward the center of the field. Meanwhile, the striker's midfielder teammate dribbling along the near sideline booted the ball diagonally toward the goal line.

On the second weekend of the Valley Mirage Soccer League fall season in September 2006, Diaz saw the well-coached play the other side was serving up. He didn't like it. Not one bit. A short, stout 49-year-old East Los Angeles native with an already thinning shock of black hair, Diaz made up for a certain lack of natural soccer coaching skill by being possessed of a loud voice.

A very loud voice.

A voice so piercing, so grating, so foghorn-ish that when he let loose—which was a lot of the time—Canada geese flying over Valley Mirage on their southeasterly fall migration were known to suddenly tack east-southeast. Like toward the even-further-out suburb of San Bernardino, which its long-gone indigenous natives originally had dubbed Valley of the Cupped Hand of God. Near the sacred spot where Los Angeles area residents who considered the risk in their daily lives too insufficient turned north on the interstate through the mountains heading for Las Vegas and a few days of purchased risk.

Blessed with his own one divinely provided physical attribute, Diaz did what he always did in these ominous situations.

He screamed at the referee.

"Offside, ref!"

More volume. "OFFSIDE, REF!"

Maximum force. "*SHE'S* (pause) *OFF* (pause) *SIDE* (pause) *REF!*"

This time Diaz actually managed to send a startled gaggle off on a due east trajectory. Sort of like more toward Barstow, the remote Mojave Desert crossroads town that singer Jay Farrar once lyricized as "More Than Halfway to Hell."

Diaz was considerably less successful with Rick Hermannik, the portly referee lumbering along the field trying to keep up with play, and with the assistant referee already up along the sideline. The AR had a perfect angle and did not raise his flag to signal the violation of offside, the long-debated, much-misunderstood soccer rule variously described as a stroke of strategic brilliance or a guarantee of boring low scores.

In this instance, a good non-call. For the other team had timed it perfectly. The striker stayed even with the fullback, who was the last defender in front of the goalkeeper—meaning no offside—until the midfielder sent the ball, then bolted toward the net to take the pass all alone and poke in an easy goal. Hermannik whipped out his $24,000 Grayson Tighe fountain pen—his one pride and joy, which he bragged about all the time—and with a flourish added another vertical mark on the game card kept in his jersey pocket.

Diaz had been riding Hermannik the entire match, his decibel level rising like the national debt with each of the other team's goals—this was the third—and decreasing with each of his own team's goals—zero so far. Now, the rules of soccer—pretentiously called the Laws of the Game, as though they had been enacted by some parliament of sport—specifically forbid the expression of dissent. That's a throwback to the myth, even putting aside the aforementioned gender discrepancy, that soccer was a gentleman's sport. (Then again, it wasn't until 1997 that the obscure British-created panel that set the rules for world soccer—and which over a century and a half never had had a female member—finally changed the name of one yellow-card offense from "ungentlemanly conduct" to the gender neutral "unsporting behavior."

A year earlier, in another burst of sexual equality, the lawmakers changed the title of the flag-carrying officials running along the sideline from "lineman" to "assistant referee.")

But a certain degree of tolerance on this point was traditionally afforded coaches. Especially volunteer coaches of youth teams. Especially volunteer coaches of youth teams in the many, many affluent Los Angeles suburbs like Valley Mirage often populated by two-income families whose guilty parents were simply too busy making money to devote the time themselves, forcing the leagues in some measure to take what they could get.

Especially volunteer coaches like Diaz, who had been around for a while and were as much a part of the local youth soccer scene as, say, the yucky, half-empty Starbucks coffee cups strewn about the sidelines after a full Saturday of matches.

Diaz didn't even have a kid playing anymore; his only child, Dora, now 23, had stopped nine years earlier when she entered high school in 1997 and started finding boys a little more sporting. But Diaz continued coaching either gender—he didn't really care which. There were a number of reasons. He liked soccer and coaching. He cared about children. Coaching afforded him a certain sense of status and self-esteem. With a wife who had divorced him, and Dora shacked up in Valley Mirage with her boyfriend—Hector Rivera, her high-school sweetheart and also a coach—Diaz had a fair amount of time on his hands. He ran a garbage collection truck in Los Angeles starting early in the day. That meant he could be done work and back in Valley Mirage in time for early evening practices while the sun was still able to peer through the ever-present smog, first identified by an early European explorer nearly five centuries earlier.

Diaz's work schedule was in sharp contrast to the many soccer parents working insane hours for insane money in Hollywood, Downtown and the West Side. That's where the terrific jobs were. Such lucrative gigs required soccer parents to spend as much as three hours a day to and from their nice homes, riding in their Priuses, Lexuses and BMWs, or slumming it in a Honda Accord. They traveled on clogged freeways that were central to the Southern California way of life and even akin to family. The official numerical designations were never uttered without a preceding article connoting their essential singularity and even personification.

The 5. The 405. The 10. The 210. The 101. The 118.

And now The Diaz. "Ref, you blew that! She was offside by this much!"—Diaz held his hands apart about a yard—"Not even close!"

Referee Rick Hermannik was a quiet, introverted fellow in his 40s—a bit of a dandy, actually, even though in his standard yellow referee jersey he looked more like that Big Bird character on *Sesame Street*. He also had no children playing; Hermannik was single. Like all the semi-volunteer referees in Valley Mirage (he was paid a measly $20 a game), he dreaded drawing a match involving Diaz; experiencing one of California's frequent earthquakes was far less stressful and over a hell of a lot faster. Hermannik eschewed unnecessary conflict. He also knew league officials did not really like coaches to be disciplined for anything short of, say, pulling a knife, which had never happened, at least in Valley Mirage.

Fortunately, Hermannik was a veteran real estate appraiser. It was a lonely calling, but one that required a certain set of accommodating people skills as he went through a house to determine its value for a buyer taking out a mortgage to assume new ownership. Frequently present during his inspection was the seller, the longtime owner who would be leaving soon, often emotionally but, thanks to the white-hot California real estate bubble, considerably richer as he prepared for retirement in Sun City, Arizona, or some other such cheaper venue. Hermannik often had to listen patiently to tearful recollections of piñata smashings at backyard birthday parties 35 years earlier.

"Coach, you may be right," Hermannik half-shouted as he trotted past Diaz for the kickoff. The outwardly self-deprecating referee smiled at the coach. "Your only problem is that I have this," he said, holding up his whistle. "Otherwise, I'm just a nobody."

Even Diaz, who in many ways *was* a nobody, had to suppress a chortle.

"Well," he finally boomed, "good thing it's not decidin' the match."

Indeed. Diaz's team, the Aardvarks, later coughed up two more goals.

Watching the Diaz-Hermannik byplay with interest while waiting for the match to end was Rivera, the 24-year-old boyfriend of Diaz's daughter. He was the coach of one of the teams of 12-year-old boys in the next match. Rivera sighed heavily as he watched coach Diaz go after referee Hermannik. *Diaz someday might be my father-in-law, if he doesn't first die of a heart attack*, he thought.

Rivera got along reasonably and even surprisingly well with Diaz, even though they had little in common beyond Dora, soccer and a Latino heritage. Whereas Diaz was outgoing, loud and a tad contemptuous of authority, Rivera was quiet, almost shy and respectful. Diaz strutted; Rivera sort of glided. Diaz rarely gave any thought to his future. Rivera brooded about his life's lack of purpose and motivation.

Diaz and Rivera did share a love of soccer, but on far different levels. Diaz knew enough to coach youth teams. Rivera had been a star high school soccer player. He was in excellent shape, still played in a Sunday-night indoor adult league and had a deep knowledge of the game, its history and its strategies—all reasons his teams rarely lost.

In fact, it was Rivera's fascination with the Laws of the Game and all the supplemental materials constituting the governing rules of the sport that made him think at one point—before dropping out of college—he might want to be a lawyer. Rivera liked to hit the fridge and watch those decades-old black and white TV reruns of *Perry Mason*. He was the fictional defense lawyer played by actor Raymond Burr who always managed to reveal in the final courtroom scene that the killer was someone other than his accused client. A client who sometimes had threatened earlier in the episode to kill the deceased. The series was set in Los Angeles. Rivera didn't like the more modern *Law & Order* shows because the episodes depicted everything from the point of view of prosecutors and cops. Few Latinos growing up in Southern California saw much merit in the point of view of prosecutors and cops.

By his second beer, Rivera himself often figured out the murderer. But he marveled at the ability of Mason to make his case without the aid of a PowerPoint presentation. Since *Perry Mason* conflicted with Dora Diaz's favorite show, *America's Next Top Model*, the couple sprung for a TiVo.

A college dropout, Rivera was hardly headed to law school. But at least he wasn't unemployed. His business card grandly styled him a technology consultant. That sounded as though his calling was to help important organizations evaluate and even fashion cutting-edge solutions for some of mankind's greatest dilemmas, like nuclear proliferation or global warming.

However, what Rivera actually did was go to people's homes and repair their pricey TVs, video-game-playing computers, kitchen appliances and other detritus of an affluent, conspicuously consumptive consumer society. He worked for a company called WeFixThingsRightNow. The firm was based in the upscale beachfront city of Santa Monica. WeFixThingsRightNow was one of many firms specialized in repairing home appliances that were out of warranty, meaning upset owners couldn't go back to the original manufacturer for a redress of grievances.

This was an especially lucrative business to be in across Southern California, for several reasons: (1) Manufacturers had become skilled at rolling out new kinds of expensive devices people never knew they needed, and, through the power of marketing and advertising, convincing potential buyers of their essentiality and trendiness; (2) to boost profits, many makers had lowered the quality of their products, insuring they would break down a lot faster; and (3) above all, residents of the Southland fancied themselves trendy and big spenders.

The boom, the bubble and the bust.

Accordingly, WeFixThingsRightNow fielded an army of repair technicians roaming most of Southern California (combined population 22 million, or one out of every 14 Americans). They traveled in a squadron of turquoise-blue vans festooned with the company's name-says-it-all moniker, a somewhat superfluous corporate slogan ("When You Need It to Function Now") and an 800 number to call for service. The vehicles also sported a large image of the corporate logo: a short fat man jumping up and down in anger at an apparently overheated screen attached to a computer or TV.

The bread and butter of WeFixThingsRightNow was the repair of bigger-ticket electronic items like large-screen TVs and computers. But the company advertised that it would take a stab (once its service fee was paid upfront) at working on just about anything that could be plugged into an outlet around the home. That's why in the course of the last week—and for that matter, every week—Rivera had to deal with an astonishing array of what could only be described as the electronic manifestation of the American dream.

One customer was in the San Fernando Valley part of Los Angeles just off Nordhoff Street, named for a 19th-century propagandist secretly paid by railroads whose lie-filled book, *California for Health, Pleasure and Residence*, attracted hoards to relocate to a region utterly unequipped to handle them. The owner needed help for a $350 laser hair restoration device that supposedly stimulated long dormant follicles in the scalp but kept shutting off.

Rivera went to Burbank, the suburb named for dentist-turned-real-estate-developer David Burbank, where lots were sold by advertising that many passenger trains a day passed through town but conveniently omitting the fact that none of them stopped. Rivera fixed a jammed $450 automatic cat bathroom, a box with a motor that was supposed to effortlessly change the kitty litter without human intervention. Another call took Rivera past Olvera Street, the Mexican-themed tourist attraction in downtown Los Angeles falsely promoted as being historically accurate (it actually only dated back to 1929 and before that was a dingy alley), to a swank high-rise condo nearby. He fixed a popcorn machine—not the little dinky kind that fit on a kitchen countertop but a full-scale version nearly the size of a refrigerator, worthy of the nearest multiplex movie theater—that didn't heat up. It had set back its owner $1,400.

Another call took Rivera to the Los Angeles port area of San Pedro, where crusading novelist Upton Sinclair was arrested in 1923 at a union rally for reading the Bill of Rights, and his brother-in-law for reciting the Declaration of Independence. Police Chief Louis Oaks, who lauded the arrests, quit three months later after he was found in the back seat of a car with illegal whiskey and a half-naked woman. Rivera was in San Pedro to repair a computer keyboard made out of leather that had cost $600.

In his three-plus years with WeFixThingsRightNow Rivera learned a lot of easy shortcuts. If the gizmo included a balky motor, a touch of oil often would do the trick. Many customers threw out, lost or never read the original instruction manual, meaning they hadn't reviewed the chapter in the back entitled "Troubleshooting." It would have told them, for instance, that the malfunctioning electronic circuitry could be reset to its default and presumably working state if someone would push the on-off button and hold it down for 10 seconds. So Rivera would push the on-off button and hold it down for 10 seconds. Voila! He would then leave with his fee and heartfelt praise that he was another Einstein.

While customer pleasure brought Rivera genuine satisfaction, the declaration of his brilliance simply increased his melancholy. Somehow, he didn't think Einstein had facilitated the excretory function of felines before coming up with $E = mc^2$.

Even as he fixed the many California computers that helped allow him to make a living, Rivera couldn't help but notice how a large number of customers, particularly the elderly, who otherwise seemed frightened by new technologies, bought a lot more firepower than they needed. All most of them did was communicate with grandchildren and check the AARP website for the latest deals on insurance and travel. Yet they frequently paid up for computers so loaded with storage capacity and other bells and whistles that government restrictions would have barred their export to North Korea. They also paid extra for a super-speed Internet connection that processed each of the handful of e-mails they sent and received daily in one-one thousandth of a second, instead of a mere one-one hundredth of a second.

Still, computer prices had come down and it was hard to spend more than $1,500 on an oomphy box. Not so the big flat-screen TVs, which could cover most of a living-room wall. Some of them still went for $10,000. Rivera long thought that was an outrageous price for what amounted to new wallpaper. *But hey*, he thought, *a living was a living, and no one was forced to call.*

One such repair trip a couple years earlier in 2004, shortly after Rivera started with WeFixThingsRightNow, was to the Valley Mirage home of Harry and Lita Smithfield. Their kids were among the seemingly few in town not into soccer. She was an office manager at a local firm; he was a nurse at a hospital. But despite at best two middle-class incomes, Rivera thought they seemed to live extremely well. Two BMWs sat in the driveway of their home, which they had bought two years earlier. Of course the house had gone up in value, like all the homes in Valley Mirage and everywhere else in the world, it seemed, except maybe Darfur.

As he performed his repair—which consisted of locating and pushing the tiny button on the TV's backside to reset the hair-trigger circuit breaker that had been tripped by an electrical surge—Harry sang the praises of home ownership and modern forms of financing.

"Those fuddy-duddy old rules about 20% down, a loan no more than three times your yearly household income?" Harry said. "Out the door. Now, next to nothing down. Adjustable rates so low anyone can qualify for a loan.

"When the teaser period is over, your income will be higher, and you can refinance into a low fixed rate forever. You don't even need a top credit rating anymore."

"Dunno," said Rivera. "Seems like you're assumin' everything'll go right. Suppose something goes wrong?"

"Like what?" Smithfield demanded.

"Oh, I don't know. Someone hit by a bus. You work at the hospital: a bad illness. Someone out of work. Anything that lowers family income. Crap happens."

"Ha," replied Smithfield. "Gotta have a positive outlook. Without that, you can't go anywhere."

But Smithfield didn't dispute the conceit of Rivera's concern, nor his sincerity. "If worse came to worse," Smithfield said finally, "we'd sell the house, take our big gains and rent for awhile."

"Sounds like a plan," Rivera said affably, collecting the WeFixThingsRightNow fee for the three second use of his right index finger.

That was nearly two years ago, and Rivera hadn't seen the Smithfields since. But for some reason that encounter kept coming up in Rivera's mind from time to time. And it came up while he was waiting for the finish of Diaz's game. Maybe because of Harry's strong advocacy of home ownership. Maybe because of his aspirational lifestyle amid all the other aspirational lifestyles in Valley Mirage.

Or maybe because of how unattainable it all seemed. Rivera's job title at WeFixThingsRightNow—consultant—was a technical term for "no benefits." He was an independent contractor essentially working on commission; the company provided him with training and the vehicle, but took most of the fees paid. Rivera had no paid vacation, no health insurance and no pension. The whole set-up skirted California and federal employment law so that WeFixThingsRightNow's owners wouldn't hurt their profits by having to pay unemployment insurance or the Social Security match. There was a 401(k) retirement savings plan, but WeFitThingsRightNow made no contribution. Rivera could put away what he pleased, but that assumed there was anything left over to put away, which there wasn't.

Finally—mercifully—Diaz's match came to an end. The teams, coaches and referees exchanged handshakes. Diaz grimaced as he gripped the hand of Hermannik, who was none too thrilled either. The squads returned to their sidelines and gathered up their things to leave.

Diaz saw Rivera come onto the field and sidled over.

"Damn ref," Diaz groused. "Second week in a row we got him. I hate him."

"Ah, Diego," Rivera said gently. "Sorta hard to blame the ref in a 5 to 0 loss."

"Whatdidyathink of that offside call?"

"Well, it was close. I was way back here. But the AR was in the right spot to see it. Striker wasn't clearly offside when her midfielder punched it over to her."

"*Baboso*. Still hate the ref."

Suddenly, Diaz clasped his hands in front of him and raised his head skyward.

"Dear Lord," he intoned. "In the past year you have taken away my favorite comic, Richard Pryor. My favorite actor, Don Knotts. My favorite singer, Lou Rawls.

"Dear Lord, I just wanted to tell you that Rick Hermannik is my favorite referee."

Even Rivera had to laugh. "You're a funny guy," he told a now-grinning Diaz. "But be careful. Someone could take that wrong."

The conversation between Diaz and Rivera almost passed in Southern California for reasoned discourse on a great issue of the day. It took place amid the usual collection of spectators surrounding the field, one of 10 laid out in a confusing pattern behind Valley Mirage Elementary School. The sunup 'til sundown weekly matches pitted players segregated by gender in divisions ranging in age from 6 to 18. The spectator group consisted primarily of the following: (1) soccer parents, (2) soccer siblings, (3) soccer grandparents, aunts and uncles (4) soccer players and coaches getting ready for the next match, and (5) members of categories (1) through (3) trying to locate the correct field to watch their beloveds.

This somewhat limited universe was noteworthy for its underrepresentation of minority players and minority soccer parents and minority soccer siblings and minority soccer grandparents, aunts and uncles—not surprising, since hardly any minorities lived in Valley Mirage. Still, the community soccer matches brought together a large number of people—thousands in the course of a Saturday—in what amounted to a very noisy open-air town hall meeting and debating society. An eavesdropping Margaret Mead would have been in her element.

Sure, most of the spectators did watch the matches. They tried to comprehend the goings-on and appropriately cheer or groan—with frequent exhortations of dubious value to their flesh and blood. A certain percentage of these advisors could be classified as hard-core soccer parents. A few even knew something about the game beyond the fact that Italy had just won its fourth men's World Cup, on penalty kicks over France, and the U.S. had been eliminated after winning none of its three matches.

There also were outliers.

Those in the know called her The Spy. The M.O. of Helen Miller in support of her children's soccer endeavors in Valley Mirage was cunning. A slim, nondescript woman, she lurked the opposing sideline hoping to pick up actionable intelligence—No. 10, the star player, would be leaving at halftime to attend a family wedding, No. 3 had complained to his mom about a hurting right leg—that she could report back to her coach. In the course of a single match she might move back and forth a half-dozen times, almost like she had a bladder problem but couldn't find the restroom.

Then there was the fellow known as The Optometrist. Not because he was a trained medical practitioner, which he wasn't. And not because he wore glasses, although he did—big thick ones that resembled the bottom of old-fashioned Coca-Cola bottles. No, Harvey Richter was called The Optometrist because of his one constant refrain standing on the sidelines watching his kids play. "Ref, are you blind?" he shouted after almost every adverse call, which meant he did a lot of shouting. "Ref, are you blind?"

Max Morris was The Evil Eye. Sitting the entire match in his carefully positioned portable chair midway between the halfway line and the goal, he glared. At the players on the other team. At the players on his son's team. At the referee. At the assistant referee running along his sideline. At the assistant referee running along the opposite sideline. At other parents. At a bird flying overhead. At a piece of trash blowing across the field. Morris just glared. He didn't cheer, he didn't root, he didn't boo, he didn't say a word, he didn't stand up. He just glared, his lips pursed tighter than a mountain climber's grasp, nary a sound escaping. If looks could kill, he'd be on San Quentin Death Row. Yet when the match was over and Morris left the sideline, a smile often creased his face, as though he had just endured some kind of an exorcism or purging of bad spirits within his soul that allowed him to cope for another week.

Besides the outliers, there were clones.

Expectant Fathers, not with pregnant wives but with unreasonably high aspirations for their kids. Gossip Girls, who viewed the matches more as an opportunity to gad about and catch up on local happenings. Rambos, dads who played tackle football in high school before soccer became more popular and still couldn't understand why a defender can't just take out the player with the ball. Julia Childs, moms who spend the first half preparing the half-time snack for the players (usually little more than quartered oranges and small water bottles) and the second half cleaning up, largely oblivious to the match.

But in the rare bouts of fall rainy weather in Southern California, the personalities merged. Huddled under their hoods, everyone looked like a Unabomber.

Still, a fair amount of the adult sideline activity on the many fields of Valley Mirage was not about the sport or the match at hand. It was talk about a universal theme far more important.

It was about money. Or real estate. Or both. Continuation of a conversation pretty much going on since Spanish forces came in nearly two-and-a-half centuries ago to grab land from Indians, loot where possible, and keep out other foreign powers to prop up a bankrupt monarchy back home.

And in 2006 there was plenty to chat about, as evidenced by the many discarded *Wall Street Journal*s littering the sidelines. Times indeed remained pretty good. The stock market was back on a roll— an all-time high—above where it was before the tech crash of 2000 and nearly 40% above its low in the dark days after September 11, 2001. Mortgages interest rates were still low by historical standards. Southern California home prices had just doubled again over a five-year period. Sure, prices were stagnating a bit, but, hell, even the housing market needed a rest now and then.

"Gotta hand it to Bush and Greenspan, but more Greenspan," Richard Fosdick said after checking his cell phone for the score of the USC-Stanford football game. "I know Alan stepped down earlier this year from runnin' the Fed. But he was there nearly two decades and knew somethin'. Bush, not the brightest bulb on the front porch."

With his goatee and sharp angular features, Fosdick bore a remarkable resemblance to Osama Bin Laden—so remarkable his appearance sometimes drew gasps. Which in his day job worked to his advantage. Fosdick was a lawyer at a big downtown Los Angeles firm that got most of its revenue defending big companies against lawsuits brought by consumers deluded into thinking they had a right to safe products. Intimidation of the other side was a key defense tactic. His forceful opinions did not stop along a soccer touchline. "Housing market wouldn't be this good with Kerry," he said. And definitely in the tank with Global Warming Gore.

"KICK IT, SUE! NOW!"

"Hey, what about the Democrats?" piped in Harry Rather, a skinny, whiney Hollywood sound technician. He wore a T-shirt proclaiming "Soccer Rules." "They whacked the red tape, got those government mortgage outfits buying stuff and rolling out new kinds of loans.

"BACK! BACK! DESTINY, GET BACK!"

"Look," Lois Bransom interjected after another sip of coffee. "We bought in '04. Just after Greenspan made that speech talkin' up adjustable-rate mortgages over fixed-rate. We took his advice. And boy, we're happy! Got an adjustable rate note with a low teaser. Think we're payin' now maybe two-and-a-half percent. A lot cheaper than my parents. Our credit wasn't the highest, but the lender was willin' to work with us. Sweet!"

A portly lady who had had children later in life, she worked for a major west-side-of-Los-Angeles entertainment company in human resources. Since the economy was still expanding, HR was an easy stress-free job, helping employees file paperwork for health insurance claims rather than, say, explaining their layoff severance packages and how to sign up for overpriced health insurance, which is what happened in a recession. "I just love that extra equity boost every year!" she declared.

"LOOK OUT! LAURA. LOOK OUT!"

"Paper. All paper profits." The speaker was Barry Sutton, a dour East Coast transplant who taught history at a community college. He looked a little bit like the crazy Kramer character on the TV show *Seinfeld.* "Gains aren't real 'til you cash out. And if everyone tries to cash out at the same time, when interest rates go up, there won't be any buyers. At least at prices you want.

"Look, Greenspan lowered interest rates after 9/11 solely to keep the economy from tanking and the stock market up. Maybe he also wanted to catch Bin Laden shortin' stocks. But what I can't understand is why Greenspan recommended ARMs to everyone when fixed rates were so low. Folks missed an easy chance to lock in cheap. Hell, he's raised rates a bunch of times since. Betcha Alan never used adjustable rate loans for himself.

"DEFENSE, CHELSEA, DEFENSE!"

"Paper, hell." Branson again. "That annual appreciation came in pretty handy when we needed a home equity loan to pay for summer camps and vacations an' stuff like that. This time is different.

"KICK IT HARD, LAURA!"

"Loans have to be repaid," Sutton retorted. "Booms come to an end. All booms. The teachings of history.

"GO FOR THE BALL!"

Random news items also provided grist for the sidelines mill—with that unique Southern California cultural perspective on the interpretation.

"Still can't believe Haley Joel Osment," said Rather, who grew up in West Los Angeles. "Ya know, played that scary little kid seeing dead people way back when in *The Sixth Sense?* Now he's 18. Just arrested. Charged with drunk driving near the 210 in a '95 Saturn. Hit a mailbox. Flipped the car. Went to the hospital.

"Can't believe it. A star with an 11-year-old car! A Saturn! What is Hollywood coming to?

"NOW, DESTINY, NOW!"

While all this weighty chatter was going on, referee Hermannik weaved between the fields and headed for the referee tent to sign the game card and turn it in to the league officials sitting there. He used, of course, his fancy pen. "Cost more than my car," Hermannik proudly told them.

But he voiced a complaint.

"Don't get it," Hermannik said. "Second week in a row I sign up for specific matches on the online computer scheduling system. Get switched to a Diego Diaz game. Life is just too damn short. Who's switching me?"

The officials at the tent just shrugged their shoulders. "We didn't change anything," one of them said finally. "Probably just a glitch. "Our systems never seem to work right, anyway."

Meanwhile, Hector Rivera's Artful Dodgers took a nearby field and beat their opponents 3 to 0, even though one player, a chubby fullback named Colt Samuels, failed to show up. Rivera had a rule that parents call ahead if the player was going to miss a match, and he hadn't gotten a call. So that evening, Rivera telephoned the family, but the line was disconnected. He had a cell phone number and called that.

Colt's dad, Bill, answered and immediately started apologizing. "We lost our house this week," he said. "The interest rate, like, tripled, and we just couldn't afford it. Guess we didn't know what we were getting into. Moved in with my sister in Redlands. Just too far away for us to get Colt to practices and games. I should have called you. Sorry."

Rivera hung up the phone. *Damn*, he thought, *that's too bad*.

Coincidentally, Rivera had been noticing some changes as he drove around Valley Mirage, and indeed, Southern California, in his WeFixThingsRightNow truck. In previous years, for-sale signs usually disappeared by the end of July or early August, when buyers eager to settle their families for the upcoming school year moved into the homes they had contracted to buy in the spring or early summer. But here it was after schools had opened, and for-sale signs—a lot of them—were still dotting front yards. Many of the signs sported red stickers trying to catch the eye of passersby. "PRICE REDUCED!" "BACK ON MARKET!" "SELLER WILL DEAL!" Plus one sticker that Rivera didn't recall before but now saw more often: "REPO."

"It's a little nicer than posting, 'Repossession and foreclosure due to stupid lender and stupid buyer.'" The speaker was Gary Holchek, answering Rivera's questions a few nights later in the Valley Mirage bar they sometimes frequented.

A husky man with a nervous twitch in his right eye, Holchek was nearly 25 years older. Rivera had gotten to know him because his 12-year-old son played soccer. Holcheck was a high-level back-office manager for one of the many large, national mortgage companies based in Southern California. That made Holchek a real estate expert, at least in the dark confines of the Dos Hombres Saloon. The combination of his naturally cynical nature, his world-weary demeanor and several rounds of Coronas made him a more candid real estate expert.

"But that's what it is," Holchek declared. " 'Repo' means that someone who had no business buying a house got a loan funded by someone who should have known a lot better.

"Look, every mortgage company officially believes in home ownership for all. It's crap."

Rivera looked at Holchek in shock. *What is he saying?*

"Frankly, not everyone's cut out to own a home," Holchek said. "It takes responsibility. Have to keep a job. Gotta pay utilities, taxes, insurance. Other costs. A lot of people ought to have 'tenant only' stamped on their ID."

"That'd be me," Rivera laughed. "But why do homes for sale seem to be sitting longer on the market?"

Holchek leaned forward. "So you noticed," he said. "Pretty simple. Prices are almost flat now, but they had gone up way too much. Nearly 400% in 10 years. People's incomes sure haven't gone up anything like that. But greedy sellers, they don't want to bend on price. And at these levels a lot of buyers are tapped out. So the homes sit. 'Specially when banks are willing to cut prices to unload their repos.

"Course, the high prices were due mainly to easy-credit policies of lenders like mine, implementin' the low-rate policies of central bankers like Sir Alan and politicians like Big Barney Frank. They think home ownership is the end-all. Hey, if you're a seller and you know a potential buyer has access to a pot of cash, you'll hold out for a higher price, too. You don't care if that pot is all borrowed, so long as you, the seller, get cash and don't have to pay it back.

"But the high prices in Southern California were also due to the fact so many of the large national lenders are based here talkin' up loans every day in ads. Us, Countrywide Financial, New Century Financial, WaMu's Long Beach Mortgage, IndyMac, Fremont, Downey."

Holchek chuckled. "Pretty funny these firms pretty much are in or near Orange County," he said. "A decade ago the county government went bust 'cause the county treasurer made a wrong bet on where interest rates would go. Biggest municipal collapse ever! Turns out the treasurer was usin' an astrologer and a psychic to forecast rates. He went to prison.

"What a great financial environment for mortgage companies to work in!

"Anyway, when I started out at my firm in the mid-1990s, it was a pretty conservative company. Buyers needed a decent down payment. A job. Good credit. Proof. Never lent more than three times yearly household income. Loan payments included principal. Appraisals were honest. Conservative lending, it was called."

Rivera cocked his head. "Still that way?" he asked.

"Nah," Holcheck said. "Since the 1980s, we and almost everyone else had been selling off the loans we originate. In big bundles called securitizations. We made a little of our money on the upfront fees from borrowers for new loans and a lot of our money by selling the bundles to Wall Street. It's called gain on sale. In effect we get a cut now of what Wall Street expects to collect down the road from borrowers. Wall Street then sold pieces of the bundles to investors looking for steady income.

"More new loans mean more fees. More gains on sale. More income for us. Higher price for our shares. So of course we do everything we can to make new loans. And if the loans are for higher amounts, we make more fees and more gains on sale.

"But here's the rub. By 2000 there wasn't much growth left in conservative lending. 'Cause everyone who already qualified had a loan. The only real growth left out there was folks with lower income. Lower credit. Not such a great market, frankly. But a huge one. We got roughly the same fees from these crappy borrowers. But then we and everybody else discovered something. We could sell these higher-interest loans to Wall Street for a lot more. A whole lot more.

"Remember what I said about gain on sale?"

Rivera nodded.

"Eight times as much on these lousy loans! It's the main reason why mortgage company stock prices have gone up so much.

"We could've called these 'loser loans,' 'cause that's who the borrowers were. Or 'subpar loans,' 'cause that's what they were. But that wouldn't sound so good. So we started calling them 'subprime loans.' A wonderful name. Some borrowers even thought that meant the interest rate was way below the prime interest rate. But what it meant was that the borrower's credit-worthiness was sub.

"Like I said, subprime wasn't such a great market. So to keep it going we had to make it easier and easier for borrowers to borrow. Even if they ran the risk of getting in over their heads.

"One thing about those simple, one-figure FICO credit scores we all rely on is that you don't need wealth or even a job to have a high score to get a big mortgage. You just have to avoid a history of unpaid bills. Hell, your score will go up just by getting more credit cards with higher credit limits and not buying stuff. FICO scores can be gamed.

"Now? We make loans to people who put nothing down, might or might not have a real job, so long as their credit isn't in the tank. We'll lend them four, five, six times the annual income they list, not a max of three times like the old days. Since we'll lend them the closing costs, the loan's often higher than the house is worth. We even allow 'em to pay back just a portion of what they really should. That just pumps up the loan balance and cuts their equity. It's called pay option.

"We qualify borrowers for adjustable-rate mortgages on the teaser opening rate. Not the three or four times highest it could go to, and which they can't afford. Will go to. Did go to. That's a big reason you see all those 'Repo' signs."

"We take their word on almost everythin'. Sure, we know the real estate agent's often lyin', the borrower's often lyin', the mortgage broker's often lyin', the appraiser's often lyin'.

"But lyin' is the American way of business. Lyin' is the grease that keeps the American economy movin' along."

Holcheck took another swig.

"We encourage people who originate these crappy loans for us to do this by paying them bonuses," he said. "Big bonuses. That's why all these kids two years out of college are earnin' $100,000, $150,000. Drivin' fancy cars. Of course, we don't call it a bonus. Since we're puttin' people into such lousy loans, that wouldn't look so good. No. We call it a 'yield spread premium.' Sounds a lot more high-falutin'. The borrower doesn't know what it means. Which is good, because no matter what you call it, the borrower is payin' it.

"It's all about paperwork. Not accurate paperwork. Just paperwork that looks good. Doesn't really matter who's the borrower, so long as there's actually a house at the given address and the paperwork is consistent. It's that way for everybody."

Holchek belched.

"Why? Because someone else will take the hit. Especially since Fannie Mae and Freddie Mac, the government big boys, are now buying all this lousy paper to gin up their own results and qualify their own bosses for big bonuses like the Wall Street crowd. Monkey see, monkey do. You know how smart government is.

"We're not really the lender, so long as we bundle the loans for others to buy fast. Just the facilitator. It's not our money. We get paid up front.

"Everyone's doin' it. None of us admit our standards are falling. Noooooooo way. Countrywide Financial is the largest of us all. Last week it staged a high-falutin' conference in New York City. Fixed Income Investor Forum, it was called. Fancy venue, too, Metropolitan Club. Lasted all day. One of the speakers was Angelo Mozilo. He's the head of Countrywide. We watched it out here on a closed-circuit hook-up. With a straight face he said Countrywide remained a role model of responsible lending."

Holchek let out a loud, long laugh—so long he almost couldn't breathe.

"God!" he said after finally catching his breath. "Even the double whoppers at Burger King aren't that big. Boy, did we have a good chuckle at the office 'bout that. Misery loves company. Everyone in subprime lending's doin' what he's doin' and we're doin'.

"Sure, there are some noisy prosecutors and investigators out there tryin' to make a reputation for themselves. But there's no way they can do anythin' more than scratch the surface. Too complicated."

Rivera took this all in. *Lots of people certainly should be in jail!* he thought. "You're not describin' a terrific situation," he said. "Won't something have to give?"

"Sure, something'll have to give," Holchek readily agreed. "We had a boom. It's clearly turned into a bubble. Pretty soon we'll have a bust."

"Aren't you worried?"

"Nah," Holchek shrugged. "The history of America is nothing but a succession of booms-bubbles-and-busts. In a little over two centuries we've had more than a dozen. Hell, the first came when the country was only a decade old. The republic will survive.

"So home prices slide 5, 10, 15%. Big deal. Some people who shouldn't have owned a home in the first place will hand it back and return to renting an apartment. At least they will have gotten to live in a nicer place for a while.

"Wall Street, they know how to protect themselves. They make big campaign contributions. Provide nice jobs for out-of-office politicians and regulators who will have to put their kids through college. The old revolvin' door.

"The government'll arrange a bailout. Just like it did for the S&L industry in 1990. And every other financial crisis before and since, too. Hell, that's why Countrywide gives the politicians mortgages on easy terms without making 'em jump through the normal hoops. It's called the Friends of Angelo plan. Sort of like insurance. Frankly, I wish my company had something similar.

"The bust, it won't be pretty. They never are. It's like the beach in Malibu. When the tide goes out, ugly stuff gets revealed on the sand. But then we'll just start all over. Just like the tide comin' in and coverin' up everything again and makin' the shoreline look pretty again."

Holchek patted Rivera on the back. "You just don't want to be the last person in this line," he said, "the one who takes the hit. Like musical chairs. Don't buy anything over the next few years. You'll be fine."

"Thanks for the advice," Rivera said. *I think.*

"No problem," Holchek said. "Barkeep, another Corona."

Driving home later Rivera pondered Holchek's words. *If even half of what he said is true, Southern California, the towns in it ...Valley Mirage will be the worst place to be in the country,* he thought.

Aw, he was just drunk. The liquor talking.

CHAPTER 2

BESIDES PLAYERS, coaches, referees, parents and other spectators, one other sub-category of people populated the soccer fields of Valley Mirage: league officials and board members walking around and acting very important. They comprised a varied group that, however, shared certain characteristics. Most of them had local jobs—necessarily, because they couldn't carry out their volunteer administrative soccer duties if they wasted time on the long L.A. commute. And voluntarily, because the exposure they got to thousands of soccer families wouldn't hurt their business prospects.

For instance, there was Manny Whitney, the tall league commissioner, genial to the point of being unctuous. In real life he was a funeral director. Whitney viewed every person he met, one way or the other, as a potential new account. He often had to leave the fields on short notice when his pager went off signifying a grieving family and a body pickup at the local hospital. This usually was the result of old age or a horrible illness but not infrequently a car wreck.

There was E. George Brennan, the league's assistant commissioner. He was a lawyer with a small civil practice based on the nuts and bolts of everyday suburban living: wills, tax returns, modest civil cases and the occasional big car-accident case that kept him going and put the new room on his house and the pool in his backyard. A small man with black-rimmed glasses and an ill-fitted toupee, Brennan always had a zillion business cards in his pocket to hand out.

There was Mark Rigas, another board member and a very successful real estate investor and broker. (He had donated the 10 sets of heavy goals that parents struggled to put up and take down every Saturday.)

Of wiry build, he was one of the few people around the soccer field in casual Southern California who often wore a suit. An extremely confident, forceful person with a military bearing reflecting Vietnam War service, which he hinted at but didn't discuss, he was used to getting his way. Rigas credited his prosperity to DNA. He told people he was a direct descendant of a major, long-ago landowner.

There was Janis Johnson. She was that increasingly rare creature in American life, a stay-at-home mom, bucking the necessity for two-income households to maintain an appropriate standard of living. Johnson's husband owned a small insurance company, so she didn't have to work. But Johnson hoped to parley the contacts she was making as a soccer board member and champion schmoozer—she seemed to belong to every Valley Mirage civic group—into a race some day for public office like that soccer mom she read about in New Mexico a few years earlier who got elected to the state legislature. In the grand style of Southern California, she was more successful keeping her hair blonde than her body thin. No one knew with any certainty Johnson's age; she had had some work done.

There was Sidney Keating. He was the tanned president of Valley Mirage National Bank, the only one in town still locally owned after Wells Fargo, Bank of America and even far-away Citibank gobbled up all the rest. A star badminton player at UC San Diego, he was a true believer in the ability of sports to build character. As well as capital, since nearly $300,000 dollars of Valley Mirage Soccer League player fees sat on deposit in a non-interest-bearing account at his small institution.

Besides burnishing their own brands, what did soccer board members do? A lot of the time, diffuse or mediate terrible important soccer issues.

Like team names.

These monikers usually were determined by a vote of the players after the season's first practice. Mirroring many soccer leagues around the country, Valley Mirage had a politically correct but probably reasonable rule prohibiting names invoking religion, ethnicity, race or nationality—essentially, anything conjuring up identifiable groups of people. Hence, the Smashing Pumpkins, Militant Mutants and Bumble Bees. Hence, no Battling Baptists, Ragin' Cajuns or Awesome Armenians (even though the Los Angeles area actually has a large Armenian population).

But what a slippery slope.

After 9/11, the league vetoed a team cheekily calling itself the Jumping Jihadists.

Wait a second, the coach said. You allowed Canny Crusaders. That's religious, too.

Ah, quick-thinking lawyer Brennan replied for the league. Jumping Jihadists was nixed not because it connoted Islamic warriors but only because jumping at an opponent is a direct-kick foul under Law 12 of the soccer rules, and we can't ever suggest that.

The Canny Crusaders moniker remained intact—until the coach pointed out these ancient Christian warriors trying to recapture Jerusalem used lethal weapons, "a clear ground if I ever saw one for a red card and send-off also under Law 12."

So largely on the basis of millennium-old hostilities, the Canny Crusaders were reconstituted as the Intelligent Designers, while the Jumping Jihadists morphed into the Nuclear Attackers. Subsequently, the board tried to expand the prohibited team-name rule but gave up after the number of suggested banned categories topped 350.

The fact that Rivera's team was called the Artful Dodgers passed muster with the soccer league thanks to the proximity of a certain professional baseball team, even though the actual inspiration was the pickpocket in the movie musical *Oliver*. One of the kids had seen it on DVD and talked it up the day his teammates voted on the team name. Rivera was aware of its Dickensian origin but considered it harmless.

Another issue causing occasional consternation was religious headwear. Aside from the general prohibition against players wearing anything unsafe, the soccer laws were silent on the point. Which left a lot of discretion to the league. But post-Jumping Jihadists, board members didn't want to come anywhere near the topic. So that meant the poor referee had to deal with the issue on a case-by-case basis on the spot when he checked in both teams before a match looking for equipment compliance.

Yarmulkes worn by Jewish boys. Hijabs worn by Islamic girls. Turbans worn by Sikh boys.

It was far from clear that the Talmud or the Koran really required the wearing of such garb on the soccer field (Sikh tradition provided more spiritual justification). But woe to the referee who, perhaps thinking such headwear provided some kind of an advantage in heading the ball, tried to bar such an adorned player. The outcry from the targeted player's parents, grandparents, aunts, uncles and siblings resembled the opening volley of yet another of history's many religious wars. Usually the referee backed off.

Fortunately, religious headwear issues didn't come up all that often in Valley Mirage because there weren't all that many Jews, Moslems or Sikhs living there. Unfortunately, one other issue did come up all the time and sometimes was surprisingly contentious.

Earrings.

The first sentence of Law 4, which governs such matters, really couldn't be plainer: "A player must not use equipment or wear anything that is dangerous to himself or another player (including any kind of jewelry)." The Valley Mirage soccer board repeated this in e-mails to all participants. Yet this simple language caused all kinds of problems, mainly among girls.

"I just had my ears pierced, and they'll close up if I take out the studs!" was the usual plaint.

Followed by, "The referee last week let me wear them, and you gotta be fair."

It didn't matter that the only purpose of the law was to keep a hard-hit soccer ball from acting as a hammer and punching a hole in the side of the wearer's head. Nor did it matter that not a single pierced ear ever has closed up in the short span of a soccer match. Nearby parents often spoke up loudly in defense of a daughter's right to bring bling. Once in Valley Mirage, an aggravated parent actually threatened to sue the referee over the issue.

Generally, though, this was a fight from which referees didn't shy away from. Over time they learned a simple non-confrontational, two-sentence way to handle it, especially with the parents.

Yes, she can wear the earrings.

No, she just can't play.

The earrings always came off.

Another issue that kept coming up like the Loch Ness monster was the wisdom of implementing a blowout rule, also known as a mercy or slaughter rule. The question was whether something should be done when one team mounted such a large lead that the match ceased to be competitive, let alone interesting or even fun (for the losing team, anyway).

This topic was hardly unique to soccer in Valley Mirage. A number of other amateur sports in the United States, such as softball, had blowout rules that were widely accepted. But this was always a more touchy topic in soccer. This was due largely to the perception in some quarters—often parents new to soccer—that the sport's European lineage already had given it an anti-American spin with rules that reduced the advantage of athletic ability in the ominous name of equality or at least a uniform disability (no hands). In what already was the lowest-scoring major sport around, the better a team got, the less it tended to score. The Marxist theory of the value of labor applied to sport, some said. The triumph of European socialism—much effort, little results—opined others.

These factions held it was no coincidence whatsoever that the United States' greatest hotbed of enthusiasm for youth soccer was in the suburbs of Washington, DC—especially on the Democratic Maryland side. This was viewed as an area populated by gung ho unelected civil servants used to imposing their own notions of liberal egalitarianism on a population forced to pay their undeservedly high salaries. For such zealots, soccer was the Holy Grail, the Great Equalizer, the Big Thumb in the Big Eye of the Big Tackle Football Establishment. With overlapping fall high school seasons in most of the country (California, where high school soccer was a winter sport, was a notable exception), they drew quiet glee from the fact some high school soccer teams had nearly gutted old-line football programs, which competed for the same talent pool, especially at smaller schools.

Thus, Jack Kemp, himself a former pro (tackle) football player, actually once took to the floor of the US House of Representatives, to which he had been elected from the blue-collar Buffalo area as a conservative Republican, to oppose a resolution supporting a US bid to host the World Cup, which was only the world's most popular sporting event. His thoughtful, well-reasoned plea was duly recorded in the *Congressional Record*:

> I think it is important for all those young out there, who someday hope to play real football, where you throw it

and kick it and run with it and put it in your hands, a distinction should be made that football is democratic, capitalist, whereas soccer is a European socialist sport.

Kemp's subsequent efforts to run for president and vice president were colossal failures, just like his campaign to keep the World Cup from invading these shores.

Valley Mirage carried the additional complicating factor of being in Southern California. It was a region that long prided itself for its humanity and compassion, although many of its most prominent municipalities, including Santa Monica and even Los Angeles, quietly harassed poor homeless folks for the high crime of being poor and homeless. Such mixed signals—coupled with the dominant entertainment industry's fervent belief in free speech, including that crucial First Amendment right to make porn movies in the San Fernando Valley— guaranteed a hot debate on almost any issue, consequential or not. Anti-slaughter rules in Valley Mirage soccer were no exception.

The debate began yet again at a Valley Mirage soccer board meeting. "Kids have to learn how to cope with losing; you can't bail them out," declared Keating, the bank president whose first job, as a lending officer at a failing savings and loan, was saved by a federal government rescue a quarter-century ago.

"It's bad enough at the end of the season we give a trophy to every player, as though each one is above average."

"But it's only a game," protested Johnson, the would-be politician who wanted to be everyone's friend and who fancied herself a caring soul. "At that age, wins by such huge margins are hollow, unfair, maybe even unethical."

"Unethical?" The almost-sputtering speaker was lawyer Brennan, brought up before the State Bar more than once on minor disciplinary matters.

"What's this got to do with ethics? Ethics!

"You've been listening too much to that old guy on the all-news radio station in Los Angeles. You know, the fellow who preaches in those commentaries about ethics that character counts.

"Character counts. Character counts. Yada, yada, yada. That's all he ever says.

"Look, it's not unfair to play as well as you can and hard as you can so long as you follow the rules and don't cheat. There's nothing in the laws of soccer saying the winning team has to take a dive."

"That's just my point," replied Johnson. "In youth soccer there should be some kind of rule when the match becomes so lopsided. We got the power to put one in place for our league right now.

"Move for its adoption."

An uproar ensued. "You can't move for its passage until you specify the terms," Brennan said. "Is it triggered by a lead of four goals? Five goals? Ten goals? And what's the sanction? Suppose the losing team eventually pulls within, say, three goals? Does the advantage go away? How the hell are you going to enforce this?"

"Uh, trigger at 4 to 0," said Johnson, thinking quickly. "Winning team plays a player short. If the lead falls to 3, player comes back. Referee enforces the rule."

"That's not fair to the player forced off the field just for being on a good team," said Rigas, the real estate man. "Much better the losing team gets to add another player."

"I could go with that," Johnson said.

"But it's all so just un-American!" Brennan exclaimed. "Teams will have less incentive to get better!"

"Yeah, like teams really like losing 6 to 0," Johnson retorted. "Get real!"

As it so often did, the peacemaking role fell to Whitney, the commissioner who never liked being forced by law to break out the cost of every item and service and let customers pick and choose. "We don't need more rules here," he said. "We need more common sense."

What eventually emerged was agreement not on new mandatory rules but on "guidelines." When a team got a five-goal lead—raised from four as a sop to Brennan—the winning coach would be "expected" to put all the players who had scored back on defense. Every time the ball crossed into the losing team's half of the field, the winning-team players on offense would be "expected" to pass the ball among themselves a minimum of 90 seconds before taking a shot on goal. The referee would be "expected" to declare existence of a blowout situation by shouting out "restrictions in force" before whistling for the ensuing kickoff.

"It can be 'expected,'" groused Brennan, "that this won't work." But he voted for it anyway. The policy passed unanimously, although it wouldn't take effect for another year.

Another contentious issue: team banners.

They were a combination art form and anything-you-can-do-I-can-do-better. In the old days they were home-made and painted on part of an old bedroom sheet, meaning they cost next to nothing but had a quaint amateur charm (along with the occasional misspelled word). But as time went on, they morphed (with the help of all that creative parental talent driving to Hollywood and back) into elaborate, professionally made designs. Some—almost worthy of the Rose Parade in Pasadena—cost hundreds of dollars. The banners got bigger and bigger—first four feet across and three feet high, then five feet across and four feet high, then six feet across and five feet high. The soccer league finally had to impose a size limitation and require small holes cut for ventilation. What inspired this rule was a gust of wind one day that blew a banner like a kite nearly a third of the way across the field, nearly clocking a midfielder.

Part of just about every board meeting dealt with what to do about errant coaches (almost all of them male), a thankfully small but still statistically significant group. Loud ones, like Diaz, who berated referees. Over-the-top coaches like Matthew Hannigan, a retired corporate executive who had e-mailed all the parents of his team of 13- and 14-year-old boys that "winning is fun and losing is for losers."

Game-the-system coaches like Lew Colson. He was a stockbroker with one of those famous national firms advertising incessantly about its smarts in all things financial, even though its analysts completely missed predicting every single stock market crash and decline in the past half-century, including the big one six years earlier in 2000. In preparation for the annual sight-unseen player draft, and figuring that, all other things being equal, older players in each age bracket would be bigger and therefore stronger and better, Colson got caught peeking at highly confidential player registration data and writing down dates of birth to grab the oldest.

Abuse-the-system coaches, like Dennis Manning. He was fond of muttering "Let it go" when an opposing 12-year-old player chased a ball last touched by a teammate as it headed toward Manning's own sideline. Hearing the voice of an authority-figure adult coach like Manning—even if he coached a different team—the opposing player often stopped, allowing the ball to go out of bounds and the throw-in to be taken by Manning's team. Manning was careful to try to speak out of earshot of the referee, who theoretically had the authority to expel him from the field for such irresponsible conduct. The parents of one snookered player complained to the league. Coincidentally, Means was a lawyer.

Sometimes the board officially suspended a coach for a week. But soccer coaches were needed—in short supply, even. Volunteers all, they shouldered most of the burden and devoted more time to soccer than the other adults. So more often the outcome was a formal "private admonition." Whitney called up the offender and in his best funeral director manner told him how much he was valued, but there was this one little thing that maybe he should give a small amount of thought to for the future. Over the years some coaches—like Diaz—had been admonished a dozen times. Of course, everyone heard about the sanctions, if they could be called that, so they really weren't all that private. But the discreet manner in which they were administered allowed for a certain degree of face-saving—and an adequate inventory of coaches.

There also were plenty of complaints about referees, those omnipotent authority figures whose title came from the fact that in the 19th century, on-the-field soccer disputes were "referred" to them by other officials for decision. (In 1891, the referees themselves were largely put in charge.) Referee gripes were a lot easier for the board to handle. Most were of the he-missed-the-call variety (again, there were very few female referees, or at least female referees who missed calls). Every once in a while, some upset coach would bring in and play camcorder video shot by a parent showing conclusively that the referee *did* blow the call—not declaring holding even though the offender had a handful of his opponent's jersey, calling a trip when there had been no contact and the falling player took a dive, and so on. Often the bad call was the result of an out-of-shape referee being out of position. But even these complaints were quickly dismissed because the Laws of the Game stated clearly that the decision of the referee—including fat ones—on "facts connected with play" was final.

The rules of soccer were surprisingly sparse. But then again, how much regulation was really needed when the sole objective was to try to kick a small ball into a big box at the end of a large field? Few sports were more primeval than soccer. Or easier. Using a foot to whack the hell out of a ball required less effort, pain, equipment and skill than many of the other things that could be done with a round object. And that was a rather long list: throwing, batting, bunting, catching, bouncing, stroking, spiking, striking, serving, hitting, slinging, slamming, hurling, putting, dribbling, passing, bowling and fetching (if you were a dog).

In soccer there were only 17 rules, or Laws as their snooty English originators dubbed them way back in the 19th century when the British Empire was riding high and whatever London said was—well, law. For the most part the rules were simple, boiling down to this: feet were good while hands were bad.

There was even a divine logic to the progression of the 17 Laws reminiscent—not surprisingly, given the Christian environment of the London lawmakers who reordered them in 1938—of biblical storytelling. In the beginning, the First Law created the earthen firmament styled the field of play. The Second Law fashioned the form called ball. The Third Law populated the space with human creatures, while the Fourth Law decreed their garb. The Fifth and Sixth Laws brought forth the beastly referee and his helpers. The next three Laws established the elements of duration and inception and repose.

Whence came the mighty Tenth Law, thundering in its stark command: "A goal is scored when the whole of the ball passes over the goal line, between the goalposts and under the crossbar." The Eleventh and Twelfth Laws defined sin and punishment.

While the last five Laws brought the ball back from the dead.

Collectively, the Laws created an unmatched fluidity for a team sport, especially compared with basketball, baseball or that other kind of football played in America by athletes who knock one another to the ground while lugging around more equipment than Lewis and Clark. In soccer, the referee and his assistants rarely handled the ball when it became dead; players usually could put it back into play as quickly as they wanted, strategically catching opponents unaware. This was so unlike basketball, which anally required a referee to handle the ball every single time there was a foul or the ball went out of bounds. Or even worse, American tackle football, where two or more officials anally handled the ball after every single play, not to mention upon a foul or out of bounds. The lines around the soccer field were in, not out, providing a few crucial inches for a streaking attacker dribbling the ball down the edge of the field. Step on a sideline with the ball in tackle football or basketball, and the officials got in the way again.

In soccer the matches were timed, but the clock didn't pause, even when the ball was out of play or a goal was scored. The referee alone decided how much "added time" to tack onto the end of the contest for certain interruptions. That was quite a contrast with tackle football or basketball, sports where it could take 20 minutes to play the last five minutes of official time, and longer if there were a lot of television commercials.

Nevertheless, there was one soccer Law that has caused the most complaining and even confusion even as it, along with nonuse of the hands, utterly defined the character of soccer and the people who partook of it.

Offside.

Law 11, its modern-day number, was possibly the most maligned rule in any major sport, and, though running fewer than 200 words, certainly one of the most misunderstood. This was especially so by soccer parents—not only in Valley Mirage, everywhere—who couldn't fathom why their team's sure-thing breakaway toward the goal was canceled by the hated referee, and the ball given to the opponents for a free kick in the opposite direction.

At its heart, the offside rule was simply a prohibition against unfair advantage. On the original theory a shot on goal had to be earned, soccer almost always had some kind of rule about offside. As the prohibition evolved, no attacker in the attacking half of the field ahead of the teammate with the ball could play it from a pass unless two or more defenders (one usually being the goalkeeper) were between that forward attacker and the goal. Borrowing a military term, that lead attacker was off his side, or offside (without an ending S so often mistakenly added by frustrated soccer parents unduly influenced by American football). Offside at least sounded a lot better than the name used in one set of early rules: "sneaking."

The complexity of offside was due to the fact that the rule was accompanied by numerous definitions, conditions precedent, inclusions and exceptions. "It is not an offence in itself to be in an offside position," Law 11 began. That meant it wasn't enough for an attacker simply to be ahead of the second-to-last defender. For offside to be called, that attacker also had to become involved in the play. This happened most commonly by touching the ball. But it also could happen without the ball being touched if the attacker interfered with or drew an opponent going for the ball, or was the only attacker with any reasonable chance of playing the ball himself. On the other hand, an attacker in an offside position could avoid a referee's whistle simply by moving off to one side or otherwise staying out of the way.

Also, whether an attacker was in an offside position was judged not when the attacker played the ball, but at the earlier point when a teammate last passed the ball to him. While this allowed strategy and plays based on clever timing and precision movement, it also had the effect of confusing or infuriating the hell out of soccer parents. Sprinting players who looked way offside when they received a pass might have been non-offside when the teammate booted it. No call. Similarly, alert players who looked okay when they retreat back past opponents to control a slowly moving ball might have been offside when the teammate weakly kicked it. Loud whistle.

Offside typically was signaled by the assistant referee running up the sideline keeping even with the defender in front of the keeper— the theoretical offside line. The AR was usually the only person around the field with a perfect view of whether an attacker was on- or offside, a situation that often did not sit well with parents and coaches.

Yet for all the personnel problems regularly tossed to the Valley Mirage board, there was one segment of the Valley Mirage youth soccer community that rarely caused any problems at all.

Youths.

In most years the board went the entire season without having to handle a single disciplinary issue concerning a player. Sure, there were occasional incidents. The 15-year-old kid shown a red card and sent off by a referee for a slide tackle, a theoretically legal attempt to dispossess an opponent of the ball with a lunging kick that in this reckless instance caught 0% ball and 100% opponent. The 12-year-old Latino player—one of a very few in Valley Mirage soccer—who during the traditional post-match handshakes at the center of the field muttered "*Te odio*" ("I hate you" in Spanish) to each of his opponents, ratted out by an equally rare bi-lingual assistant referee standing nearby. The 13-year-old caught sneaking a smoke behind the trees lining the fields. The

11-year-old boy who threw a shin guard at the referee after a 2 to 1 loss in a tournament match.

Indeed, the largely privileged children of largely privileged Valley Mirage found the soccer fields a refuge of sorts from the rest of their lives. Lives being battered earlier and earlier by coming-of-age issues — thanks to no small part to new technologies like cell phones, text messaging and a fledgling service called Facebook. Lives requiring quick peer-pressured decisions without the benefit of life experience and therefore with scant regard for consequences. Lives amid the rat race of a modern-day America in which two-worker families often had more than sufficient economic resources but — thanks to longer workday responsibilities — less than sufficient emotional ones, and time to spend together.

Privileged indeed.

For most kids in Valley Mirage, soccer remained a pure sporting endeavor. One with minimal rules — but rules nevertheless — that allowed the exuberant and guiltless expression of sheer physical effort without the need to explain or justify or even think, except in a strategic sense of, say, trying to figure out where the ball was going. And a family endeavor, too, with parents and siblings and grandparents and aunts and uncles lining the sidelines and cheering even when there really wasn't much to cheer about.

Although the youth soccer coaching books all said knowledgeable soccer parents made better soccer parents, Rivera, now in his third year of coaching, wasn't so sure that was a universal premise. A certain percentage of those who considered themselves graduates of the University of Soccer Parents — that is to say, they had older children who had played the game — fancied themselves expert on the strategy and stationed themselves along the sidelines to call out "encouragement." But their shouts often contained coaching advice of dubious value.

"Kick it!"

"Get back!"

"Defense!"

Even "Now!" — simple and harmless as this might seem — could prompt a player used to hearing a parent's orders to conclude something should be done immediately, when doing nothing or standing still might be the better course of action. Such instructions drove Rivera crazy, but there was only so much he could do.

Rivera made extremely good use of his low-key demeanor to calm down irate parents, often by explaining the relatively simple laws of soccer. Yes, it is legal for a big opponent to bump a smaller player with the ball. No, it's not handling unless the player deliberately touched the ball. Yes, a goalkeeper can dribble the ball back into the penalty area with his foot and pick it up, so long as a teammate didn't kick it to him. No, it isn't a foul every time someone falls down.

Rivera also had negotiated positioning along the sidelines with bitterly divorced parents (she stayed at the north end, he at the south). He helped hyperventilating parents, well, ventilate normally. To a couple upset that their kids were playing simultaneously on different fields, Rivera suggested they use their cell phones to call match updates to each other: "Pretend you're both Vin Scully." He gently reproached a lawyer parent bragging openly about teaching his son to fake injuries in the penalty area to draw a penalty-kick call from the referee: "Would a judge let you get away with that kind of stuff in court?"

With parents like these, I should become a psychologist 'cause I've already done the clinical stuff, Rivera thought more than once as he guided the fortunes of his team.

Still, his life was certainly a better existence than might have been predicted at its outset. Rivera also thought about that a lot.

He had spent his first 11 years in the down-and-out Pacoima district of Los Angeles in the San Fernando Valley. His mom, Elvira, had come to the United States from Hermosillo, capital of the Mexican state of Sonora and one of North America's most ghastly heated places. She arrived in the late 1970s, back before everyone got hot and bothered about illegal immigration and undocumented workers, and it was a lot safer to cross the border at an unapproved spot. Elvira was 16 and had some family in the area, and the economy looked a lot more promising than back home.

Barely two years later she was pregnant with Hector. He never knew his father, and his mom didn't talk much about him, perhaps because she might not have been sure about his identity. Hector thought his mother might have been a hooker—she looked like a hot number in a couple of old photos he had of her. But that would have been a hard life, too.

After having Hector, Elvira went legit, eking out a living as a cleaning lady, seamstress, anything. Along the way she managed to get a green card. But she never took US citizenship, maybe because her English had improved only a little. Having been born in a Los Angeles charity hospital, Hector was automatically an American.

Pacoima was one of the many areas in Southern California that took its name from the language of Indians, areas now populated by people who say there's no evidence Indians were ever there in significant numbers. The profusion of Indian names certainly suggested the one-time presence of an awful lot of natives: Castaic, Simi, Coachella, Yuma, Lompac, Topanga, Cahuenga, Malibu.

Hector and Elvira ended up in a unit of San Fernando Gardens, a sprawling public housing project along Van Nuys Boulevard. The Gardens, a collection of one and two-story buildings each holding as many as a dozen apartments, was built in the 1940s for workers making World War II planes at the Lockheed manufacturing plant in nearby Burbank and was originally hailed as a model of racial integration.

But over the next four decades it became almost exclusively Latino, and pretty run down despite occasional efforts to spruce up building exteriors with pastel-colored paint. The Gardens were next to Whiteman Airport, a small private aviation facility. That meant low-flying planes annoyingly buzzed overhead at all hours, adding to a depressingly melancholy atmosphere that included large "no trespassing" signs plastered on each building and a foreboding tall, black iron fence surrounding the Gardens.

The housing project had become a poor area —by official statistics just about the poorest in all of Los Angeles. Yet a surprising number of expensive cars lined the Garden's curving streets and tiny parking lots, suggesting substantial sources of undeclared and perhaps illegally earned income.

Without a father figure—not that it necessarily would have made any difference in this environment—Rivera grew up somewhat aimlessly and thus even more susceptible to outside influences. Like gangs, which had become an integral part of many Los Angeles neighborhoods. Pacoima had its share of Latino outfits, with names like Terra Bella, Latin Kings and Project Boys. Wearing the wrong color shirt or giving the wrong answer to the feared question "Where ya from?" had life-threatening consequences. So did another developing Los Angeles phenomenon: drive-by shootings, in which a house was riddled with bullets fired from a passing vehicle.

The gangs drew new members by ticking off the benefits of affiliation, almost like door-to-door salesmen hawking goods. Peer recognition. Easy money. Strength in numbers. Just like the US Army or the Marines, they said, playing down the surprisingly similar prospect of violence and sudden death. They also didn't say much about *El Juvy*—Juvenile Hall, the youth detention facility not far from Pacoima in Sylmar. Like any business organization—and make no mistake about it, each gang had a strong economic aspect to its operation, especially the drugs they sold—the gangs were big into recruitment.

Real big. Since there was no minimum age limit, gang members started approaching boys young. Anywhere they could. Hector was first solicited as he walked along the edge of the Gardens on Norris Avenue and then across the street to Pacoima Elementary School. He was 11 years old in fifth grade. Shh, don't tell your parents. Boys who were a little older had to walk five blocks up Pierce Avenue to Charles Maclay Middle School, named for the 19th-century politician who made a killing by taking advantage of distressed sellers and buying the 56,000 acres of then-undeveloped Pacoima for the dollar-an-acre price of $56,000. The longer route—past troubled David M. Gonzales Park as well as a mobile home park completely enclosed by a wall topped with barbed wire in an effort to create a crime-free zone—gave the gang recruiters a longer shot at their prospects. Shh, don't tell your parents.

Despite this uncertain environment—and the nightly gunfire and drive-by shootings that made it advisable to sleep in rooms away from the street side—it was still a big surprise to Elvira in 1993 when she answered a knock on the door to find Julio Morales, a Spanish-speaking Los Angeles policeman. He was a member of the anti-gang unit that all the politicians were talking up after the last effort at brokering a gang truce—there was even a football game between the rivals—broke down in a hail of gunfire.

Morales said he wanted to question Hector about the killing a few nights earlier of a gang member on Herrick Avenue just outside the Gardens.

"*¿Por qué Hector?*" she asked.

"He's got some connection with the other gang," Morales said. "We heard he might know something."

"Hector in a gang?" Elvira exclaimed. "He didn't tell me that."

"They never do."

Hector wasn't home. But when he returned later that night he was subject to an extreme maternal grilling. Mama didn't have to give any Miranda warnings.

The gist of what she squeezed out of Hector was this: Yes, he had become friendly with some members of the other gang who were trying to recruit him and hung out with them. No, he wasn't an inducted member, meaning he hadn't yet shot anyone or committed an armed robbery. Yes, he found the prospect of gang life interesting. No, he wasn't anywhere near the killing and had no direct knowledge. Yes, he was sorry.

Elvira realized her son—her only child—was at the brink, but still on the good side of the law. She also realized she was fighting a losing battle in the environment of Pacoima. So she made a quick decision.

To move. Away. Fast.

Within a week she found an apartment for Hector and herself many, many miles out in Valley Mirage. Despite its boom-time growth, Valley Mirage was one of the relatively few Los Angeles suburbs old enough to have a section of town with a supply of aging, and therefore cheaper, apartment complexes.

The rent still was nearly double what Elvira was paying in Pacoima for a two-room flat. She wasn't near her family, meaning she'd have to find someone else to look after Hector when she worked (not that her relatives were very good at that, anyway). But Hector was away from those gang influences, because Valley Mirage didn't have gangs, or at least not quite as many as the gangs in Pacoima, nor as vicious. And the schools were considered pretty good. Despite the dreary academic environment of Pacoima Elementary School, young Hector had turned into a decent student and, as it turned out, an even better soccer player when he wasn't out sampling the gang life.

Elvira's strategic decision saved Hector. He lost touch with old acquaintances—especially the ones who ended up in prison, or dead, or both. This, of course, was exactly what Elvira wanted. He stayed clear of the law.

In Southern California there seemingly was a rule requiring towns to have three times as many dry cleaners as daycare centers and churches combined (the same multiple went for sushi bars). Valley Mirage was no exception. Elvira got a job at one such establishment as the resident seamstress. She mended torn shirt pockets, let out pants a lot more often than she took them in, put on buttons and performed similar tailoring services. Her customers came of age in the 1970s and 1980s when they had no time or inclination to learn any of these mundane skills, and thought a sewing machine had something to do with the propagation of seeds in farming. Which, of course, was very good for Elvira. Much of the American economy was based on the inability of Americans to be economic.

The shop owner, an Armenian who lived in Glendale and frequently railed on about the Turkish genocide of his ancestors during World War I, took a cut of her fees in exchange for providing space and a sewing machine. So for big jobs—say that rare person who had lost 30 pounds—Elvira had the work brought to her apartment at night. Over time she developed a fair bootleg clientele.

At first the move to Valley Mirage was rough on Hector. He didn't know anyone, which, of course, was precisely the reason that Elvira relocated there. She kept a lot closer eye than she did in Pacoima on whom he hung out with, and did not go out of her way to take a message when one of his old "buddies" called from Pacoima. Southern California's historic aversion to mass transit since the advent of automobiles made it difficult for Hector to catch a bus back to the old 'hood. Elvira had scraped up the money to buy an old car, and occasionally she and Hector went back on weekends and holidays to visit family. But Elvira rarely let Hector out of her sight.

In many ways, though, what saved Hector in Valley Mirage was soccer. He found himself in a town with an established youth soccer program, initially centered around the Valley Mirage Soccer League. The coaching was a little spotty—there were plenty of Diego Diazes before Diego Diaz—but at least there were coaches. Valley Mirage High School had a full sports program and a full set of reasonably competent coaches. And in sports, at least, competence trumped the color of your skin or what kind of car your family drove.

Reflecting back on all this as he drove to yet another soccer practice, Rivera for some reason started wondering what it was like to be a big shot—at least in the context of Valley Mirage—like some of the soccer board members. He didn't know any of them very well. Mortician Whitney was friendly to Rivera, but then again, he was friendly to everyone. Banker Keating tended to gravitate along the soccer field sidelines to others of perceived wealth, which meant he was rarely near Rivera.

Real estate man Rigas seemed by nature to be a little more aloof. But once, when he and Rivera pulled up in their vehicles at the same time, Rigas, rather than pulling rank, waved him into the one remaining open parking spot on the street. Rivera had remembered that.

At heart, Rivera was a team player, always willing to help out. That is why he found himself after work one night as the season began at the offices of the Valley Mirage Soccer League. It was a donated two-room suite in an office park owned by a soccer parent who took a big tax write-off for his gift. The larger room served as a classroom for coaches and referees. The smaller room was used for storage, some soccer gear but mainly paperwork. Lots of paperwork, some going back years, much of it unneeded now, demonstrating the powerful force of inertia.

It was the job of Rivera and two other volunteers to sort through the stuff and toss what could be tossed to make some room. They came across several boxes full of game cards for the previous season. With the results stored online, the hard copies could go. Other boxes contained soccer law tests. The league had a rule that every adult who held a formal position with the league—coaches, referees, even league officials—had to take a rules test every year as a refresher. The tests weren't graded, so it was pretty ridiculous they even were kept around.

Because it was after normal working hours, the office park's refuse bin was padlocked shut (to keep Valley Mirage residents from dumping stuff they couldn't put in their own trash like batteries and light bulbs with mercury), so there was no place to toss the trash. Not a problem, Rivera told his colleagues; he'd just put the four boxes in the back of his truck until he found a place to dump them. Rivera would do anything for soccer.

CHAPTER 3

A FEW DAYS LATER, it happened again to Rivera, as it did just about every month for several years. He was returning home in his WeFixThingsRightNow van just after dusk at the end of a very long day. The last assignment, repairing a cooling unit on a walk-in wine vault in someone's basement, was in Arcadia. That was an affluent San Gabriel Valley town famous for the Santa Anita Park race track and infamous for an old written pledge by city leaders to stay "Caucasian forever."

Rivera had just come off the freeway and was heading down Valley Mirage Boulevard. Suddenly, flashing lights appeared in his rearview mirrors. He pulled over to the side. The Valley Mirage Police Department was fulfilling its sworn mission of guarding The Third Safest City Of Its Size In The West.

Wearily, Rivera rolled down his window. "What's up, officer?" he said pleasantly to whomever was holding the flashlight blindingly shining in his face.

"Your vehicle was weaving a bit as you were coming down the road," Rivera heard, still not able to see the face behind the light. "I, uh, wanted to make sure you were okay."

"I think I am, officer," Rivera said evenly. "Just on my way home from work."

"Lemme see your driver's license, registration and insurance."

"Here you are, officer," Rivera replied, handing over the documents.

The cop took the flashlight's beam off Rivera's face and scanned the back of the van, looking for contraband but uncovering only a jumbled combination of electronics parts, tools and soccer stuff.

"Back in a minute," he said, a tad disappointed, walking to his cruiser parked behind the van. Rivera caught a glimpse of a dark-haired man maybe in his late 30s with a crew-cut and a wide derriere.

Rivera actually heaved a sigh of relief. Just about any time a cop said a driver had been pulled over for "weaving a bit," Rivera knew it was a pretext. *The cop just wants to have a closer look at me*, he thought. *Maybe get a chance to run my ID through the warrant database on the laptop computer in the cruiser.*

One of Rivera's buddies, whose father was a cop, had told him in a bar one night about the ruse. "Weaving a bit" was a ploy taught at some police academies (or in police station locker rooms), a way that a policeman could pull over a driver without being accused of an utterly lawless stop and without losing face. Such phrasing fell considerably short of alleging the driver failed to stay in his lane, which would be a ticketable offense but one easily disproved by the always-on camcorder atop the patrol car dash. Of course, a weaving-a-bit stop when the driver wasn't weaving a bit was obviously lawless, but a lot less provable.

In some cases the cops actually did see some real weaving, and stopped the car figuring there might be a drunken driver behind the wheel. However, DWI—driving while intoxicated—was unlikely to be a major law enforcement concern at 8:12 on a Tuesday night, which was the precise moment Rivera was stopped. He had been pulled over for DWL—Driving While Latino. Or maybe its more precise offspring, DWYLM—Driving While a Young Latino Male.

In a region like Southern California, where the Latino population topped 40% and included many leading politicians, the presence of a Latino anywhere might seem pretty unremarkable. After all, it was the huge Latino working class (mostly from Mexico, but also hailing from Guatemala, El Salvador and other countries south of San Diego) that kept the economy running for the better-heeled non-Latinos. Often taking the jobs others didn't want. Even going so far as to stand on street corners offering their services as day laborers in a simple trade: an honest day's work for an honest day's pay.

In the pecking order of things, Latinos as a class might even be viewed as the new Southern California Indians. This perception lacked no irony given the key role that Spanish-speaking settlers played over the centuries in ridding the region of its original non-Spanish-speaking Indian inhabitants. Yet the specter of Latinos—or more particularly, young Latinos, or even more particularly, Young Latino Males—created a certain amount of fear in certain affluent Los Angeles suburbs that saw their prime mission as preserving a certain way of life, and, not incidentally, keeping up property values. One of those factors was a lack of crime, or at least so little crime that the suburb stayed off the front page of the *Los Angeles Times*.

What Rivera was experiencing along Valley Mirage Boulevard was simply part of the marketing of Valley Mirage. Despite the staggering population of Southern California, there remained a remarkably huge amount of undeveloped land. Land waiting to be subdivided, graded, laced with streets, electrified, gasified, watered, built upon, populated and, of course, taxed. That put more than 200 incorporated cities and seven county governments that oversaw all the unincorporated land into a rabid competition to attract developers and the people who would buy the homes or work in the buildings the developers produced.

Except for location there wasn't a whole lot else to distinguish the real estate. It pretty much all was earthquake-prone, flood-prone semi-desert backed up against fire-prone mountains and foothills, themselves prone to mudslides sweeping down into the subdivisions that often shouldn't have been built where they were in the first place. Obviously, calling attention to the earthquakes, the floods, the fires and the mudslides was not a good selling strategy. (It was no coincidence that the world's best-known measure of earthquake intensity was co-developed by Charles Richter, a Los Angeles resident trained at the California Institute of Technology and, in the grand tradition of Southern California individuality, an avid nudist and womanizer.) So some of the suburbs focused on stressing bells and whistles. Our schools are new. There are bike paths. You can see mountains.

And in the case of Valley Mirage, the self-proclaimed "Third Safest City of Its Size in the West."

How did such a claim come about? It helped, of course, to have low crime, and Valley Mirage, like many of the richer suburbs, really wasn't all that dangerous. As Rivera knew all too well, the police department did its best to hassle Young Latino Males. But the city council had made it clear to the police department leadership that it wasn't necessary that every crime be charged like it was the outrage of the century. These sentiments were conveyed in meetings held behind closed doors, with the press and public excluded on the stated but bogus grounds that litigation issues were being discussed. Not much could be done about clear, cold-blooded murder. And for politically correct reasons, rape couldn't be minimized, either. But maybe a burglary could be called a trespass. Or an aggravated assault simply an assault. And even a driver whose recklessness resulted in someone else's death might escape vehicular homicide charges, on the theory that such a case was best handled by the victim's family in a civil lawsuit for damages, which would keep it out of the crime stats.

After all, even if murder and rape went up but all the other categories measured went down, the overall crime rate would go down, too.

City Hall functionaries had spent a fair amount of time and money data-mining crime statistics and census results trying to figure out the most expansive claim about Valley Mirage public safety that could be justified. Some of that research was funded by a federal Safe Cities grant, even though it didn't improve safety. Ideally, for crime stat comparisons Valley Mirage wanted to be put in a national class along with bigger problems like Detroit, St. Louis, New Orleans, Memphis, Philadelphia, and Camden, New Jersey. But intellectually, there was no convincing way to do that. There were plenty of safer places bigger than Valley Mirage and smaller than these six.

Hoping to strip out pockets of law-abidingness, the city planners then started looking at geographic qualifiers—"in the West," "on the West Coast," "in the Mountain West," "in California," "in Southern California," even "Coastal California." But every time they ran the numbers, 10, 20 or more other cities came out better. Eventually, using "the West" as their universe, they started scrutinizing population bands. The standard broad ones—like, say, 50,000 to 100,000, 100,000 to 200,000, and 200,000 to 500,000—did not produce the desired superlative outcomes. So they looked at smaller and smaller population bands— 40,000 wide, then 20,000, then 10,000, then 1,000, then 500 and finally, one that was just 300 people wide.

Ta-da! In that narrow range—19 people below Valley Mirage's exact population and 281 above—there were only 13 cities across the entire West. But only two had better crime statistics. Thus was born the "Third Safest City of Its Size in the West" —along with strict orders to keep secret the fact that the peer group was a mere baker's dozen of towns.

As a largely upscale community, Valley Mirage had a large local corps of financial services professionals —real estate agents, stockbrokers, financial advisors and accountants, aided by lawyers —with more than its shares of finaglers. Fortunately, as the Valley Mirage city manager explained to the city council at one of its closed-door meetings, "FBI statistics don't include white-collar offenses when computing local crime rates. You can have all the fraud and forgery in the world, and we'd still be among the country's safest city."

To which one sharp-tongued council member muttered under his breath, "Not to mention the poorest."

The Valley Mirage municipal game plan was to "wall off" troublemakers. It long has been illegal (although not always) to prohibit residency on the basis of race and ethnic origins. So the strategy was to keep a close, close eye on elements deemed suspect, along the lines of imparting this message: "Don't even think about doing anything here." And few elements were deemed more suspect in Valley Mirage than Young Latino Males.

The chosen vehicle of such municipal enlightenment was the Valley Mirage Police Department. The agency enjoyed resources all out of proportion to the city's size or even needs, plus political support such that Young Latino Males could be stopped on the street or in their cars for the slimmest of reasons. Drive past a car pulled over to the side with a Valley Mirage patrol car behind it (lights still flashing, of course), and it was far more likely than not that the driver slumped behind the wheel looked Latino. Elected officials bragged about their "strong" police department. They pretended that such racial profiling didn't run afoul of various US Constitution provisions prohibiting searches without probable cause and differing treatment on the basis of race.

There was also a secondary economic motive. California law permitted municipalities through their police departments to "impound" vehicles driven by someone without a valid registration or driver's license or charged with driving under the influence. That meant the vehicle was seized on the spot and towed to a guarded lot. The law also allowed the municipality to set whatever fee it wanted that the owner had to pay to get back his vehicle. Unlike traffic court fines that essentially went to the state, the city could keep 100% of these fees.

The city fathers of Valley Mirage saw a two-pronged golden opportunity to suppress Young Latino Males while bringing in good coin. Even though they weren't supposed to make money in this way, they set the impound fee at $400, about four times the Southern California average. In the latest year nearly $1 million of impound fees came into the Valley Mirage city coffers. The city denied that police officers had to meet a daily impound quota, but the city manager reported at every city council meeting (behind closed doors, of course) exactly how many cars had been grabbed in the previous month and how much loot that brought in.

Occasionally, however, such forceful policing policies led to unfortunate results.

A year earlier, a group of Young Latino Males was attending a party one weekend night at a Valley Mirage home. Notwithstanding the apparent belief of city officials and the Valley Mirage Police Department, most of the Young Latino Males in Valley Mirage didn't belong to gangs. But at this particular party a gang member was present. At some point a car pulled up out front and someone in the vehicle—probably a member of a rival gang—fired a gun. The shots missed the sole gang member present but hit another one of the Young Latino Males, Antonio Garcia. His buddies quickly put him in a car and started driving toward the nearest hospital.

Two minutes later, officer Arthur Goetz, a member of the ever-vigilant police department, pulled over the vehicle—for weaving a bit, of course. Goetz radioed for backup, convinced he had encountered the leadership of a gang of Young Latino Males fleeing some as-yet unreported crime scene. He approached the car warily, hand on his holster.

"Everyone keep their hands in sight," Goetz ordered. "Out of the car."

"Tony can't!" shouted Pedro Rodriguez, the driver. "Shot at a party! Hurt bad!

"Gotta get him to the hospital!"

"Sure," said Goetz, eyeing with scorn the bleeding Garcia in the back seat. "What was *he* doing when he was shot? Knocking over a liquor store?"

"Nothing, officer," Rodriguez said, ignoring the insinuation. "Just standing around at a party. He needs a doctor now!"

"Tough," said Goetz. "Everybody but him out."

Goetz retreated to his cruiser. Garcia lay alone moaning on the back seat for four more minutes until the arrival of other squad cars. A sergeant took one look at Garcia and—unlike Goetz—called immediately for an ambulance. That took another five minutes. The ride to the hospital consumed six minutes. The ambulance arrived at the hospital 24 minutes after Garcia was shot.

Sadly, 90 seconds after Garcia died from a loss of blood.

Garcia's anguished family sued the Valley Mirage Police Department—meaning the City of Valley Mirage—for wrongful death. His parents said officer Goetz contributed to their son's demise by deliberately delaying his medical treatment due to a mistrust of Young Latino Males and a belief he was in a gang and thus would not be missed by law-abiding society.

City lawyers fought the case on grounds Goetz under the circumstances did nothing wrong and any lawsuit should have been brought against the real perpetrator—the killer firing the gun, who was never caught. Lawyers for the city—or more accurately, its well-heeled insurance carrier, which would be on the hook for any judgment—used their UCLA and USC law degrees to file motion after motion to dismiss or at least delay the case. The result was it was nowhere near trial. And by delaying a case, the insurance company could invest and get a return on money it otherwise would have paid out.

At the insistence of city fathers, the lawyers also won court orders to keep secret much of the evidence against the city—including Goetz's failure to call an ambulance after inquiring about a nonexistent liquor store robbery. That helped keep the case out of the *Los Angeles Times*, which despite a much-shrunken staff delighted in printing stories about trouble in suburbia.

Back in the present, the officer returned to Rivera, this time with the flashlight off. "Here're your papers," he said, in a manner vaguely equating Rivera with a participant in the Westminster Kennel Club dog show. "Free to go. But watch that weaving a bit."

"Okay, officer," Rivera replied, thinking, *I've come up clean in the computer check.*

"Hey," the cop said, "your name's familiar. Weren't you on that championship high school soccer team here a few years ago?"

"Yes, officer," Rivera replied, pleased but also surprised and even a little wary that the cop remembered. "The school's first SoCal title in any sport. Still the only one, I think."

"Yeah, the high-school sports around here stink, especially football," the cop said. "Me, I don't get this soccer thing. Boring, no scoring. But it does seem to be popular" — he paused — "in certain quarters."

"A lot of quarters, officer," Rivera said brightly. "The world's most popular sport. Lots of kids play it every week right here in Valley Mirage."

"Guess so," the cop muttered. Then he asked, "Did you learn to play in Valley Mirage?"

Rivera, whose prowess on the soccer field, both as a player and as a coach, came partly from an ability to stay calm under pressure, sensed a bit of a trap. "Some of it, sure, officer," he said. "But I started playing soccer as a kid in Los Angeles" — he paused — "where I was born."

The cop looked at him in surprise. "You're a US citizen?" he asked.

"Yep," Rivera said, looking up. "Probably just like you."

"Well, of course just like me," the cop said, a bit flustered. "I mean, yes, I was born in the US."

"Where?" Now Rivera was asking the questions.

"Moreno Valley. Inland Empire."

"I moved to Valley Mirage 'bout 12 years ago with my family," Rivera said. "You?"

"Can't afford to live in Valley Mirage," the cop said. "No one on the force can afford to live here. We're all just hired guns." He laughed. "I live over in Simi Valley."

"I sometimes go over there on repair calls, officer. Long commute."

"You got that right," the cop said. "But you gotta do what you gotta do."

He stopped. "Hey, how can *you* afford to live in Valley Mirage?"

"Small rental apartment, cheap part of town," Rivera said. "No back yard. Split rent with a roommate. Try to work hard. Live modestly."

He glanced at the clock on his dash. "You said I'm free to go," Rivera said. "If that's still true, I should be getting home."

"Okay," the cop said. "But remember, watch that weaving."

"Yes, officer."

Rivera drove off. Even though he had never gotten a traffic ticket, Rivera found all of these police encounters stressful. But he had been stopped enough times for DWYLM that he knew what to do. Practice makes perfect. Sort of like soccer.

He was still steamed about his encounter when he arrived a few minutes later at the tiny one-bedroom apartment he shared with Dora. She was sitting on the sofa watching yet another top-model show. He kissed her, then went over to the fridge for a beer and sat down beside her.

"Cop stopped me again. Sayin' I was weaving," Hector said. "Let me go again after checking my ID."

"Here in Valley Mirage?" Dora asked.

"Yep," Hector said. "Happens to me elsewhere, but mainly here. Course, I'm here more. They're afraid I'm a gangbanger."

"Sure, a gangbanger who fixes massaging easy chairs," Dora said, somewhat lightly. "Such a danger to society. Boy, are they barking up the wrong tree." She rolled her eyes.

"Why do you watch those kinds of shows?" Hector said, changing the topic. "Want to be a top model?"

"Mainly an escape," she said. "But there's nothing wrong with hoping. Gotta have hope. 'Specially when you're young. Who knows? Someday I might run that damn company where I work. Couldn't do it any worse than the asshole boss runnin' it now."

"America is full of asshole bosses," agreed Hector. "I think it's required by the Constitution."

Dora sat up.

"There you go with that law stuff again," she said. "When you're not working or at soccer, you sit around here drinkin' beer and moping about how your life isn't going anywhere. So finish college and go to law school. Isn't that what you really want? Why else would you watch those old *Perry Mason* re-runs? One of which, by the way, I'm TiVoing right now for you."

"Thanks, sweets," Hector said. "You know, a lawyer over in Ventura wrote the *Perry Mason* novels the shows're based on. Law is interesting. But I'm not sure I have what it takes to stick at something that long. At least when I go to fix something, job's usually over in an hour."

"Hey," Dora said, "you've stuck with soccer all these years. A lot longer than it would take to become a lawyer."

"Yeah, but that's just a sport, a hobby." Hector said. "Not a job or something serious like that."

"Tell that to my dad," Dora said. "Sometimes I think it's the soccer coaching that keeps him going. Certainly not his trash job. And not, from what I see, his personal life.

"In soccer he gets excited and all gung-ho. He lives for it. Probably not good for his heart he yells at referees like he does. But it gets him charged up. Gets his mind off other things.

"He can't wait for day's end so he can hold a practice. Or for the week to end so there will be a match. Look, I know he isn't the best of coaches. But that doesn't bother him. For him, hope springs eternal. One game at a time."

"Diego's dedicated, no question," Hector acknowledged. "But it might be a little better if he would, uh, work at improving his coaching. You know, read a book, take a class. He'd have better outcomes."

"Definitely not into learning," Dora agreed. "But you are! You read more than any college dropout I know. So start reading law. Then we can move to a nicer pad."

"Only if you'll be my Della Street," Hector said, referring to the fictional Perry Mason's fictional secretary.

He leaned over and kissed her. She kissed him back. Pretty soon no one in the Valley Mirage apartment was watching the top-model show or Perry Mason.

The tiny minority population in Valley Mirage dated back to the early days of World War II when workers were desperately needed for nearby military industries. Deed restrictions prohibiting residency by non-whites were ignored in apartment buildings rapidly going up as housing. This did not sit well with long-time Valley Mirage residents who had moved there partly because deed restrictions *were* enforced. But judges had started refusing to honor such covenants around Los Angeles. One highly publicized case was won by Hattie McDaniel, the Academy Award-winning servant in *Gone With The Wind*. The jig was up in 1948 when the US Supreme Court ruled courts could no longer uphold such provisions.

Or was it? Valley Mirage city leaders couldn't do anything about home sales, but they could get out the word to such groups that the environment might be better elsewhere. Over the years this was done in a myriad of ways, and with more than just an overbearing police force. The city levied parking fees on nonresidents—especially, it seems,

Spanish-speaking nonresidents—who used gated city parks. After the 1965 riots in the black Los Angeles neighborhood of Watts, the city successfully pressured Los Angeles County to shut Wellmount Pool, a public swimming facility to which Watts kids long had been bused for "a day in the country." Sensitive about image, the city said it sought the closing only because the pool was prone to storm runoff that expensively clogged municipal sewer lines.

Still, over time some of the racial and ethnic barriers weakened, especially with the influx of higher-income families of Pacific Rim extraction—Koreans, Japanese and Chinese—led by breadwinners drawn to the high technology industry springing up across Southern California. This was on top of the jobs created by the ever-expanding entertainment juggernaut centered in Hollywood and West Los Angeles. Valley Mirage started popping up on lists of best places to raise a family (which generally did not take into account efforts, or lack thereof, concerning racial diversity).

With soldiers returning, the end of World War II had accelerated the building boom in Southern California. Across Valley Mirage, small subdivisions—15, 20 homes—started appearing. By the 1970s, the pace of development quickened. In fact, for developers the development process itself almost became effortless. Thanks in part to large "political" donations to council elections, developers easily got municipal approvals. They then easily cleared their tracts of most of that desert vegetation they considered pesty but was essential in anchoring sloped ground during those not-so-rare bouts of excessive rain. They easily graded the slopes, easily installed streets and easily put up homes.

There once had been a not easily surmountable obstacle in the LA suburbs—an insufficient supply of water. But then along came completion of several branches of the California Aqueduct. This state-government-built system—basically a very long straw—brought water generated by the mountains of Northern California hundreds of miles south to the deserts of Southern California. Now all developers had to do, easily and at minimal cost, was tap in. Which they did, like USC frat brothers on a Saturday night. As a result, new subdivisions in Valley Mirage got larger and larger—50, 100, 200 homes at a pop. The homes, too, got larger and larger—four bedrooms, five bedrooms, six bedrooms with a media room—as the California economy thrived and mortgage loans became easier to get. Valley Mirage gradually became positively upscale, with the ritzy newer homes outnumbering and relegating to inferior status the older section of town where Latinos like Rivera were clustered.

The next morning, sitting at the kitchen table, Rivera scoped out the upcoming weekend match. His team was playing a weak opponent. Rivera's biggest problem would be making sure he put his best players on defense to avoid running up the score. His next biggest problem was a topic of obsession everywhere but especially to those living in Southern California.

The weather.

For all of Southern California's vaunted reputation worldwide as being possessed as a pleasant climate, the truth was that the environment was subject to violent exception and unexpected peril. That's not counting air quality problems so predating 20th-century auto-generated smog—problems that some 19th-century developers slyly labeled as "fog-laden sea breezes"—that in 1542 Juan Rodríguez Cabrillo, exploring for Spain, dubbed the waters off Los Angeles Baya de los Fumos, or Smoke Bay. That was due to the presence of what would become known as the Santa Monica and San Gabriel Mountains trapping overhanging haze from Indian village fires.

It was mid-September. That meant that it hadn't rained in Southern California since early March and wouldn't again until the short rainy season began again in November. The vegetation on the foothills and mountains was drier than a bond prospectus. A spark—from a car's underside, a thoughtless smoker, a bird's fiery final fall of revenge after hitting a high-power line—easily could trigger one of those infamous California wildfires.

And fanning one of those infamous California wildfires could be the infamous dry seasonal wind called the Santa Ana. Where the name came from remained uncertain. But the effect on places and people was well known and even immortalized in literature. "There was a desert wind blowing that night," pulp fiction writer Raymond Chandler began one of his famous novellas. "It was one of those hot dry Santa Anas that come down through the mountain passes and curl your hair and make your nerves jump and your skin itch. On nights like that every booze party ends in a fight. Meek little wives feel the edge of the carving knife and study their husbands' necks. Anything can happen."

They couldn't predict specific earthquakes, but California authorities had gotten pretty good at predicting specific Santa Anas and wildfires. There was even a formal mechanism to inform the public of this prospect. It was called a Red Flag warning. Formal criteria, too—15% humidity or less with sustained winds of 25 miles per hour or more for at least six hours. The authorities, of course, didn't actually hoist flags somewhere; they just sent out weather bulletins and put up the advisory on websites.

The radio on the kitchen counter was bleating a Red Flag warning would be posted for Saturday. Rivera smiled. He was a little more strategic than most of his rival coaches. Under the Laws of the Game, the pre-game coin-flip winner chose which way to go during the first half; the other side (referees were taught to avoid the term loser) kicked off. Everything was reversed for the second half. Most coaches told their captains if they won the toss to play into the wind during the first half, counting on the physical and even psychological advantage of having it at their team's back for the second.

Rivera saw things quite differently. *Wind can change direction or even die out*, he thought. *Just because it's blowing strongly in one direction at the start doesn't mean it will keep up that way for the whole game.* Figuring that a near-certain half-game of wind advantage was better than the chance of none, Rivera told his captains if they won the coin toss to go immediately with the wind. The result was that Rivera's teams got the wind advantage for nearly 100% of their first halves, and the wind disadvantage a lot less than that during the second.

The Santa Ana is my friend, Rivera thought. But then he remembered all the past damage from fires. *On the soccer field, anyway.*

As usual, the authorities had the wind and fire prediction nailed when Saturday came around. By 10:00 a.m. wildfires had broken out on the sides of three mountain ranges, the San Gabriels, the San Bernardinos and the Santa Monicas. And also as usual, a plethora of governmental agencies mustered an impressive amount of counter-power. Helicopters dropping water. Fixed-wing planes unloading red fire retardant. Fire fighters advancing on foot. A military assault missing only guns. With some notable exceptions, such efforts usually stopped the fires dead or at least confined them to the surprisingly large amount of Southern California that was steeply mountainous and therefore unbuildable and unpopulated. This afforded a certain sense of comfort, almost like what transpired was a part of Disneyland.

"Boy, that's somethin', ain't it," Loretta Patterson, one of Rivera's soccer moms, greeted him as he arrived at the fields early for his match. She hooked her thumb over her shoulder toward a ridge line a safe 10 miles back but clearly in view. An eerie orange glow peeked out from just behind the top like a solar eclipse that had gotten too low and too close.

"So far I don't smell smoke," Patterson continued. "The wind seems to be going parallel to us, not toward us. Hope it doesn't change."

"Hope it doesn't, either," Rivera said, although he really was thinking something else. *If the smoke stays away, it's okay by me if the wind changes 180 degrees at halftime.*

Then Rivera noticed trouble. Big trouble. And not the fire, although the trouble also involved sparks. Rivera heard the trouble before he saw it. A match involving Diego Diaz's team, the Aardvarks, was under way on Field No. 8. And hoofing it down the center of the pitch: Referee Rick Hermannik.

"HANDBALL REF! HANDBALL!" Diaz screamed, waving his arms up and down in front of his body like a Watusi dancer. "GIVE US A BREAK!"

Hermannik didn't respond. Then:

"SHE'S PUSHIN', REF, PUSHIN'!" Diaz yelled, mimicking the offense with his arms like a bouncer forcing back the crowd outside a hot West Hollywood club. "Where's the call?"

Hermannik ignored him. Then:

"HOLDING!" Diaz hollered, thrusting his arms above his head, right hand grabbing the left wrist, like he was crowning himself a champ. "EVERYONE SAW THAT!"

Hermannik again paid no attention.

Asking around along the sidelines, Rivera learned to his considerable surprise that the score was 3 to 2 in favor of the Aardvarks, with only a minute or so left. Rivera was surprised not only by the fact that Diaz was ahead—itself an unusual occurrence—but also by the level of his discontent. *Diaz sounds like he's down three goals,* Rivera thought. *He ought to focus on coachin', not complainin'. His game to lose.*

A number of league officials had gathered to watch the end of the match. Rivera learned that before the game Hermannik had complained about again being "switched by the computer" to the Diaz match.

"Boy, was he unhappy," Janis Johnson told Rivera. "I thought he was just going to leave."

"Why didn't he?"

"Manny talked him into staying. 'For the good of the game,' he said over and over. It was like a chant. And you know how soothing and persuasive Manny can be."

Rivera laughed. "Well, he hasn't sold me a casket yet, but I'm still young."

Johnson looked at him. "Just wait," she said.

Suddenly, nearby parents around them—Rivera was standing on the side of the opposing team—erupted in cheers. The Sweat Tarts (the league had vetoed Sweet on grounds that was sugar leading to tooth decay) was mounting a final offensive to try to tie the score. The ball was bouncing around midfield in sort of a kickball scrum, surrounded by three or four players from each side. Then the ball squirted out and a Sweat Tarter with a good foot laid into it, sending it arching toward the Aardvark goal. Normally, the uncontested Aardvark goalkeeper simply would collect the ball with her hands, run up to the front of the penalty area, and punt up field, or at least to one side. That would blunt the challenge and in this case maybe run out the clock for an Aardvark win.

But this time was different. Instead of letting the ball roll to the keeper, one of Diaz's fullbacks swung in front of her, got control with her feet and started dribbling upfield herself. She got about 30 yards in front of the goal when she, too, decided to send it.

Except that one of the Sweat Tarters managed to get her long leg in front of the ball an instant after it was kicked. So what was intended to be a long pass up field instead turned into a boomerang, bouncing back over the Aardvark fullback's head toward her own goal.

With two Sweat Tarters in alert hot pursuit. They had a breakaway. The two of them versus the one Aardvark keeper.

With everyone around the field screaming, the pair streaked toward the Aardvark goal. They started out even with one another about six yards apart. The girl who had blocked the kick got control. Without passing, she dribbled the ball. That slowed her down a bit such that her teammate drew maybe a yard in front of her off on the left flank. Instead of charging out to confront the attackers, the Aardvark keeper hung back, not knowing exactly what to do.

Bad move. Just inside the six-yard line—the front of the small box surrounding the goal—the girl with the ball whacked it into the net just past the keeper's outstretched hands for the game-tying goal.

"NO GOAL!" Diaz screamed as the Sweat Tarters leaped around the field in joy and geese in the skies scattered. "OFFSIDE!

"NO GOAL, REF! THE OTHER PLAYER WAS OFFSIDE!

"SHE WAS AHEAD OF THE BALL! INTERFERIN' WITH MY KEEPER!"

Hermannik looked over at his assistant referee, who had the best view. He hadn't raised his flag, which would have been the signal for offside. And he was running back up the touchline, the normal signal for a goal. But just to be sure, Hermannik beckoned him over, out of earshot of everyone else.

"What did you see?" Hermannik asked quietly.

"Well, the other player was ahead of the play, in an offside position 'cause only the keeper was in front of her," the AR said. "But she was over on one side and not involved. Didn't block the keeper's view. She was just there. Dribbler never passed it. Just drilled it into the net. Good goal, I say."

"Fine by me," Hermannik said. Except, of course, it wasn't because he knew what was coming. Gamely, Hermannik turned and faced the field, which meant he sort of had to face a faraway Diaz, too. "Goal stands," he shouted, giving a signal.

"WHAT?" Diaz exploded across the pitch. "HIGHWAY ROBBERY! YOU DON'T KNOW OFFSIDE! YOU DON'T KNOW SOCCER! YOU DON'T KNOW NOTHIN'." The wildfires in the distant mountains seemingly bellowed from his blast.

By then, playing time had run out on Hermannik's watch. He was in no mood to add some time and extend the match, a prerogative he had under the Laws, and certainly in no mood to go closer to Diaz if he could help it. So he blew his whistle the traditional three short toots. "GAME!" he shouted.

CHAPTER 4

THE FRONT DOOR was unlocked two days later when Rosa Caldera arrived, as she had every Monday morning for years, to clean Hermannik's house. The lack of security was not unusual. Hermannik ran his real estate appraising business from his home. Unless out on an early assignment putting a formal value on yet another highly appreciated house in the process of being bought with borrowed money and hardly any down payment, he always unbolted the door before she came. Since Caldera had a key, it was no big deal, but a nice gesture, anyway.

A stoutly built woman in her late 40s with a weathered face, Caldera had a Mother Hen quality about her. In addition to cleaning Hermannik's two-story house, she changed his sheets and made him *huevos revueltos* if he hadn't eaten. Caldera also did his wash, which included his soccer referee uniform, often steeped in sweat for two days. Hermannik was pleasant but made little chit-chat; his Spanish, and her English, weren't too good. For her three-and-a-half hours of labor, Hermannik paid $75 in cash. The mutually beneficial arrangement allowed him to avoid paying his share of employer taxes like Social Security and her to avoid paying taxes altogether.

Hauling her cleaning equipment, Caldera entered the house.

"*Buenos días,*" she said.

No answer.

"*Buenos días,*" she called out somewhat louder.

Still no answer.

"*¿Cómo está?*" she shouted.

Silence.

Caldera knew that Hermannik always returned in time to pay by the end of her shift. So she started on her appointed rounds through Hermannik's home, not one of the mansions in Valley Mirage.

Going into his first-floor bedroom, she took his clothes piled in a hamper—his yellow jersey on top—to the washing machine in an alcove and started a load. Caldera scrubbed the kitchen and mopped its floor. After scouring the bathroom, she dusted the rest of the first-floor furniture, then vacuumed. While working she liked to hum and sort of mouth the Spanish words to various children's songs. Her favorite was "Itsy Bitsy Spider":

> *"Araña arañita, sube la escalera*
> *Araña arañita, súbela otra vez.*
> *¡Pum! se cayó. ¡Pum! se cayó*
> *Vino un sapo gordo y se la comió."*

She tried to time it so she sing-songed the final line—"There came a big toad that swallowed it down"—as her vacuum hose sucked up something crawling across a floor or wall. Caldera didn't mind being the *sapo gordo*. Still, she was always amazed how one person living alone could attract so many bugs.

Struggling with her clunky ancient Hoover, Caldera waddled up the stairs to the second floor where Hermannik used one of the bedrooms as his office—desk, computer, printer, all that stuff—and a second to store files. Putting down the vacuum, she opened the door to the office.

In front of her was Hermannik.

On the floor.

Motionless.

Caldera screamed.

She screamed again.

Caldera kept screaming as she ran down the steps and out the door. Her screams were heard down the street, around the corner and then some. Ricocheting off home facades with faux columns, designer garage doors, gargoyle-topped fences and finally a lumbering brown UPS truck passing by, which screeched to a stop. The driver took one look at Caldera—yelling, *"¡Está muerto!"* over and over while standing in front of Hermannik's house—and dialed 911 on his cell.

"Look, my Spanish ain't the greatest," he told the operator. "But there's a woman here I think is yellin' there's a dead body in a house."

Valley Mirage cop Harold Fitzpatrick wasn't too far away, questioning a Latino driver stopped out of concern he had been weaving a bit. Hearing the alert, Fitzpatrick let the driver go, hopped back into his squad car and raced over. Still, he was beaten to the scene by a crowd that had gathered on the opposite side of the street. No one wanted to get too close to the still-screaming Caldera, who for all they knew had just killed someone and was confessing, or who could even kill again.

Fitzpatrick's supervisor, Sergeant Mark Emerson, rolled up. Since neither spoke any Spanish beyond what was needed to order tacos, they patched in an interpreter on a police radio who questioned a somewhat-calmed-down-by-then Caldera. The interpreter then told the cops Caldera said she had found the owner of the house dead in his upstairs office. With guns drawn, Emerson and Fitzpatrick entered the house. A few minutes later they emerged, guns holstered, as a city EMT crew arrived in an ambulance. It was part of a rapidly growing armada of other vehicles massing along the street, including several private ambulances hoping in the era of government downsizing that their wildly overpriced services could be of use.

The cops beckoned over the EMTs.

"We'll take you upstairs," Emerson said, "but I don't think you'll be needed. He's dead. Body's stone cold on the floor."

"Heart attack?" asked one of the techs.

"Doubt it," Emerson said. "There's a cord around his neck."

The sergeant looked at the tech. "His pants were pulled down, too."

The tech flinched. The world-weary Emerson did not.

"Once you confirm he's dead, don't move or touch anything," he said. "Could be murder. I'm callin' in detectives and the coroner."

Meanwhile, word already had begun to spread to the gaggle across the street that there was a death under very suspicious circumstances. With home-owning neighbors long departed for their well-paying jobs in Los Angeles, most of the people there were hired help—other cleaning ladies, gardeners, nannies, a plumber and the UPS man—with no idea who Hermannik was.

But one person did. Jay Evers, who lived four doors down across the street, was a very rare stay-at-home dad in a very equally rare single-income household; his wife had a high-powered job with a national cable network based in Los Angeles, one that specialized in UFO programming ("All Roswell, All The Time" was one of its slogans). He took care of their two kids. They both played soccer. This was why Evers knew Hermannik, who otherwise pretty much had kept his distance from neighbors. Evers walked over to Officer Fitzpatrick.

"You know, officer, the guy who lives there, Hermannik, he referees youth soccer," Evers said. "Had a run-in on Saturday with some coach. Big run-in. Coach threatened him. I heard it. Everyone heard it."

"Oh?" said a suddenly interested Fitzpatrick. "What kind of threat?"

"Coach didn't like his calls," Evers said. "Something 'bout shoving his whistle somewhere."

"Wait here!" Fitzpatrick ordered. He walked away and had a whispered conference with Sergeant Emerson, who had just been briefed by the EMTs. Then Fitzpatrick turned and strode back rapidly to Evers. "Come with me," he commanded. "The sarge wants to talk to you."

For it turned out that the EMTs just discovered that in fact a whistle *had* been shoved someplace, specifically, up Hermannik's ass, or at least a little way in. That presumably was after Hermannik had been strangled. Presumably why Hermannik was missing his pants. And presumably connected to the reason he was killed.

"Who was the coach?" demanded Emerson, who saw himself cracking his first murder case.

"Not sure," Evers replied. "Don't know everyone out there for soccer." He paused, thinking. "Maybe San Diego."

Emerson frowned. "That's a city," he said.

"Well, something like that, then," Evers said. "Ask around. Plenty of people know his name."

That knowledgeable group quickly expanded to include Valley Mirage Police Department detectives once they arrived and started going through the death scene. The screen on Hermannik's office computer was dark. But one detective noticed the power button was glowing, meaning the computer was not turned off completely but was in some kind of sleep mode. So stepping over Hermannik's body—it hadn't been moved so the death scene could be photographed in its gruesome entirety—he gently pushed one of the keys on the keyboard. The screen suddenly lit up. And on it was what looked like a half-written Microsoft Word document. With these words:

> Formal report to the league on threatening telephone call received 30 minutes ago from coach Diego Diaz. Diaz

continued complaining about the no-offside call yesterday.
Diaz cursed and threatened me with violence

The writing stopped there. As though the writer had been interrupted suddenly.

But it was more than enough for the detectives to figure out the identity of their top suspect. It was more than enough for them to figure out a motive. And it was more than enough for them to get a search warrant 90 minutes later to enter Diaz's empty apartment nearby and look for evidence.

Diaz came home from work in the afternoon and got out of his car in the parking lot. He was met by Sam Wormsley and Harry Fuhrman, two uniformed Valley Mirage policemen who had been on a stakeout for him. They approached him with guns drawn.

"Mr. Diaz?" Wormsley asked.

"That's me," Diaz said. Then he saw their hands. "Hey, why you pointin' them at me?"

"Police officers," Wormsley said. "Turn around. Arms on the side of the car."

"Why?" Diaz protested.

"Do what we say. We want to frisk you."

"Why?" Diaz again asked as he was sort of spun around by Fuhrman.

"You're under arrest for suspicion of murder," Wormsley said.

"Murder?" Diaz shouted over his shoulder as Fuhrman patted him down. "Murder of who?"

"Rick Hermannik," Wormsley said.

"What?" Diaz exclaimed. "How can he be dead? Son of a bitch just refereed my game on Saturday."

"Found dead this morning. Strangled in his home."

Diaz flinched like he had taken a punch. "What?" he exclaimed. "You're kiddin'!"

"Put your arms behind you," Fuhrman said, followed by the click of handcuffs.

"Hey, what's this?" Diaz said, struggling because the cuffs hurt.

"You're coming to headquarters," Wormsley said.

Fuhrman leaned over and whispered something to Wormsley, who pulled out a laminated card and started reading.

"Tienes el derecho de permanecer en silencio," Wormsley said in halting, badly mispronounced Spanish. *"Cualquier cosa que digas puede—"*

Diaz cut him off. "Hey, I know my Miranda rights," he said. "Why the Spanish?"

"Well, uh, uh," Wormsley said, fumbling. "You're, uh, Latino."

"Yeah, but you're not," Diaz retorted. "That's the problem 'round here. You sound like a three-year-old! Stick to English!"

"Okay," said a suddenly chastised Wormsley, flipping over the card to the other side and reading again. "You have the right to remain silent. Anything you say can and will be used against you ..."

After he was taken to the Valley Mirage Police Station, Diaz was allowed the traditional one telephone call. He made it to Dora.

"Honey, been arrested for killin' a soccer referee I yelled at on Saturday," he told her over a phone line undoubtedly monitored by the police.

"What?" Dora screamed into the phone. "You killed someone?"

"No, honey." Diego said. "Didn't kill no one. Had nothin' to do with it. Didn't know anything 'bout it 'til the cops arrested me when I got home from work. Cops say the ref was strangled in his home. Found this morning by his maid."

"Oh my God!" Dora exclaimed. "Who was the ref?"

"Fellow named Rick Hermannik. Don't know much about him 'cept he reffed a lot of my games and was lousy." Diego paused, chuckling despite his plight. "Guess I think all refs are lousy."

"You're charged with murder?"

"I'm charged with something bad. Cops searched my apartment. Look, Dora, I need a lawyer here. Fast. Call Bruce Horning. Represented me in my divorce. Haven't seen him in a while. If he can't come here, ask him for names. The cops have been trying to question me. I talked a little. Want to see if I can get out of here on bail."

"Okay, I'll call him."

"Haven't done anything, honey. Police told me the body was found next to a computer. Said he was writin' an e-mail saying I had called to threaten him."

"Did you?"

"Course not."

"Daddy, I love you!"

"Love you, too, Dora!"

"What happens now?"

"Not sure. That's why I need a lawyer. Dora, please find one."

"Okay, Daddy."

When she hung up, Dora called Rivera at work on his cell.

"Daddy's in jail charged with murder!" Dora shouted.

"Murder?" Hector repeated. "Of who?"

"Dunno," Dora said. "Some soccer referee named Herman or something."

Hector gulped. "Rick Hermannik?"

"Yeah, that's the name. How'd you know?"

"Didn't. But he reffed Diego's match on Saturday. Diego really screamed at him. Saw it myself. What happened to Hermannik?"

"Daddy said he was found strangled today at his home. Daddy called me from jail. Needs a lawyer."

"Did Diego, uh, have anything to do with this?"

"Whose side are you on?" Dora demanded, forgetting that she had asked Diego pretty much the same question. "Of course he didn't. Daddy's crazy at times. But he's no killer."

Her tone softened a bit. "He told me he knew nothin' 'bout this 'til the cops arrested him when he got home from work. Searched his apartment, too."

"Does he have an alibi?"

"We didn't get that far. He wants me to find a lawyer. Told me to call his old divorce lawyer. I'm doing that now."

"I'll try to get home as soon as I can."

"Please do. Bye."

By this time word had started to spread about Hermannik's death. To some degree this was due to the fact that the major Los Angeles news organizations subconsciously had a tendency to pay more attention to killings that take place in fancier white neighborhoods than an ethnic lower-class venue, like a street corner in East Los Angeles or South Central Los Angeles. Of course, this was true across the country and not just around Los Angeles. Killings just weren't supposed to happen in those nicer white areas. And when they did, they were unexpected and hence news, unlike the poorer minority neighborhoods where such endings were expected and hence not news. It essentially was the same difference in coverage between man bites dog (news, except it never happened) and dog bites man (not news, except when the man was rich and famous or died from rabies).

Media outlets that monitor police radio frequencies heard the call to go to Hermannik's house. Several of the freelance camera crews that constantly cruise the Los Angeles area hoping to get video they can sell to television stations showed up. They'd much rather have footage of a Hollywood star in a traffic accident. But on a slow day they took what they could get, in this case the body bag being wheeled out of Hermannik's home into a waiting coroner's van. The *Los Angeles Times*, which to save money had cut back on its bureaus in the suburbs, worked the story on the phone. Only the local *Valley Mirage Daily Post* sent an actual reporter to the scene outside Hermannik's house. He was a young fellow barely one year out of college by the name of Jeff Berman.

It was cub reporter Berman's great luck to encounter Jay Evers and start talking to him. Evers told Berman just enough to plant in his mind the angle of a berserk soccer parent taking the ultimate revenge.

The perfect suburban crime story! Berman thought. He just hoped it was true.

Evers still couldn't remember Diaz's full name, so he didn't give it to Berman. The reporter asked around, but none of the other spectators present knew anything about the soccer clash. The cops had no comment. So Berman hurried back to his office to see what else he could develop on the story.

Meanwhile, Evers went home and called both of his children's soccer coaches, who also had witnessed the confrontation. They knew the name—"Diego Diaz, not San Diego," the first told Evers. And like Evers, they put two and two together. Word *really* started getting around.

Still, at that point no one outside of the official investigators—not Evers, not Berman, not the body-bag photographing camera crews and certainly not the public—knew anything about the message on the computer screen mentioning threats from Diaz or the unusual position of Hermannik's whistle. However, those informational deficiencies were cured soon after Diaz was taken into custody. The search warrant affidavit by the detective with the reasons for searching Diaz's apartment became a public record. So did the charges that were filed against Diaz: (1) murder and (2) desecration of a corpse.

Then Berman, who was sitting in the newsroom trying to write his story, got lucky for the second time that day in his short journalistic career. He got an e-mail from Evers, to whom he had given his business card.

"Jeff, click on this YouTube link," Evers wrote, referring to the one-year-old video sharing website started above a Silicon Valley pizzeria that already had become a household word. "Some parent uploaded a video from Saturday of the coach threatening the dead ref. It's already the talk of Valley Mirage soccer." Indeed it was; Evers had been alerted to it in an e-mail from a coach.

Berman quickly clicked on the link. He sat in amazement at the images and audio emanating from his computer.

Even though other news organizations were onto the story, Berman knew he had a scoop if he got it out fast—maybe even scooping the cops, who were not too Internet savvy. After calling over his editors, Berman played the clip two more times, taking notes, then resumed rewriting his story, a lot more feverishly.

Ninety minutes later—and after much scrutiny by his worry-wart editors, always afraid everything in the paper will lead to a libel lawsuit against them personally—the story was posted on the paper's website. With a few modifications it was typeset for use in the print edition that would be thrown on front steps across Valley Mirage in the morning.

VM Soccer Referee Murdered, Coach Charged

Internet-posted video shows anger police say led to killing

By Jeff Berman

A Valley Mirage referee of youth soccer matches was found strangled in his home Monday, and police accused a coach whose angry rant about weekend officiating was captured on video.

Authorities said the body of Richard Hermannik, 47, was found with a cord around his neck in his home in the 23100 block of Hummingbird Lane early Monday by a maid who had come to clean. Later in the day, police arrested Diego E. Diaz, 49, of the 27400 block of Tukupar Avenue. He was being held without bail on Monday night; it was not known if he has a lawyer yet.

Police said it appears Hermannik was killed sometime late Sunday. According to papers submitted to obtain a search warrant, Hermannik was found dead in front of a computer by his maid. The computer screen contained a partially written report stating Diaz had called less than an hour earlier to continue complaining and that he had "threatened violence." The full text of the search warrant affidavit can be found at this link.

Diaz was formally charged with an open count of murder—and also one count of desecration of a corpse. According to court filings, a referee's whistle was found inserted into an unnatural position in Hermannik's body.

The whistle's location took on added significance in light of a tirade Saturday by Diaz after the end of a Valley Mirage Soccer League match behind Valley Mirage Elementary School. Police Detective Reynolds Wolfington cited Diaz's comments in a sworn statement submitted midday Monday to obtain that warrant to search Diaz's home.

As it turns out, the *Daily Post* has learned, Diaz's highly charged comments were videotaped by someone holding a camcorder and uploaded hours later to YouTube, an Internet-based video sharing service that began last year and has become very popular worldwide. As of Monday night, the clip had been viewed 621 times, according to a counter on the website. The video can be seen by clicking on this link. There was no mention of the video in Detective Wolfington's search-warrant request, raising the possibility authorities then were unaware of its existence.

Diaz, who coaches a team of 12-year-old girls, was upset that Hermannik, the match referee, allowed a last-second break-away goal tying the match for the other team. Diaz argued vehemently that the goal should be canceled because the attacking team had a player who was offside.

Offside is an offense in soccer that occurs under certain circumstances when an attacking player without the ball is in front of a teammate with the ball and there is an insufficient number of defenders between the forward player and the goal. A declaration of offside, which costs the attacking team possession of the ball, is sometimes a close judgment call for the referee and his assistant referee along the sideline.

In the YouTube-posted video, Diaz can be seen after the disputed play expressing strong criticism of Hermannik. "Highway robbery!" he says. "You don't know nothing!" Hermannik then blows his whistle and shouts "Game!" to end the match.

An extremely agitated Diaz continues to berate the referee. "You and your game!" Diaz can be heard shouting. "You and your whistle! Someone should shove it where it belongs!"

In charging Diaz with murder and desecration, the police are alleging in effect that he followed his own suggestion. It is likely the video will become evidence against Diaz. The video went up on YouTube under the headline, "Soccer coach tells referee to shove it in Valley Mirage, California."

Still unknown is the identity of the camera person, who posted the video using a made-up identity, as is common on the Internet.

Also captured in the background as Diaz vented his anger was smoke billowing from the big mountain wildfire.

"Boy, was he really yelling at Hermannik," Jay Evers, a neighbor of the dead referee who witnessed the soccer-field confrontation, said Monday. "Everyone could hear it."

Hermannik was a self-employed real estate appraiser who worked out of the home in which he was killed. Details on Hermannik's next-of-kin were not immediately available. Neighbor Evers said that Hermannik was a quiet fellow who kept largely to himself and lived alone.

Diaz works in the garbage hauling business.

The violence against Hermannik comes amid a national backdrop of growing complaints about aggressive "soccer parents," which in some quarters has become a pejorative label. News reports across the country have recounted a number of verbal incidents among parents at youth soccer matches, often directed against referees.

Berman's story went up on the *Daily Post* website by 7:30 p.m. Within minutes, it caused a sensation.

Like an earthquake along the Whittier Fault, the rumble started in the Los Angeles area as other news outlets routinely trolling the web saw the story. Especially excited were the assignment editors of the six Los Angeles TV stations with local newscasts. TV—everywhere, not just in Los Angeles—gave inordinate coverage to crime, often to the near exclusion of everything else except weather, sports and stories about animals, which bizarrely were considered human interest. "If it bleeds, it leads," the mantra went. Yet the truth of the matter was that most after-the-fact crime stories on TV generated lousy after-the-fact video. For every one riveting clip like Rodney King being beaten to a pulp by police in view of a witness running a camcorder—the acquittal of his uniformed assailants triggered the deadly 1992 Los Angeles riots—10,000 boring clips got air time showing bored cops looking boringly official as they boringly walked behind boring yellow "do not cross" tape too far back from the actual crime scene to see anything.

It wasn't the fault of the TV crews, of course, that they weren't present when the crime took place, like they were when pre-empting regular programming to televise live from helicopters the many car chases in the Los Angeles area involving police and suspected felons. But the Diaz clip was the next best thing. Video of what might have led to the killing! In the perp's own words! And thanks to YouTube and the Internet, free!

The development didn't leave the stations with much time before their late newscasts. They all immediately dispatched trucks equipped with remote satellite transmission capabilities to Valley Mirage so reporters could do live "stand-up" reports, brief words cribbed from the *Daily Post* sandwiched around the damning video. Three went to the Valley Mirage police station where Diaz was still being held; three went to the soccer fields. The results were pretty much the same.

"In Valley Mirage tonight a referee of youth soccer is dead, a coach of youth soccer stands accused of his murder, and there is video." That was how Hal Fishman, the 75-year-old, plane-piloting, Ivy League-educated anchor of KTLA, the independent TV station that first broadcast that beating tape of Rodney King, began the 10:00 p.m.

newscast from his studio in Hollywood. "Let's go live to where it may have begun in Valley Mirage." The screen cut to a reporter waving his arm and pointing into the darkness toward what presumably were the soccer fields, then to the clip. Then back to the reporter, waving a copy of the search warrant affidavit and paraphrasing the part about the message on the screen and the location of the whistle.

Watching the TV in their apartment, Dora winced. "This is the first I've heard about a whistle," she said. "What's that all about?"

"Don't know," Hector said, frowning. "Did the lawyer say anything about it?"

"Not to me," Dora said. She had reached Bruce Horning, Diego's divorce lawyer. He didn't practice criminal law but referred her to Charles Gramm, who did. Gramm had gone to the police station jail and met with Diaz. Afterwards, Gramm called Dora and said there was a lot of work to be done, but first he had to be paid. Dora had written him a check.

Fishman, who possessed excellent news judgment, was just the vanguard of the media sensation. For on top of the universality of any crime, this touched upon soccer—the sport so many Americans loved to hate. And soccer parents—the population subset so many Americans loved to ridicule for their helicopter characteristics (they liked to hover about). And an upscale suburb—the paradise so many Americans loved to trash. Valley Mirage quickly became the center of the media universe. By the next morning the major networks—ABC, CBS, NBC, CNN—had crews in town. Even Fox News, much better at in-the-studio ranting than on-the-spot reporting, sent a truck.

Variations on a theme.

"The world's most popular sport, soccer, is viewed in the United States as a quirky, unpopular aberration...."

"The aggressive image of soccer parents, not great to start out with, is taking a blow...."

"Here is this idyllic Los Angeles suburb full of BMWs...."

Lost in much of the early coverage: Soccer actually was pretty popular in the United States, Diaz was no longer a soccer parent, and a lot of people in Valley Mirage drove lesser cars.

The next night, the image-conscious Valley Mirage City Council convened an emergency meeting behind closed doors—posting a notice on its website saying the purpose was to discuss litigation matters. That was a lie. The real purpose was to discuss hiring a public relations consultant to help spin the media coverage in a positive direction—less *Paradise Lost*, more *Ozzie and Harriet*. Or at least away from Valley Mirage, whose very name (bestowed decades earlier by a cynical developer) suggested an optical illusion not comporting with reality. The council members debated retaining Harold Myers Gunnell. He was a well-known, rather sardonic specialist in crisis publicity whose unofficial slogan, inspired by a Mark Twain saying, was, "Truth is a precious weapon; use it sparingly."

Gunnell's usual M.O. in these kinds of situations was to blame the victim, and he often did so by playing to the considerable vanity of journalists. Off the record and therefore leaving no visible fingerprints, he or his partners quietly whispered into the ears of a willing reporter where old public records could be found casting aspersions on the victim's character. It could be an ancient arrest record, a yellowing newspaper clip about something embarrassing, or a suggestion to see if the victim really had that claimed college degree.

Gunnell was thrilled when an obliging reporter took the evidence and trumpeted it as an exclusive based on solid, intrepid investigative reporting. Such a news presentation had far more credibility with the public, and therefore far more persuasive power, than if the story sourced the information directly to Gunnell. Unlike the journalists he fed, Gunnell had no trouble keeping his own ego in check. Indeed, such self-control had helped him buy a get-away home near Palm Springs.

In the end, the city council decided the best course of action was to do nothing. It was certainly cheaper than Gunnell's big fees. The hope expressed was that over time, things would blow over—the police, after all, considered the case solved with the arrest of Diaz—and at some indefinite point in the future a marketing campaign could be mounted touting Valley Mirage as a good place for children (if not for soccer referees).

The soccer league board, which also held an emergency meeting, had been thinking about canceling its scheduled matches the next Saturday as a sign of respect. But anxious to quickly project an image of a return to normalcy, city officials urged that the games take place. For the kids, they said. As a way of reinforcing the notion that the case was solved, they said. To help keep pumped-up property values pumped up, they thought but didn't say. The board acquiesced.

The media onslaught continued, especially the talking heads of the national electronic variety. Larry King and Anderson Cooper on CNN. Sean Hannity, Alan Colmes and Bill O'Reilly on Fox News. Keith Olbermann and Chris Matthews on MSNBC. Rush Limbaugh, Glenn Beck, Michael Savage and a flock of others on the radio. Show after show after show. Conservatives (many of whom never much liked soccer because of its foreign origins) said the situation showed the failure of permissive liberal thought. Liberals (many of whom liked the relatively nonviolent egalitarianism of soccer) said the situation showed the failure of conservative law and order. Caught in the middle, the just-the-facts interview shows equivocated ("Tonight, soccer violence: Too much?").

The "Whistle Up the Wazoo"—the actual headline in one New York City tabloid—became a symbol of run-amok soccer parents, who found themselves likened to Al Qaida, killer bees, and the Charles Manson gang. Al Capone got better press.

One beneficiary of all the media attention was YouTube. Within two days the clip of Diaz providing whistle storage advice to Hermannik had been viewed more than 1 million times.

Another result of all this notoriety was an intense amount of national media interest in the rather ordinary and even boring life of Diaz. His ex-wife, remarried but still living in Valley Mirage, had the grace to decline all interview requests. Furious at the disparagement of her father, Dora cursed at a broadcast network camera crew that cornered her leaving her father's apartment, which she was taking care of during his incarceration. Her beeped-out epithet aired nationally.

Diaz's neighbors were more accommodating, regaling reporters with accounts of other over-the-top screaming fits. Almost universally, the object of his anger was animals: stray dogs, slinking cats, burrowing squirrels, foraging raccoons, the odd possum. "He got really worked up whenever he saw a wandering creature not on a leash," Harry Cisneros, whose apartment faced Diaz's across a courtyard, told reporters. "I remember one time he yelled at a raccoon near the trash cans, 'Get out before I get you!' And boy, did that coon hightail it outta here."

Had the reporters asked a few more questions of Cisneros and other neighbors, they would have learned that Diaz never actually did anything to the animals that so bothered him. He just yelled at them. He didn't set traps, lay out poison, or shoot them, and he certainly didn't strangle them or stick things in them. Indeed, neighbors were never on the receiving end of Diaz's verbal abuse. (Granted, that may have been because they weren't soccer referees.) But the reporters didn't ask about that, either. So the result was more bad press for Diaz.

"Ref murder suspect threatened to kill wildlife." *So what?* Hector Rivera thought as he stared at the *Daily Post* headline over the second-day front-page story by Berman. *Diego is all talk, no action. Everyone knows that. He didn't do anything to animals. He never does anything. Why doesn't the story point that out?*

The next day, Berman had a better front-page story: "Ref killer suspect was investigated for gang murder as youth." The article recounted how, nearly 35 years earlier as a 15-year-old kid in the East Los Angeles barrio, Diaz had been questioned because he belonged to a gang thought to have killed a 16-year-old rival gang member named Marco Olivia. The case was never solved and no charges were brought. Berman, who clearly had gotten a tip, had managed to track down Mike Sibley, a retired Los Angeles County sheriff's deputy. Sibley had worked the case and was mad that someone had gotten away with murder— so mad that when he retired, he took along a copy of the file, which he happily shared with Berman. Reading him parts of the file, Sibley listed the gang members who had been questioned, a list that included Diaz. A typewritten one-page in the file said Diaz denied knowledge or involvement. "Seems scared," someone—probably Sibley—had scrawled in a margin. More luck for the young reporter.

Suggesting as it did a long history of violent tendencies, this Berman story, too, immediately got noticed after the paper put it online in advance of the morning print publication. That prompted another rush of stand-up TV reporters to Valley Mirage. On top of the field video, their reports all but convicted Diaz.

One reason for this added burst of media excitement was Southern California's long and even storied history of gang activity. What began nearly a century earlier as social clubs formed along ethnic lines had morphed first into defensive organizations—blacks, Latinos and even whites protecting their own—and then into offensive organizations grounded on crime. This being Southern California, much of the gang culture was celebrated in movies, television and even popular video games like Grand Theft Auto, which featured murderous gang members and cops cavorting around a West Coast city called Los Santos.

So that's what the gang stuff was, Rivera thought after reading Berman's story. He had heard vague hints from Diaz of some dark incident in his long-ago past. Rivera thought it likely that at most back then, Diaz was a follower, not a leader, just as, when it came to stray animals now, he was a talker and not a doer.

By contrast, the life of Hermannik drew far less intrusive media scrutiny. That was partly because of the solicitousness normally afforded victims of violent crime. It was also partly because he grew up somewhere else (in the Midwest, apparently), kept to himself and didn't seem to have a circle of friends who could talk about him. His line of work—real estate appraising—wasn't terribly sexy. And since he worked for others on a per-job basis, Hermannik didn't have a single employer who might have been able to say what a terrific guy he was. Jeff Berman had asked around, but couldn't find out much other than he always showed up on time. The best Berman could muster was a short story. The headline read, "Slain ref was reliable worker."

CHAPTER 5

DORA WAS OFF seeing her father in the Valley Mirage Police Department lock-up during the evening visiting period on Wednesday, two days after Hermannik's body was discovered. So Rivera returned from running his team's soccer practice to an empty apartment. A very empty apartment.

Then the doorbell rang. Followed by a sharp rap on the door. Then the doorbell again. Then another sharp rap, more insistent.

Rivera frowned. *Too obnoxious to be the door-to-door Mormon missionaries trying to save me with their talk. Or the door-to-door Jehovah Witnesses trying to save me with their booklets,* he thought. *Maybe more reporters looking for Dora.* But when he opened the door he encountered not friendly disciples in the immediate service of the Lord nor even friendly members in the immediate service of the Fourth Estate.

"Detective Captain Reynolds Wolfington, Valley Mirage Police," said the shorter of the two men before him, holding out something that looked like a police badge from a TV show. "This is Sergeant Mark Kelly," who nodded. "We'd like to have a word with you."

Rivera had never met Wolfington but knew all about him. All the Young Latino Males in Valley Mirage knew about Wolfie, as they called him behind his back. He was no Joe Friday, the polite, just-the-facts-ma'am cop in those old *Dragnet* TV shows that gave the Los Angeles Police Department a far better image than it deserved, particularly in light of numerous later cop scandals and unwarranted killings.

Wolfie liked to harass anyone he thought was a gangbanger. And he defined gangbanger as any Young Latino Male under the age of 25. Since most of the Young Latino Males in Valley Mirage were not gangbangers, this meant Wolfie performed a lot of unnecessary work.

On the other hand, it gave him a prestigious and even easy job heading a detective unit in a police department that really was too small to support one.

Rivera also knew from the paper that Wolfie was working the Hermannik murder. So he had a pretty good sense of what was coming.

"Sure," he said, standing in the doorway. "How can I help you?"

"May we come in?" Wolfie asked in a tone suggesting it was an order and not a request.

Given the attitude of the Valley Mirage Police Department toward Young Latino Males like him, Rivera thought it a better idea to remain in a place visible to witnesses like neighbors and passers-by. "Uh, the apartment is a real mess, Detective," he said, standing his ground in the doorway. "Happy to speak with you here."

Wolfie wasn't thrilled about that, but there was little he could do.

"Okay," he said. "You can tell me everything you know about the murder of Rick Hermannik."

"That's easy, Detective," Rivera said. "Nothin', 'cept what I hear on TV, read in the papers."

"Where were you?" Wolfie asked, a tad accusingly.

Rivera looked at him. "Where was I when?"

Wolfie's face went blank. "During the murder."

"Well, when was that?"

"'Bout 9:15 on Sunday night."

"Right here with Dora, my girlfriend. Watching TV together."

"Here with the murder suspect's daughter," Wolfie said sarcastically. "What a convenient alibi."

Rivera felt a rush, but—like in soccer—tried to keep his emotions under control. "Why do I need an alibi?" he asked. "Haven't done anything."

"He doesn't have much of an alibi," Wolfie said, trying to provoke a response. "Told us he got a phone call shortly after nine from a man whose name he said was Jerry. Diaz said 'Jerry' said he had found a check with Diaz's name and phone number. Was calling from a fast-food joint 'bout 15 miles away. Diaz said Jerry told him he would wait in the parking lot for him to come pick it up.

"Diaz said he got in his car, drove to the joint, but no Jerry. In fact, he said, the joint was closed. No one was there. So he drove home.

Says he was away maybe 40 minutes. Doesn't seem to have anyone able to verify his alibi."

Rivera pursed his lips. "That's what he told Dora," he said. Then Rivera recalled a TV episode he had seen. His face brightened. "Since when does someone get convicted just on the basis of an alibi he can't verify right away?" he asked. "How about scientific evidence linkin' him to the murder scene? Fingerprints, blood, DNA. Stuff like that."

Wolfie frowned. "Nothing scientific," he said. "Not yet, anyway."

Rivera pressed Wolfie. "You searched Diego's apartment," he said. "Find anything interesting?"

Wolfie frowned again. "More empty pizza boxes than a Pizza Hut," he said. "Nothing. He has a computer. But the only thing on it were e-mails 'bout scheduling soccer practices.

"But don't forget Hermannik left that note on his computer screen saying Diaz had just called and threatened violence."

Rivera cracked a half-smile. "It's not really like Diego to stew for a day, then sound off on the phone," he said. "I know he denied to Dora he's called Hermannik. That day or any other day. But suppose he did? Isn't it sort of a leap to assume he carried out what clearly wasn't a serious threat?

"I mean, half of Valley Mirage heard him say it on the field. Hell, I heard him say it. No way he meant it."

"Not such a leap," Wolfie quickly interjected. "Don't forget the tape on YouTube. To us, it's his ahead-of-time confession. And then there's the, uh, final position of the whistle."

"Hmm," Rivera murmured. "Look, I'm no cop. But if I understand your theory, Diego announced to the world he was going to assault Hermannik over a call he didn't like. Then proceeded to do it. Under circumstances guaranteein' his arrest for murder."

Wolfie stared at him, then laughed. "Not a bad closing summation, counselor," he said mockingly. "Clearly, what happened wasn't smart. But a lot of killers aren't smart. And we see crappy motives for murders all the time."

Rivera nodded. "I'm only 24," he said. "But I've been around soccer a long time. Never heard 'bout a ref being physically assaulted. At least 'round here."

Wolfie looked at Rivera. "It seems to me that you and Diaz have something in common other than Dora and soccer," he said slowly.

"What's that?"

"Gangs."

Boing! Rivera thought. Wolfie obviously had read the *Daily Post* story about Diaz's distant past. But it was now clear the detective had been poking around about Rivera, probably by reviewing secret files some police agencies had of names associated with gangs. *Wolfie is sure he's onto a squad of Latino hit men,* Rivera thought.

"Not sure what you mean, Detective," Rivera said, a little less confident than before. "I never belonged to a gang here. Nor in LA. They tried to recruit me when I was 11. But my mom moved out here from Pacoima to get me away. That life's long behind me."

"Do you ever really leave a gang?" Wolfie asked.

Rivera just looked at him. "Wasn't in one, so don't know. But what does Diego's maybe once being in a gang have to do with Rick Hermannik's death?"

"A little more prone to violence, maybe," Wolfie said.

Rivera shrugged. "Wouldn't know," he said. What Rivera thought but didn't say: *Wolfie should talk. The police are their own gang.*

Wolfie tried to catch Rivera unaware. "So you were watching TV here on Sunday night." he said. "What shows?"

Rivera sighed. "*Extreme Makeover,*" he said. "Followed by *America's Next Top Model.* Reruns. Hate 'em both. Dora loves 'em. But it was her night to choose. I was mostly reading."

Wolfie took this all in. "I gather you two aren't married?"

"No," Rivera said. "Not yet, anyway. Not rushing into things. But she sure needs support over this stuff with Diego. It's tearin' her up."

"Probably not as much as it could be tearing up Hermannik's friends and family," Wolfie said. "As I see it, Diaz had the means, motive and opportunity."

Means, motive and opportunity, Rivera repeated silently to himself. He had heard that phrase. It was some kind of legal test for guilt, that someone who met each of the criteria probably did the crime. Rivera knew the presence of all three factors greatly excited law enforcement.

"Don't know anything 'bout the opportunity angle," Rivera said. "But disagreein' with a referee's call doesn't strike me as much of a motive. As for means, the papers said Hermannik was strangled. I would think that takes a certain degree of finesse. Diego is an overweight klutz. He can lift trashcans, but he has trouble tying his shoelaces."

Wolfie looked at him. "Diaz may be a klutz," he said, "but you aren't. You're still a soccer player, I hear. In fact, I hear you're quite coordinated."

Rivera felt the heat rising on the back of his neck again. It was all he could do to not erupt. *That's what Wolfie wants me to do,* he thought. "You hear right," he said. "Sure, I'm athletic. But I harbored no grudge against Hermannik. And I was sittin' right here with Dora. So no means, no motive and no opportunity. Not a one."

"The killer maybe needed a lookout," Wolfie said.

"Now there's a great theory," Rivera said. "Diego killed a referee out of blind emotional rage. Yet waited a day and also arranged for a get-away driver."

"So who did it?" a miffed Wolfie persisted.

"Told you I have no idea," Rivera said.

"Okay," Wolfie said. "We have our suspect. Case closed."

"Hmm," Rivera murmured. "If the case is so closed, why are you even here right now?"

Now that question caught Wolfie by surprise. "Uh, uh," he stammered. "Just tryin' to tie down some loose ends."

"Aha," Rivera said. "So the case isn't closed."

Wolfie exploded.

"Lying to a cop is a crime, you know," the detective said, pointing his finger and moving his face closer to Rivera's. "So is obstruction of justice. Like tryin' to lead me in the wrong direction.

"And so's helping someone else murder someone."

Rivera moved back a half step. Intimidated as he was, it was his turn to explode. But in his usual quiet way.

"Detective," he said, "I'd say you've convicted Diego for being a loud soccer coach. That ain't no crime. If it was, a lot more people would be in jail. Especially parents in Valley Mirage."

Rivera's sudden assertiveness startled Wolfie; he wasn't used to that when cops in Valley Mirage faced a Young Latino Male. But this wasn't a car stop. And without a search or arrest warrant in his pocket—Wolfie didn't have a scintilla of evidence to support either— there wasn't much more he could do. Rivera, taking none of the offered bait, had called his bluff. Wolfie had been told that under soccer fire Rivera was a smart, cool player. *I can see that*, the detective thought.

"You're free to go," Wolfie said, forgetting that Rivera by then in the doorway of his own apartment. "But we're not finished with you."

"Fine, Detective," Rivera said. "You know where I live." He then gently closed the door and threw the deadbolt. Through the cheap wood used for the apartment house he heard the sidekick sergeant tell Wolfie as they walked away, "Boy, that was useless."

A little while later, Dora came home from visiting Diego. She was depressed. Hector told her about the visit from Wolfie. That made her even more depressed.

"Daddy's not doing well in the lock-up," Dora said. "And he may get moved to one of the larger county jails, which are a lot worse."

"Any chance he can get bail?" Hector asked.

"His lawyer, Charlie Gramm, said unlikely," Dora replied. "He was there when I was. Said it's tough to make bail on a murder charge."

"So what happens now?"

"Well," Dora said. "Charlie wants to push hard for a preliminary hearing. You know, where a judge has to decide if there's a decent case worth sendin' to a full trial with a jury. Charlie says that'll get the case away from the frickin' cops here who've made up their minds. Force prosecutors to take a close look.

"He's counting on the fact prosecutors are overworked from bigger crime and budget cutbacks. Said that faced with the need to prepare quickly for a preliminary hearing, they might agree to bail to get the hearing put off."

"Perry Mason won a lot of his TV cases during preliminary hearings," Hector said. "But by then he usually had a pretty good idea of who the real killer was.

"I guess it would help Diego if there was another suspect to suggest. Does he have any idea who did this?"

"No," Dora said. "He doesn't know much about the dead referee. Doesn't know any of his friends, either."

Dora looked at Hector. "Did Wolfie come here to interview you or me?" she asked.

"Don't know," Hector said. "Probably mainly me. I don't think the cops see too many father-daughter hit squads. But they know Diego and I are both involved in soccer.

"Talk to your mother about this?"

"Yeah," Dora said. "She doesn't think he had it in him, but she doesn't care. They've been divorced 13 years. She has a new life, new family. They run into each other sometimes at the store, the odd family function. Civil to each other. That's 'bout it."

Hector said he'd call Diego's lawyer to tell him about the encounter with Wolfie.

But first he had to help his players. It was Friday night. Thanks to the business-as-normal decision of the local soccer powers-that-be, game time was barely a dozen hours away.

On Saturday morning, Rivera drove to the soccer fields a little earlier than he had to. *Probably be good to hear the buzz about Hermannik and Diego*, he thought. But he was not prepared for what awaited him.

The streets adjoining the fields were lined with rows of TV station news trucks present to cover the day's big story: Soccer After Death. Citing the potential for disruption, league officials had banned camera crews from the actual fields. But they simply remained on the public sidewalk buttonholing those entering and exiting. Parents, coaches, even players.

They were asked what they thought about the murder of Hermannik, the arrest of Diaz and the fact matches were taking place less than a week after the killing. Most of the soccer community members confronted had the good sense simply to decline comment and continue on their way.

But TV cameras are an irresistible lure to some, especially in Southern California's personality-driven economy. And if enough cameras are stuck in front of enough people, some very silly things get said. On this Saturday in September 2006, Valley Mirage was no different.

"Well, I don't understand the offside rule, so I can see why the coach got mad," opined parent Penny Richter, combining soccer ignorance with a suggestion of contributory culpability on the part of Hermannik.

"It was terrible, but nobody likes referees," declared Mark Mills, a rock musician on the way to coach his 11-year-old daughter's team.

"Referee whistles are too loud!" cute-as-a-button Christine Walsh, age 10, said, clasping her hands over her ears Shirley Temple-style as her approving parents watched.

Rivera managed to slip onto the fields without catching the attention of the cameras, not all that surprising since he was unknown to the media, at most a sideshow in this soccer saga. But as he crossed the fields, Rivera became immediately aware he was being watched. By huddles of parents pointing at him not so discreetly. By fellow coaches looking curiously in his direction. Of course, by referees murmuring about their own fates.

And by Manny Whitney, the mortician league commissioner, who had been watching for him. Whitney quickly walked over.

"Hello, Hector," he said in his best comfort-the-bereaved manner.

"Hi, Manny," Rivera replied, shaking hands. Gesturing toward all the TV trucks, he said, "Quite a scene, eh?"

"Indeed," Whitney said. "There's something I have to talk to you about."

Rivera sensed trouble. "Okay," he said. "What?"

"Look, Hector, we all know you," Whitney said. "We know you're a fine fellow and a fine coach. We don't think you had anything to do with what Diego Diaz did...."

"What he's accused of doing," Rivera interjected, almost angrily.

"Yes, accused of doing," Whitney said, barely missing a beat. "Diego is certainly entitled under the law to a presumption of innocence. Of course, since he's in jail, he can't coach. So his assistant coach is taking over the team.

"Um, um"—uncharacteristically, Whitney was almost at a loss for words—"but your relationship with his daughter is well known. There are some people here who would be very uncomfortable for the time being with your continued presence on the fields."

"What do you mean?" Rivera asked. "I'm not accused of anything."

"Indeed you're not," Whitney said. "But you're being here will be, ah, ah"—Whitney again was fishing for words—"disruptive. It will get people's minds off the game, which is why they should be here.

"The league's executive committee had a meeting. You have an assistant coach. We decided it would be best for you to turn over the team to your assistant for the rest of the season."

"I'm being suspended for doing nothing?" an astonished Rivera asked.

"Not suspended, really," Whitney said. "More like placed on temporary leave."

Rivera would have none of it. "Where does it say in the Laws of the Game that someone can be sent off 'cause a friend's father was accused of a bad crime?"

"It doesn't," Whitney agreed. "But we always have the inherent power to act 'for the good of the game.' An old principle of soccer."

"How is this for the good of the game?" Rivera demanded. "People are going to think the league thinks I had something to do with Hermannik's murder."

"Your absence will hardly be noticed," Whitney said. "We're not announcin' this or actin' like it's a big deal."

"Yeah," Rivera said. "Like all those private"—raising his arms, he used two fingers of each hand to make imaginary quote marks in the air—"admonitions you give to coaches that everyone finds out about in two minutes."

"It's hard to keep some things confidential," Whitney allowed. "Everyone knows everyone in this soccer community."

Rivera played a hunch. "Have you been in touch with Wolfie— ah, Detective Wolfington?" he asked.

"Um, yes," Whitney said. "He came to see me. Part of the investigation."

"Is he behind my send-off?"

"It's not a send-off," Whitney said. "But no. In fact, Detective Wolfington, ah, even seemed a bit worried that you might become the victim of violence yourself."

"Ha," Rivera said. "He expressed concern for the well-being of a Latino male like me? Now that's news. He probably told you I might be done in right here on the fields by gangbangers to silence me. Players could get caught in the middle."

"Um, he did indicate that gangs do not conform to societal norms."

"And what evidence did he offer of any gang involvement at all in Hermannik's death?"

"None, now that I think about it. But of course he doesn't have to tell me anything."

"Well, Detective Wolfington certainly gave me no warnin' my life's in jeopardy," Rivera said sarcastically. "So who does he think is this big threat to my personal well-bein'? The Hermannik clan? An avenging lynch mob of overweight referees?"

"I, uh, may be reading more into what he said than what he said," Whitney said.

"Okay," Rivera said. "So whose idea was it to bounce me? Yours?"

"Uh, the executive committee acts as a whole," Whitney said. "The decision was made collectively."

He looked at his watch. "You can coach today," he said. "But that's it for the season."

"This isn't fair," Rivera said, shaking his head. "Not fair at all."

"I'm sorry," Whitney said. "But that's the decision the committee made."

The walkie-talkie hanging from his belt blared. Whitney grabbed it, listened, then said into the gizmo, "I'll be right over."

He looked at Rivera. "Excuse me," he said. "I have to go deal with another problem." Off went Whitney to mediate another flare-up of that age-old dispute between referees and coaches over the important issue of preferred parking spots.

Rivera stood on the field feeling sorry for himself. *They're taking soccer away from me*, he thought. *That's all I really care about!*

Then he realized he also cared about his mother, Dora, and even Diego. *At least I'm not in jail like Diego*, he thought. Then it dawned on him that not having to run a soccer team would give him some free time to help Diego—although Rivera wasn't sure exactly what kind of help he had to offer.

In the middle of these deep thoughts, Rivera felt a tug on his shirt. "Hey, coach," said Andy Newcomb, his star striker and the unofficial captain, "time for warm up."

Rivera looked at his watch. "Okay," he said. "Get everyone over here to run a lap around the fields."

The rest of the morning passed in a blur for Rivera. Fortunately, the Artful Dodgers were well trained, and their opponents—the racy-named Deep Threat—were not. Final score: Dodgers 5, Threat 1. Rivera didn't have the heart to tell the team this could be his last game for a while. He decided he'd send an e-mail later to his players' parents and let them break the news to their kids.

Rivera drove back to the apartment. Dora wasn't there. *Probably visiting Diego again*, he thought. Being alone was good. It gave Rivera some quiet time to think. One of the first things he thought about was his ban from soccer. Rivera remembered Whitney had said he was suspended by the league's executive committee. Rivera wasn't sure exactly what that was. He turned on his computer, got on the league's website, and started poking around. Pretty soon he found a set of the league's bylaws, which governed how things operated off the field. The executive committee, he read, was a panel of the full board that made decisions that needed making between meetings of the full board.

Rivera started searching for any material in the bylaws concerning suspensions, forced leaves, discipline or whatever Whitney said had been declared. Going through a legalistic document was not exactly Rivera's forte. But reading slowly with his lips, he persevered, and on page 14 found the following language:

9.4 RIGHT OF APPEAL

A person aggrieved by any decision of a league official or of any committee of the board, including but not limited to decisions concerning disciplinary matters, shall have the right of appeal to the full board. Notice of such appeal shall be made in writing to the Commissioner. If time is of the essence and the appellant so requests, the board shall hear the appeal within seven days; otherwise, the board shall hear the appeal within a reasonable period. The person bringing the appeal shall have the right to attend the hearing and, in support of the appeal, to present evidence and make arguments. The right of appeal does not apply to routine coaching decisions. It is also limited by the Laws of the Game and does not extend to the referee's sole authority under Law 5 to determine facts connected with play in any match he or she officiated. The decision of the board shall be final.

Bingo! Rivera thought. *At least I think bingo. All the phrases starting with "if," all the sentences amendin' or limitin' previous sentences are pretty confusin'. But if I'm reading this right, I can force the full board to take a look at my case.*

Rivera went over the paragraph again, mentally checking off its various points. *Yes, I'm certainly a person affected by the ban. No, I'm not appealing a referee's field ruling. Yes,* Whitney said it *was* a board committee decision. *No, this isn't a coaching action. Yes, I'm running out of time.*

Then Rivera froze. *No! In writing! It says the appeal has to be in writing!*

Like a huge number of America's recently minted high school graduates, Rivera was a poor writer. Facing a David Beckham penalty kick as a goalkeeper was far more inviting. Indeed, the prospect of having to write up appeal grounds made Rivera think of abandoning his plans.

But he took another look at the appeals clause. He realized the only thing that had to be in writing was the notice of the appeal, not the appeal itself. And another section of the bylaws said the definition of "writing" included words sent by electronic means other than voice. *Okay,* Rivera thought. *I probably shouldn't send this via text messaging. But an e-mail should do.*

So Rivera slowly typed out his message. He found Whitney's e-mail address on the league's website, typed that in, and hit the send button. His text was brief.

> Commissioner Whitney:
>
> Pursuant to section 9.4 of the Valley Mirage Soccer League bylaws, I appeal to the Board the decision of the Executive Committee to relieve me of my coaching duties for the rest of the season. The season is underway, so time is of the essence. I request my appeal be heard within the seven-day period specified in the bylaws.
>
> —Hector Rivera

Two minutes later, Rivera's cell phone rang. Whitney. He was still at the fields but had picked up the e-mail on his Blackberry, which was always with him in case his bereavement services were needed.

"What's this all about?" he asked in a tone not quite as comforting as his normal demeanor.

"Uh, the league rules say I have the right to appeal somethin' like this and have a hearing if I so request," Rivera replied. "So I requested."

"You have to put your appeal in writing," Whitney said.

"I did," Rivera said. "Under the league rules an e-mail is writing. Section 13 Point 2."

"I see," Whitney said. "You also have to write out your grounds."

"Ah, that's, ah, that's not what the league rules say. The only thing that has to be in writing at this point is my notice of appeal. You got that. The rules say I can present whatever evidence I have at a hearing and make my arguments then. I can read you the section 'bout this if you want."

"Hmm. Didn't know you were a lawyer."

"Nope, not me," Rivera laughed. "All I did was look at the rules."

"Okay," Whitney said. "I'll put this on the agenda of our next board meeting in three weeks."

"Excuse me," said Rivera. "Rules say the board has to hear my appeal within seven days of my appeal if time is of the essence. Which it certainly is with the season running. That means seven days from today."

"Seven business days," Whitney said, stalling for a little time.

"Uh, the rules don't say anything about counting by business days," Rivera said. "It just says seven days. And the rules even use the word 'shall.' As in, 'The board shall hear the appeal within seven days.'

"To my mind, 'shall' means something has to be done."

"I'm not sure a board meeting can be scheduled that quickly," Whitney said.

"Okay," Rivera said. "But you gotta understand. This's a matter of urgency. My team was expectin' me being the coach for the whole season. Don't claim to be the world's greatest coach. But I think the players think I do okay. So they're hurt by every practice, every game I miss. And I'm hurt, too. 'Cause I want to be involved.

"Look, you know I think it's unfair for the Executive Committee to suspend me on the basis of Diego. I'm just askin' for the right to plead my case to the full board.

"You expect me to play by the rules. I expect the league to play by the rules."

Whitney realized he had no grounds. "Okay," he said. "Let me see if I can schedule a meeting for next Thursday night. That's five days from now. Within your seven-day deadline. I'll let you know once it's firmed up."

"Thank you," Rivera said. "Appreciate your acting on this."

"Got to go now," Whitney said. "Another dispute over parking."

Rivera started to look for the list of people on the full board—the tribunal that would determine his soccer fate, at least for the short term. Then Dora walked in, sniffling and her eyes bloodshot red. She had been crying the entire trip back from seeing her dad again in jail.

Hector and Dora hugged.

"Look, I know this is nothing compared to what Diego is facing," Hector said, "but I was banned today from coaching my soccer team for the rest of the season. I was told my presence would upset people because of my connection through you to Diego."

Hector didn't expect any sympathy from Dora; he just wanted her to know. But she surprised him.

"Those bastards!" she spat. "You're too good for them. But you shouldn't take this lyin' down."

"Well, I'm not," Hector said. "It was a decision by the commissioner and a few of his cronies. I've appealed it to the full soccer league board. There'll be a hearing."

"Good," Dora spat again.

"The only sunshine is that I'll have a little more time for Diego," Hector said. "Except that I don't know what I can do for him. It's not like I'm a trained investigator or anything."

Dora looked at him. "I've been tellin' you for years you can do anything you put your mind to," she said. "You have more energy than anyone I know. You're a lot smarter than you think, too."

"I'm not smart enough to think like a killer," Hector said.

"That's only because you've been headin' soccer balls for too long," Dora said, laughing. Then she got serious. "I've watched you play. You're good. You chase every ball. Chase every pass. Watch everything. Hope someone on the other team will screw up. Mispass. Miskick. Stumble. Not be alert. Then you swoop in for the kill.

"So treat this like you treat soccer."

Given his life history, that wasn't such bad advice.

Like many of the Latino kids growing up in Los Angeles, Hector had gotten hooked on soccer at a young age, playing in side streets, vacant lots and, when they were available, parks. He was quicker than most of his peers—physically and mentally—and at an early age developed better instincts about the game, such as where the ball was likely to go or how to outfox opposing players. This helped compensate for the fact that many other players were bigger and stronger. Rivera learned early on that an extra step's advantage often made all the difference.

Most of the soccer he played was pick-up; opportunities were limited in the inner city for play in organized leagues where he might get the benefit of some real coaching. (It also didn't help that he had started hanging around the gang scene.)

To partly compensate for the lack of coaching, his mother took him to public library branches around Pacoima where they checked out its few books on soccer. Since hardly any of the works were in Spanish, one side benefit was that Hector got a lot better in English, and even began to enjoy reading books—especially if they were about soccer.

After the move from Pacoima, Hector quickly became a solid soccer player, first in the age-classified divisions of the Valley Mirage Soccer League, then in high school, where he made the varsity team as a sophomore. Hector generally played midfield, where his ability to anticipate play and be in the right place at the right time benefited both offense and defense.

The upshot was that Hector slid through his teenage years without much of a gang imprimatur. The biggest factors facing Hector in Valley Mirage were culture and money. Latinos were a decided minority in Valley Mirage. So were poor people. Elvira and Hector belonged to both groups. As such, they were tolerated—somebody, after all, had to take the bad jobs—but not especially embraced. As he got farther into high school, Hector took part-time jobs when he could find them— a worker in a fast-food restaurant, a counter worker at a copy shop, and his favorite job, working one summer in Valley Mirage's recreation program teaching soccer. But like so many people of his age and era, he got hooked on computers and their potential. Valley Mirage High School had a vocational-technical program. Although he wasn't a part of it, Hector took as many tech and electronics courses as he could work in. He even got a job one summer in a computer repair shop.

Like so many of the affluent suburbs around Los Angeles, Valley Mirage High School was really two schools. One consisted of the 25% or so of the student body clearly headed to four-year colleges. (That percent would be a lot higher except that many of the wealthier families in Valley Mirage sent their children to fancy private high schools in Los Angeles or even to boarding schools, despite studies showing students doing well in public high schools had no worse a chance of making it into the Ivies.) A disproportionately large amount of school resources went toward providing this group—which was overwhelmingly non-Latino white—with a full range of Advanced Placement courses of relatively small class sizes, in hopes of getting a few students into the prestigious schools. It made the local school board members feel good and gave them something to talk about when they campaigned for reelection.

The other school-within-a-school was for everyone else, which included virtually all the Latinos. That embraced a wide range: students with a shot at getting into one of the eight University of California campuses (even if it was the newest one in cow-country Merced), students who would be easy admits into the 23-college California State University system, students who would enter one of the two-year community colleges, which had an open admissions policy, and finally students who just would be lucky to get out of high school with a diploma. The everyone-else group had swelling class sizes often taught by uninspiring, burned-out teachers whose union had succeeded in getting laws and contracts making it nearly impossible to fire someone for anything short of a felony. And even then, only if there was video proof with sound.

Hector sort of fell into the Cal State tranche. Thanks in no small part to those soccer books at an early age, he had picked up the habit of reading and was able to learn from books. Rivera wasn't much of a writer, but high schools, even good ones like Valley Mirage, no longer stressed that—nor tested much for it. Rivera got through high school writing not a single paper longer than seven pages. Yet he graduated easily in the top third of the class.

One problem with playing soccer in high school is that there wasn't very much scholarship money available for college. It wasn't like football or basketball, or even, against all odds, baseball. Hector wasn't even sure he wanted to go to college; none of his relatives had. But the Cal State system was cheap enough, and Hector got a state low-income grant, so he was able to afford to attend—so long as he lived at home.

Which is why things started getting complicated. In his junior year of high school he had met Dora. Although a grade behind him, they were in a biology class together. One day the teacher started on that birds and bees stuff. There was a lot of giggling and even red faces. Hector, who had already noticed Dora—she had a dancer's figure, slim and tawny—stole a glance her way. She wasn't flustered in the slightest. One cool chick, he thought. Though shy, he summoned up the courage a few days later to ask her out, and they had been together ever since.

Unlike Hector, Dora had grown up since birth in Valley Mirage. But there was still a difficult family story. Her parents, Diego and Felisa, had moved to Valley Mirage in 1979. Diego's steady job driving a garbage collection truck allowed him to pull together the scratch for a down payment on one of the small, two-bedroom bungalows built during World War II to house those defense workers. It was in the same part of town that Hector and Elvira later settled. In fact, the street also had an Indian name: Tukupar Avenue, the Tongva tribe word for sky, although a lot of the locals in Valley Mirage thought the name was of Pacific Rim origin.

In 1993 when Dora was 10, Diego and Felisa got divorced, for much the same conduct that Diego displayed on the soccer field toward referees, a hot temper and the tendency to say whatever popped into his mouth regardless of the consequences. Diego wasn't violently just verbally abusive. Felisa got the house, which, thanks to the early stages of the California real estate boom, had become an object of value. But Diego, wanting to remain in Dora's life, rented a small apartment down the street.

All things considered, he succeeded, coaching Dora's soccer teams and trying to play the role of the doting dad. Felisa remarried and had two more children; Diego decided one wife and one daughter were enough.

Dora had no aspirations for college, but she had taken various secretarial and bookkeeping courses at Valley Mirage High School. The curriculum wasn't very challenging, but it usually assured one an immediate job at something higher than the minimum wage. Upon graduation she took a job in the front office of a small manufacturing company in nearby Rancho Viva La Vida. Dora lived at home with her remarried mother, her stepfather and her half-siblings. But that was considerably crimping her social life with Hector, who also was still living in the one-bedroom apartment with Elvira. So in 2002 they decided to get their own apartment—also in the older part of Valley Mirage—and move in together. A decade or two earlier that would have been shocking, but times had changed. Elvira soon moved back to Pacoima, where rents were still cheaper.

Even though she was working full time, Dora expected Hector to pay half the rent. As long as he was a full-time student with no family support, Hector couldn't do that. But despite pulling solid Bs, he was getting fed up with college. He was studying stuff he pretty much learned in high school. Hector didn't think he was really into serious learning and didn't know what he wanted to do in life. So after his sophomore year, he dropped out of Cal State and soon took the job at WeFixThingsRightNow. Although they both were under some vague family pressures to get married, neither Hector nor Dora was so inclined at that point. They decided to take their time and see what developed.

CHAPTER 6

LIKE A LOT of suburban dailies, the *Valley Mirage Daily Post* wasn't much of a newspaper. It was owned by one of those national chains that awarded a big cash bonus to its chief executive every time a round of employee layoffs took place among its far-flung properties. This did not have the best effect on morale of the remaining workers.

Even as its classified ad revenue—long wildly overpriced because publishers stupidly thought they had a monopoly that would never go away—was being siphoned off by an upstart Internet free-ad site called Craigslist, the *Daily Post* stayed in business mainly for one reason. It published more stuff about Valley Mirage and its surroundings than anywhere else. If you lived or worked there and wanted to know what was going on, you had to read the paper. Sure, most of its content were paid display ads and press releases by advertisers who viewed publication of their lame submissions as part of the deal for paid ads. At one point the paper had adopted the official slogan "It's news to us" until someone pointed out that also had the meaning of total ignorance.

Still, real news was printed. And when something of true significance took place—like, say, the arrest of a local soccer coach accused of killing a local soccer referee—the paper would muster its meager resources to blanket the big story.

That's why reporter Jeff Berman was on the case. The Hermannik killing had been quite a ride for him, a year out of J-school on his first job and hoping to move on as soon as possible to a big-time paper. Having broken scoops about the YouTube video and Diaz's vague gang background, Berman found himself being interviewed on national and even international TV (a crew had showed up from soccer-mad Brazil). He enjoyed the attention—who knows, it might lead to that better job.

His editors pressed him for any copy remotely connected to the crime. So Berman decided to write a long story about the history of soccer and how it eventually grew in America. *It will look good as a feature clip when I'm job-hunting,* he thought to himself. Berman searched for elements that might somehow tie into the crime and venue at hand.

His story appeared on Sunday morning, the day after Rivera's suspension as a coach (about which at that point Berman and the rest of the world knew nothing). The headline—"How Soccer Explains Valley Mirage"—was inspired to a certain degree by a two-year-old book he came across called *How Soccer Explains The World,* by journalist Franklin Foer. Berman was an extremely quick study. As it turned out, he found plenty of material, although Berman took every opportunity to "localize" the copy, as editors old enough to be his grandparents instructed. Unusual in its length, the story was spread over three pages.

In an eerie way, Berman wrote, the killing of Hermannik by an accused coach in Valley Mirage reflected a historically resonant theme of soccer. Even as the sport evolved over time and eventually spread itself upon the fruited plain of America, violence, criminality, deception and rebellion against authority—and sometimes by authority— often were not that far away.

Berman went way back. Way back. Who started the sport? He basically dissed the English. Like so many things on this planet, he wrote, the Chinese probably were first.

There actually are records suggesting a game involving kicking a ball was played in China around 300 BC, and maybe a lot, lot earlier. Its name was *tsu-chu.* No, not like our Metrolink trains. *Tsu* was Chinese for "kicking with one's foot," while *chu* meant "a ball full of animal skin." In other words, kickball.

Initially, it might have been played only one day a year, on the emperor's birthday. But it clearly persisted. A silk net supposedly was stretched between two 30-foot-high bamboo poles. The object of *tsu-chu* was to boot the ball through a tiny hole in the net. Hands were not supposed to be used.

The development of *tsu-chu* had nothing to do with creating family recreational opportunities so that, like here in Valley Mirage, peasant parents could gather on the sidelines and watch their offspring *tsu* while sipping, say, green tea instead of Starbucks. The idea was to keep young male soldiers in good physical shape so they could successfully fight the regular wars—killing people—that in those days were the principal form of government economic development and revenue rather than today's sales, income and property taxes.

Thanks to a Chinese poet named Li Yu who lived about 400 years later—that would be about 100 AD—there's even a written account of a Chinese football game. It went like this:

A round ball and a square goal
Suggest the shape of the Yin and the Yang.
The ball is like the full moon,
And the two teams stand opposed;
Captains are appointed and take their place.
In the game make no allowance for relationship
And let there be no partiality.
Determination and coolness are essential
And there must not be the slightest irritation for failure,
Such is the game. Let its principles apply to life.

Sound familiar in Valley Mirage?

Berman then started a wild journey around the world.

Now, a case of first football also can be made for the natives of Mexico's far-closer-to-here Yucatan Peninsula and thereabouts. About the same time as the Chinese, they were playing some kind of game with a ball combining aspects from what would become soccer, basketball and American-style football. It helped a lot that they knew how to use raw latex milked from plants to make balls that bounced. Some scholars believe that—gasp—even kids played.

There's also an ancient tomb in Egypt with a drawing of a man juggling a ball maybe six inches across—only a little smaller than the standard size for today's eight-year-old players who play behind Valley Mirage Elementary School. Since the Egyptian was the only one in the picture and there's no indication he was involved in a team sport, it wouldn't go down as the world's first documented example of a handball foul.

Meanwhile, the Greeks developed something they called episkros, which seems like a combination of soccer and handball. It's unclear whether episkros was an event in the big national sporting competition they had been running for a couple centuries called the Olympics. What is clear is that an Athens museum has a sculpture from that era of a man kicking the ball with his leg. The man is buck naked, not even wearing shoes.

What also is clear is that the Greek writer Antiphanes, who was known as a humorist, left behind an account of an episkros match astonishingly similar to the parental sidelines chatter that would resonate across Valley Mirage soccer fields several millenniums later:

"Pass out. Throw a long one. Past him. Down. Up. A short one. Pass it back. Get back."

But back along the Pacific Rim, the Japanese developed their own version of *tsu-chu*. It was called *kemari*. Players stood in a circle and passed the ball to one another without letting it touch the ground. A similar game called *sepak raga* was all the rage in the islands that later became Malaysia.

Meanwhile, back in Mexico, the Mayans, Aztecs and Zapotecs had developed their batting-about-a-round-ball game into a sport called *tlachtli*. Players would hit the ball with their bodies with the idea of eventually propelling it through a small stone ring. That rubber coating from the latex sure made things easier.

Besides two teams and a ball, *tlachtli* foreshadowed two other big common elements with the modern game we attend or watch on TV. The first was extremely low-scoring matches. So low, a player who made a goal was given jewelry; it was that big a deal. The second: *Tlachtli* was taken very seriously. To some zealots now, soccer is akin to religion. No fooling back then, especially for the Aztecs. Priests oversaw the matches, laid out fields—and sometimes presided over the altar sacrifice of losing-team members. Call it Darwin's survival of the fittest centuries before Darwin.

Not to be outdone by their rival Greeks but nevertheless waiting centuries, the Romans stole the concept of *episkros* and called it *harpastum*. A ball was passed among teammates while opponents tried for interceptions or tackles. Kicking didn't seem to have been an element, making *harpastum* more like rugby. There weren't a lot of rules, either, which made it violent like rugby.

Harpastum was played in the streets, which had one big plus—easy proximity—and one big negative—easy proximity. The famous lawyer Cicero wrote about one court case in which a ball accidentally kicked into a barber shop killed a customer getting a shave.

Berman then brought it to the very shores of the Atlantic Ocean.

The forces most responsible for introducing such activities to England weren't Anglo or even Saxon. Being an impressionable place, England was not immune to foreign influences, especially when those influences appeared suddenly in boats on the horizon of the North Sea armed to the hilt and commencing serious real estate annexation and wealth redistribution. It's possible that *harpastum*, or something like it, arrived when the Romans showed up in this rude fashion in 43 AD.

In the East Midlands town of Derby, the claim was made that in the year 217 AD, the locals beat a squad of Roman soldiers in something approximating a game of football. It's a nice patriotic story, based on what historians call "oral tradition." That means everyone wants to believe it except there isn't a single shred of written evidence it's true.

Still, it's a better yarn to wait a millennium and lay the inspiration at the feet of Denmark. The Baltic Sea nation didn't have much of a ball-sport reputation but it did have the father and son team of Sweyn Forkbeard and the grandly named Canute the Great. *Pere*, then *fils*, were Viking kings of Denmark—and Norway—and England. This last title they assumed around 1013 as the result of their yearly invasions across the North Sea to shore up finances back home. As one might imagine, the Brits didn't take kindly to this domination and as the century wore on the Danish influence wore out.

Here's the fun football angle. English legend holds that after Danish authority ended, a worker in an old burial ground in Cheshire accidentally dug up the skull of a fallen foreign warrior. Out of anger he started kicking it. Then his friends started kicking it. Back and forth. Get the idea?

It was not exactly the royal soliloquy in the future *Hamlet*, which, as it happened, also had a heavy Danish theme. Nor is there any real documentation supporting this tale—that old oral tradition again. But something clearly was brewing, and not just tea (which wouldn't appear in England for another 500 years). For it is an absolute fact that a century later, in 1175, a London monk named William Fitzstephen wrote about a simple sport of the local townsfolk. It went by the name *ludus pilae*—a game of ball. *Ludus pilae* was played on the afternoon of Shrove Tuesday, the hard-partying last day before Lent, the 40-day Christian period of fasting, self-denial and reflection.

This is what Fitzstephen wrote:

"All the youth of the city go to a flat patch of ground just outside the city for the famous game of ball. The students of every faculty have their own ball, and those who are engaged in the various trades of the city also have their own ball. The older men—the fathers and the men of substance—come on horseback to watch the competitions of the younger men. In their own way the older men participate in the sporting activities of their juniors. They appear to get excited at witnessing such vigorous exercise and by taking part in the pleasures of unrestrained youth."

He was writing about soccer parents just like what we have in Valley Mirage!

Time for Berman to start working in soccer-related violence— like Valley Mirage, not all of it happening on the field of play.

Ludas pilae took on a ludicrous life, not the least of which was due to a tendency of players to play without removing all their weapons. During a friendly football match in 1280, in the small village of Ulgham near the North Sea in Northumberland, a player known as Henry, son of William de Ellington, accidentally bumped up against his buddy, David le Keu. Unfortunately, Henry also accidentally bumped into the unsheathed knife that le Keu had strapped to his side. Henry died.

It happened again four decades later at the village of Shouldham in Norfolk. The knife-wearer was William de Spalding, a Catholic priest. This time the case went all the way up to Pope John XXII, who declared de Spalding not guilty.

There were more acts of sports violence. Playing football on the streets of Oxford in 1303, one Adam of Salisbury, a student, was killed by a gang of rival Irish students.

The projectile used as the ball could be a pig bladder, an animal skin stuffed with grass, an assorted fruit—or the odd skull. In one particularly ghastly episode, two brothers in the North West English town of Vale Royal murdered a servant in 1321, then used his head as a football. Such use of a human head wasn't common, although it was said the noggin of the tyrant Oliver Cromwell—in life a football enthusiast himself—performed that same function after being dug up in 1661.

By most accounts English football in these earlier years was little more than an organized riot, a mob sport pitting village against village, played with miles-long roads as fields. "Undignified and worthless than any other kind of game, rarely ending but with some loss, accident or disadvantage to the players themselves," one disapproving scribe put it. "Beastlike fury and extreme violence deserving only to be put in perpetual silence," wrote another.

In other words, violence was a tremendous part of its appeal.

Not surprisingly, British monarchs started signing edict after edict outlawing the game.

The first in 1314 was by the hapless King Edward II, who thundered, "For as much as there is great noise in the city caused by hustling over large balls ... from which many evils might arise, which God forbid, we command and forbid on behalf of the King, on pain of imprisonment, such game to be used in the city in the future." Unfortunately, the monarch was gruesomely murdered 13 years later in a plot hatched by his wife. In a further indignity of eternal duration, he was buried in Gloucester Cathedral (nearly seven centuries later the set of Hogwarts School in the four *Harry Potter* movies shown so far in Valley Mirage) very near a wood carving of two men playing soccer—the very sport he sought to ban. Some consider the engraving the world's oldest illustration of the sport.

In 1349, Edward II's far more competent son, Edward III, denounced "skittles, quoits, fives, football or other foolish games which are no use." He favored archery, which had a clear military purpose. This is believed to be the first known written use of the dreaded word "football" (as opposed to Fitzstephen's mention two centuries earlier of mere "ball.") The term was used to distinguish the game played by the masses from that other ball game, polo, played on expensive horses by people with a whole lot more money, and therefore, big proponents of the *status quo*.

In 1389, King Richard II banned football.
In 1410, King Henry IV banned football.
In 1447, King Henry VI banned football.

In 1477, King Edward IV banned football, admirably displaying a little more candor about the reason: "Every strong and able-bodied person shall practice with the bow for the reason that the national defense depends upon such bowmen." It was that money thing again.

In 1496, King Henry VII banned football.
In the 1500s, King Henry VIII banned football.

Why, you might ask, did all these monarchs have to prohibit something that already was prohibited, especially with the Tower of London so handy? Obviously, the message from above was not reaching the working class. The little people were just having too much fun.

These admonitions did tend to generate a certain amount of legal action. During the reign of Henry VIII, a man was sent to the Tower for playing football on Sunday in a churchyard. Two men were fined in Chester, near Wales, for playing football in a church cemetery during services. An Essex man was charged with playing on Easter Monday. Also in Essex, in what amounts to a conspiracy case, 10 others were charged with Sunday playing of football "whereon grew bloodshed." There were also prosecutions for staging football banquets and even—look out, Valley Mirage soccer parents—for just watching matches.

And in the distant London suburb of Brickhill, George Taylor was convicted and jailed in 1535 for being stupid enough to say within someone's earshot, "I set not by the King's crown, and, if I had it here, I would play at football with it."

Berman interjected the weekend element, followed by a change of official attitudes:

Religious authorities weighed in with their stern disapproval. There were two main reasons for this. One was competition. Today, youth soccer is played in Valley

Mirage mainly on Saturdays. But centuries ago, that was a work day. The only day off a lot of people had to play football was Sunday—when they were supposed to be in church for lengthy services that often occupied most of the daylight hours. It is similar to the rule here in nearby Pasadena that the Tournament of Roses Parade and the Rose Bowl are delayed a day if January 1 falls on a Sunday. The other reason was the sometimes frightful carnage that ensued.

Eventually, in England the mood began to change. One enlightened headmaster, Richard Mulcaster of Merchant Taylors' School, wrote that football, properly controlled, with trainers and even officials, would be a good thing. In 1580 tony Cambridge University relented and said students could scrimmage one another so long as they didn't play other schools (a limitation that disappeared within a generation).

History's greatest playwright soon took note. "Am I so round with you as you with me, that like a football you do spurn me thus?" asked a character in Shakespeare's 1592 *Comedy of Errors.* "You spurn me hence, and he will spurn me hither. If I last in this service you must case me in leather." Sixteen years later in *King Lear,* the Earl of Kent denounced a colleague thusly: "You base football player."

A bit more of an admirer, poet Nicholas Breton, in "The Honour of Valor" lauded those who can "strike a football strongly through a goal."

Politicians also started getting the word. Like King James I, who survived Guy Fawkes' villainous plot in 1605 to blow up Parliament. The activist monarch may have learned something from his long-running and entirely unsuccessful campaign to ban another popular vice, tobacco (writing prophetically it was "hateful to the nose, harmful to the brain, dangerous to the lungs"). In 1618 he allowed football after Sunday church services. In fact, clergymen increasingly came to the realization that they would lure more people to church on Sunday morning if they were allowed to play football on Sunday afternoon.

Some divine intervention helped. In 1722, a hurricane on a Sunday blew into the fishing village of East Looe, near England's southwest corner, toppling the church steeple. But, one account declared, the parishioners "happened to be luckily at a football match, by which means their lives were probably saved."

The nexus between football and political action also developed in these early times. On more than one occasion, organizers scheduled a football match, then used the concurrent mayhem to accomplish some other goal, such as tearing down nearby fences or dams that benefited the rich folk at the expense of the poor folk.

Berman headed west—briefly.

Meanwhile, stirrings of footed balls arose far, far away. From the Old World to the New. Yes, football had come to America.

Of course, it was always there, or at least—remember Yucatan and the Aztecs—had been for a long time. Pilgrims arriving at Plymouth Rock in 1620 discovered that Massachusetts Indians indulged in a historic game called Pasuckquakkohowog, local lingo for They Gather To Play Football. An inflatable bladder cleaved from an animal served as the ball. The field, a mile long and very wide, was often a beach along the Atlantic on the Cape Cod peninsula or on the mainland at places like Revere or Lynn. Entire villages competed, and much was at stake. "A large amount of property changed hands, depending upon the outcome of the game," English transplant Willian Wood wrote in 1634. Weapons were banned from the playing field.

All very civil—in sharp contrast, it seems, with the comportment of the English settlers who in 1607 had founded Jamestown, Virginia, North America's first outpost of "English civilization." It is recorded that by 1609 they were playing some version of football among themselves. It is also recorded that elders soon banned the sport. The same thing happened a half-century later in Boston, due to the propensity for street football matches to send something—or someone—through a shopkeeper's window. The fine: a hefty 20 shillings, about $125 today.

Berman crossed the Atlantic again.

Back in England, the dawning of the 19th century brought the Industrial Revolution and big changes to British society. New-fangled railroads made it easier for people—and football teams—to get around the country. Football clubs sprung up across the land. Somewhat unexpectedly, the sport went upscale, possibly due to the notion of "muscular Christianity," the theory that English religious values would best be developed by vigorous exercise.

Football found new adherents at fancy schools, which also just happened to have wide grassy playing fields suitable for playing without any of those knee-crunching cobblestones found in street football. Those adherents included school administrators eager to channel their charges' energies away from unstructured violence. One was Thomas Arnold, headmaster of the Rugby School in Rugby, Warwickshire, who made sports an official part of the educational process. A further boost came when the inventor of vulcanized rubber, the American Charles Goodyear, developed a rubberized football in 1855.

But there was one issue tearing apart the sport.

Hands.

The more violent carry-the-ball "running game" championed by Rugby School was all about the use of hands. But the more sedate "dribbling game" pushed by equally old guard Eton, Harrow and Winchester relied on the foot (and the body, including the head) to advance the ball. Hands could be used only to stop the ball and put it on the ground for kicking. The growing number of football clubs not connected with schools went both ways.

In England, everyone seemed to have their own set of rules, and variations of rules, and variations of variations of rules. With no commonly accepted protocol, matches could not take place until the conclusion of intense negotiations—just like a century later when first-generation fax machines couldn't communicate with one another until a common electronic protocol was worked out. But slowly the dribbling game gained ascendancy. This was reflected in the 1862 publication of an unofficial rule book entitled "The Simplest Game," that prohibited extensive use of those five-fingered extremities.

It became clear the next year that a sit was needed involving all of the interested parties. This being England, the venue was a bar. But not just any bar. Negotiators chose London's Freemason's Tavern, where the learned Royal Astronomical Society had been founded in 1820 to ponder the mysteries of the universe. With this omen from the heavens, the Football Association, known as the FA, was born. After five fall meetings, a set of rules was hashed out embracing the kicking-game take on things. Outvoted, the running-game adherents withdrew to pursue their vision of what would become at most a minor sport known by the name of its most prominent academic supporter, rugby. It became most popular in places like Australia, which by coincidence was significantly populated by descendents of criminals and hooligans.

On December 8, 1863, as the United States remained in the throes of the Civil War and just 19 days after Lincoln's Gettysburg Address, the FA approved its first official rulebook detailing how football would be played. Like Lincoln's brief speech, the FA's effort was extraordinarily sparse: a mere 550 words spread among 14 rules (or Laws as they would become known), taking up all of four printed pages, with another two pages of definitions. Henceforth, football would mean the dribbling game. A punchy slangy term soon arose for the sport, a diminutive derived from asSOCiation footballER: soccer.

Berman returned for good to America.

On our side of the Atlantic, things were also at an advanced, and somewhat parallel, stage. As early as 1827, the freshman and sophomore classes of Harvard, America's oldest and most influential college, vied in an annual football game. Not to be outdone, students at Princeton— still officially named the College of New Jersey—partook of a diversion called "ballown." As the game, yet another English transplant, was played, Princeton students could hit the ball—presumably "owning" it—with both a foot and a fist. One might wonder whether the fist-hitting was confined to inanimate projectiles.

Other elite Eastern colleges—Brown, Columbia, Haverford, Yale, Dartmouth and Amherst—had their own games of foot and ball. But as in England four centuries earlier, authorities were not pleased. In 1837 Columbia president William A. Duer (son of a noted New York crook imprisoned for life) banned the sport. The Harvard faculty enacted its own prohibition in 1860.

And as in England four centuries earlier, these edicts were about as successful in stomping out the game. This was especially so in Harvard's home region of New England, where something called the "Boston game" developed and drew a wide following. The Oneida Football Club, the country's first organized football team, organized itself in 1862 and on November 7, 1863, played its first match against another team on Boston Common, the famous 50-acre public park across the street from the Massachusetts State House.

But what sport was Oneida and all its school-yard predecessors playing? Soccer didn't really exist then. When

Oneida was formed, the rule makers in that London pub hadn't hashed out the official rules. The Americans likely were playing rugby, which included extensive use of hands. Oneida ceased operations in 1865.

As a Berkeley grad, Berman had no truck for East Coast colleges. So he really let it fly.

The best candidate for America's first organized public soccer match actually is a contest that long has been portrayed as the country's first college football game. It took place in New Brunswick, New Jersey, on the afternoon of November 6, 1869, just one day shy of the six-year anniversary of that Oneida dustup on Boston Common. A team from Princeton played a squad from a tiny New Brunswick college founded in 1766 by the Dutch Reformed Church with a charter from Benjamin Franklin's illegitimate son. The original name was Queen's College. Perpetually short of money, the institution had changed its name in 1825 to honor a noted New York philanthropist who donated a $5,000 bond and a bronze bell worth $200. His name was Henry Rutgers.

New Brunswick was a dank crossroads town 35 miles southwest of New York City earlier named Prigmore's Swamp and later nicknamed the "armpit of New Jersey." It was an area so prone to flooding that such a calamity would be mentioned in the lyrics of the school's alma mater song written just four years after the big match.

The contest, the first of what was envisioned as a three-game series, had been arranged by the two team captains. One was Rutgers' William J. Leggett, who would become a prominent minister. The other was Princeton's William Stryker Gummere. Subsequently, he became a railroad lawyer and after that a New Jersey Supreme Court judge. In that capacity he earned the nickname "Dollar-A-Life Gummere" in 1896 for ruling—with no expression of sympathy whatsoever and even a trace of condescension—

that the legal value of Melville Graham, a 4-year-old boy killed by a speeding Jersey City trolley car in front of his house, was only $1 to his grieving parents. For such service to corporation-friendly New Jersey protecting property rights above all, Gummere was soon elevated to the position of Chief Justice. He held that post for more than 30 years.

The rules, chosen by Rutgers as the home team, definitely were British FA, meaning soccer. Players could not run with the ball, which could be advanced through kicking or heading, although it was legal (as it was then in British soccer) to catch the ball with the hands and put it on the ground to be kicked. The goals were 25 feet wide, and the idea was to propel the ball between the uprights (whether there was a crossbar remains unclear). Teams consisted of a massive 25 players. The first to score six goals would be the winner.

The venue was a stony, empty 100-yard-wide lot along New Brunswick's College Avenue surrounded by a low wooden fence that spectators sat on top of, like pigeons on a clothesline. There couldn't have been more than 100 watching. But as the game's legend grew over the decades, so did the number of people claiming to be in attendance. Everyone played in street clothes. Since neither team had uniforms, the Rutgers players all wore purple scarves or handkerchiefs—the school mascot later became the Scarlet Knight—wrapped around their heads. This added a bizarre Middle Eastern cant to this most quintessentially historic of American cultural occasions.

Not all actions were directed toward the ball. There was a fair amount of violence to go along with the fact that players wore no shin guards. "You men will come to no Christian end!" one elderly Rutgers professor screamed. A New Brunswick newspaper account called it a "lively but rough game." That was a considerably kinder characterization than the one published in a newspaper several counties away: a "jackass performance."

Even though an unidentified Rutgers player accidentally kicked the ball toward his own goal, leading to a Princeton score, the Rutgers ragheads won, 6-4. At the rematch a week later in Princeton, using more rugby-like rules, the home team prevailed, 8-0. The third match was canceled after professors from both schools complained students were neglecting their studies.

Because it makes for a better story, Rutgers, Princeton and the rest of the US football establishment still call the November 6 encounter the first college football game. Rutgers, which eventually became the state university of New Jersey, didn't beat Princeton again in football for 69 long years. Still, the school used the spurious claim as the basis for a protracted, expensive and ultimately totally unsuccessful campaign to locate a college football hall of fame on the campus.

Berman kept pouring it on.

Despite a promising start, college soccer went nowhere. Within seven years it was moribund. The culprit: Harvard. The trigger was pulled by the same university that would lead all others in the production of US presidents, big-company chief executives—and high-end white-collar criminals. In 1873, Rutgers, Columbia, Princeton and Yale wanted to create a league to oversee a soccer-style sport modeled on England's FA, meaning the "kicking" game rather than the rugby-style "carrying" game. Harvard refused—not because the sport had been banned in 1860 but because it now was deemed not "manly" enough. Harvard chose the route of Walter Camp's tackle football.

Yet soccer in the US did not die. It just moved off the elite college campuses of the Northeast, away from the leafy greens and the ivy-clad buildings, beyond the eating clubs and fraternities. The sport found a new home in the teaming port cities and working-class textile factory towns, amid the tiny row homes with outdoor plumbing that were drawing hundreds of thousands of job-hungry immigrants a month from far-away places like Ireland and Scotland. In the space of a single decade, soccer went seriously downscale— and thanks to foreigners reached new levels of popularity on these shores.

In 1884 soccer teams meeting in Newark, New Jersey, formed the American Football Association—the first FA in the world outside England and only the second US non-collegiate sports organization (the first, created eight years earlier, being baseball's National League). And in 1885 the teams, mainly sponsored by companies, started the American Cup, a competition to determine a national champion in soccer. This was eight years before Lord Stanley's Cup first honored the continent's top hockey team, 17 years before the first Rose Bowl crowned a college football champion over there in Pasadena, 18 years before the first World Series determined baseball's best team, 54 years before the National Collegiate Athletic Association organized its first basketball tournament, 62 years before pro basketball did the same and a whopping 82 years before the first Super Bowl anointed the top pro dog in the other kind of football.

Indeed, except for seven years around the start of the 20th century there has been some kind of a national competition in soccer every single year since 1885, a longevity that is one of the best-kept secrets in all of American sport. Its duration illustrates both the enduring nature of the game and the utterly inept and pitiful efforts of its backers to promote it beyond the faithful.

What is now the United States Soccer Federation— parent to just about all things soccer in the country—was founded in 1913, but it totally failed at its stated goal of making soccer a national pastime. In many cases the team names—New Jersey Celtics, Boston Wonder Workers, Brooklyn Wanderers, Providence Clam Diggers—were more memorable than the level of play. In 1922 a touring team of women players from England played four male US teams and lost only once.

Over the ensuing decades, leagues—pro, semi-pro, amateur or something in between—came and went, due to money problems and low levels of fan interest. Some teams were owned by baseball clubs owners trying to fill stadiums on off-days, others by corporate titans who went bust. The development of the World Cup did little to promote the game in the United States, even though in the first competition for men, in 1930, the American team came in third, a high finish it has never repeated.

A bright spot came in 1975 when the New York Cosmos of the North America Soccer League signed Pelé—arguably the world's best known soccer player but nearing the end of his legendary Brazilian career—to a three-year contract for $4.5 million. Pelé later wrote in his autobiography that he took the deal only because he was on the hook for a defaulted $2 million loan he had guaranteed in his native Brazil to a company he partly owned. But the league collapsed within a decade. Among the victims was the Los Angeles Aztecs.

In 1993 a new organization, Major League Soccer, arose, staying in business but with substantive local followings in just a few markets. There are two teams around Los Angeles, Galaxy and Chivas.

Finally, Berman drove to his conclusion.

Yet while the professional game proved, ah, elusive, soccer became a widely played youth and amateur athletic endeavor in the US, as witnessed by its popularity here in Valley Mirage. Its dramatic expansion was due to the action of a single individual not associated with the sport, nor even with being terribly ethical or honest, or even a believer in fair play.

Richard M. Nixon.

On June 23, 1972, the Republican president of the United States signed what would become known as Title IX. The legislation prohibited discrimination on the basis of sex in any educational program receiving federal aid—like, say, just about every high school and college in the country.

As soon interpreted, Title IX forced thousands of schools to start more athletic teams for women. Soccer found itself the subject of a quick expansion. After all, it was easy to play, easy to coach, didn't require expensive equipment and could be staged on already existing boys tackle football fields. Within three decades, US women's teams were winning the big international titles that long had eluded the US men, including World Cups.

The fresh interest spread outside schools, and within both genders. It was this impetus that spawned the creation in the mid-1970s of the Valley Mirage Soccer League for youths from ages 7 to 19.

But signing Title IX wasn't the only momentous thing Nixon did that day in the White House. He also taped himself having a 90-minute meeting in the Oval Office with his Chief of Staff, H.R. Halderman. They discussed favorably how the Central Intelligence Agency could be used to obstruct and cover up the FBI's investigation of the break-in by Republican political operatives just six days earlier at the Democratic National Committee headquarters in the Watergate complex.

That didn't work out too well for Nixon. Two summers later, the US Supreme Court unanimously ordered him to turn over to prosecutors a group of recordings including that one. It quickly became known as "the Smoking Gun Tape." A mere three days after it became public, Nixon resigned in disgrace just ahead of certain impeachment and removal.

So throughout history, soccer was never far from the good and bad of society.

The morning his story appeared, readers posted online comments of congratulations for a story well done. Some were even from Republicans.

But one brief note stood out. It was by someone using the pen name Sleepless in Valley Mirage. "So how does the Hermannik killing explain Valley Mirage?" the poster wrote. Berman saw it while reading the website at home. *Guess I don't have a good answer to that*, he thought.

CHAPTER 7

RIVERA WOKE UP that Sunday morning determined to clear the name of both Diego Diaz and himself. He wasn't sure exactly how he was going to accomplish this. But first things first: Rivera hopped in his truck and drove to a nearby Starbucks for a mocha light frappuccino.

En route, he happened to pass the home of Harry and Lita Smithfield, whose $10,000 flat-screen TV he had fixed two years earlier. A big U-Haul truck and trailer was in the circular driveway, surrounded by pieces of furniture and a lot of boxes.

They're moving out, Rivera thought. *Wonder why?*

Then he saw Harry struggling as he carried a box out the front door toward the U-Haul. Rivera stopped his truck, got out and walked over.

"Hi, Mr. Smithfield," he said. "Hector Rivera. You may not remember me, but I'm the guy who fixed your big-screen TV couple years ago. I was just passin' by and noticed the U-Haul. Hope everything's okay."

The sweating Smithfield put down the box and looked at Rivera. "Sure, I remember you," he said, sticking out his hand. "You came on time. Pleasant, too."

Smithfield nodded toward the U-Haul. "As you can see," he said, "we're moving."

"Oh?" Rivera said.

"We're losing the house." Rivera said. "Moving in with Lita's sister's family in the Valley."

"Sorry to hear that," Rivera said.

"Combination of things," continued Smithfield, who seemed to be in a mood to talk. "Lita lost her job as an office manager. Couldn't find another. My hours as a nurse got cut way back. Economy's slowin' down, I guess.

"On top of all that, we started gettin' killed by our mortgage. Have one of those interest-only adjustable-rate mortgages with nothing down. Rate was just 2.5%. Also got a home equity loan to pay for"—he laughed, a trace bitterly—"that TV and other stuff like cars, and some nice trips. We figured the home value would keep going up 20% a year forever.

"But the mortgage rate reset to 5.5%, and we also had to start paying some principal. So our monthly payments went from a little under two grand a month to over five-and-a-half grand. Nearly tripled. Couldn't handle it.

"House value apparently went way down, too, or at least stopped going up fast. Maybe it never was worth what we paid for it. Anyway, with all that extra borrowin', we owed a lot more than the house was worth. Couldn't refinance into a lower fixed rate. Should have when we had the chance, I guess.

"So we're just walkin' away. Handin' it back to the lender. So much for our Great American Dream."

Smithfield's candor left Rivera almost speechless. "Uh, uh," he stammered. "I'm sure you'll pick up the pieces. Just have to get your bearings again."

"Probably worse on our kids," Smithfield said. "They liked livin' out here. Havin' all the latest electronic doodads. God knows what awaits them in the Valley and the LA school system, but that's all we can afford right now. Guess that's life. Boy, were we stupid.

"Thinkin' back, this house was never worth what we paid for it in the first place. I guess the seller made a killin'."

"Who was the seller?" Rivera asked.

"Some guy named Richard Stevens," Smithfield said. "Never met him. No one was ever home when we looked at the house. For the closing, we pre-signed all the papers. The deal was completed at an escrow office by one person. The way it's done in California."

"Hmm," Rivera said, who didn't know anyone by that name in Valley Mirage. "Guess the lender must be pretty upset, too. Who was it?"

"Some outfit from out of state named Associated Capital Equity. I don't know that it did a lot of due diligence on the deal."

"What do you mean?"

"Oh, we had to fill out forms listing our income and all that. But they never asked us for copies of paystubs, tax returns or anything. Pretty free and easy." Smithfield grimaced. "Too free and easy."

"From what I hear, that was the style then," Rivera said, thinking back to what Holchek told him in that bar.

He looked at Smithfield. "I know you have a lot of stuff to do," he said. "I should be going. Be thinking about you."

"Okay," Smithfield said, reaching out again to shake Rivera's hand, like the two had just done a deal. "Hey, you know, that TV you fixed never gave us any more trouble."

"Happy to hear that," Rivera said.

"We had to sell it," Smithfield said.

"Ouch!" Rivera said.

He drove away feeling sorry for the Smithfields, who seemed like a nice family even if they weren't involved in soccer. But Rivera also felt they deserved a bit of the fate that befell them. *Definitely living way above their means, and borrowing to do it,* he thought.

Sitting under a Starbucks umbrella and nursing that mocha light frappuccino, Rivera pondered the plight of the Smithfields some more. It sort of sounded familiar. Then Rivera remembered that he had lost a player on his team, Colt Samuels, for what sounded like the same reason.

The family had moved in with relatives in Redlands, east of San Bernardino, but Rivera still had a number stored in his cellphone. He called it. Colt's dad, Bill, answered.

"Hi, Bill, Hector Rivera here. I just wanted to see how you're doing. We miss Colt on the team."

"Oh, hi, Hector. We miss the team, too. Colt isn't playing soccer this year 'cause he only wanted to play for you and the Dodgers."

"Tell him it's important to play. Plenty of coaches and teams out there can use him. How is he adjustin' to Redlands?"

"So-so. He misses his friends in Valley Mirage. Hard for him."

"How are you and your wife adjustin' to Redlands?"

"Hard for us, too. Not easy losing your job, and then your home."

"Yeah," Rivera said, sensing an opening. "I remember you told me a little bit about that. Something 'bout adjustable-rate mortgage and the interest rate going way, way up."

"Well, that did happen, but it was a lot worse than that," Samuels said, more than a trace of bitterness in his voice. "We were sold a pile of crap."

"Crap?" Rivera repeated.

"The house we bought was never worth anywhere near what we paid for it. We were snookered. Ace was snookered, too."

"Ace?"

"Yeah, Ace, our lender. They took a bigger hit on this than we did."

"Is Ace a mortgage company around here?" Rivera asked.

"Nah," Samuels said. "Out of state. Ace is just an abbreviation. Full name is Associated Capital Equity."

Associated Capital Equity! Rivera thought. *The same lender as the Smithfields!*

"Oh, that Ace," Rivera said, his heart quickening as he tried to remain calm and draw out Samuels. "I think I've heard of them. Who did you buy your home from?"

"Some guy named Larry Murphy," Samuels said. "But we never met him."

Just like Smithfield, Rivera thought.

Samuels paused. Then suddenly he blurted out, "He had it coming!"

"Uh, who had what coming?" Rivera asked.

"Rick Hermannik! The guy your girlfriend's father killed. I've been reading the stories. Good riddance for the world, I say! If I'm on that jury, Diego will walk! Justifiable homicide!"

A startled Rivera knew the Samuels family had been involved for years in Valley Mirage soccer, where the connection between him and Diaz was pretty well known. But he still was astonished. "Why, why are you saying this?" he asked.

"Hermannik was the appraiser who said our house was worth way more than what it was really worth," Samuels said. "We didn't know it at the time. But we know it now. Underwater from day one! People like that don't deserve to live!"

"Uh, so you think Diego killed Hermannik?"

"How do I know?" Samuels said. "I watched that YouTube video. Diego's language sure was rough. He was a hothead from what I saw on the soccer fields. I don't know him well. Don't know his character.

"But I don't care. So what if Hermannik was killed for the wrong reason? There was a good reason to do him in. Maybe Diego got to him first. Some people just need killin'!

"And in case you're wonderin', I have an alibi. The night the newspaper said Hermannik was throttled? I was movin' a lot of what remained of our furniture and goods into a self-serve storage facility out here. Surveillance cameras everywhere. I'm sure there's plenty of tape of me strugglin' to hold onto our possessions.

"Long live Diego Diaz! If I had some spare change, I'd contribute to a legal defense fund for him."

"That's nice—I guess," Rivera said. "But if you feel this way 'bout a Hermannik appraisal after losin' your home, there must be other people out there who feel, ah, just as strongly."

"Probably so," Samuels said. "Tigers don't change their stripes. But no, I don't know of any other victims. Lots of homebuyers who lose their homes through foreclosure blame themselves for bitin' off more than they could chew. They know they signed an agreement to make monthly payments. Know those payments can go way up. Know they stopped making payments when they did go way up.

"They don't look back to see if they overpaid in the first place. They go quietly. Don't ask questions. Conditioned by the banks to be ashamed. Even though big business does the very same thing.

"Hasn't the great Donald Trump thrown his own companies into bankruptcy to get out from paying something owed? Yet he gets hailed as a great leader! A great businessman! Even gets his own TV show!

"Hell, I'm ashamed, too. So I went quietly, too. The only reason I'm telling you all this is 'cause you called. You're a good guy."

Samuels sort of ran out of air, exhausted by his rant. "Look, I'm sorry," he told Rivera after a pause. "I hope for you Diego didn't do it. It's hard for me to imagine a soccer coach killin' a soccer referee over a call. But it's also hard for me to imagine someone killin' an appraiser over an appraisal. That's just too far out there for me.

"But someone killed Hermannik, that's for sure. Someone who seriously wanted him seriously dead.

"Look around, Hector. Gotta be more than meets the eye here."

"Okay," Rivera said. "But keep in touch. I want all the best for your family. Tell that to Colt."

Rivera clicked off, his mind racing. *Too strange to believe*, he thought. Looking through his cellphone memory, he still had a number for Harry Smithfield from when his big-screen TV was fixed. Rivera called it.

"Mr. Smithfield? Hector Rivera here. I just spoke to you at your home."

"Sure."

"Look, I know that you're real busy and all that. But you would be doin' me a big favor if you could find for me the name of the appraiser on your house. I, I"—there was a limit even to Rivera's candor—"want to give it to a friend."

Smithfield sighed. "Okay," he said. "The house document box is still here by the truck. Wait a second."

Rivera heard the sounds of the neighborhood—passing traffic, distant kid voices, a bird. Then Smithfield came back on the line.

"Ah, one second. Here it is. Herman. Richard A. Herman."

"Is it Herman?" Rivera said, his heart quickening. "Or Hermannik?"

"Wait. Yes, yes, it is Hermannik. Sorry. Richard A. Hermannik."

"Okay," Rivera said, believing but not believing what he heard.

The Smithfield family was not part of the Valley Mirage soccer orbit and obviously had been preoccupied with the impending loss of their house. "Gee, that name sounds familiar," Smithfield said. "Anyone you know?"

"Uh, I used to know him," Rivera said. "Look, thanks for the information. Good luck on your move."

"Okay," Smithfield said. He paused. "One other thing, Hector. I remember when you came to fix the TV. I talked at length about the benefits of buying real estate with nothing down. No doubt I was boring and obnoxious. Just want to let you know I no longer think leveraging up like that is such a good thing."

"Okay," Rivera said before hanging up. "I'll remember that."

Rivera's head was spinning. Deals involving two wildly overpriced houses in Valley Mirage. The same obscure out-of-state lender. Mysterious sellers.

And the involvement each time of Rick Hermannik.

What does it mean? Rivera wondered. *Does it mean anything? Like Samuels said, who would kill someone over a bad appraisal?*

Rivera figured Hermannik over the years must have appraised hundreds of homes. *So what if he was off on a couple?* Rivera thought. *I made mistakes, too. Like getting involved with the daughter of a wingnut like Diego.*

That brought Rivera's chain of thought to a full stop. *I shouldn't be blaming Dora for anything Diego did*, Rivera thought. *Besides, I don't think Diego did this.*

But how to prove that?

Mulling over what he had learned, Rivera realized he didn't know enough about the ins-and-outs of real estate, even though that's what everybody seemed to be talking about around the soccer fields. Rivera knew what a mortgage was, of course. And he knew that someone could lose their home through a foreclosure if the mortgage wasn't paid. Rivera realized that the chances of a connection between Hermannik's murder and bad mortgages was remote. But he had to start somewhere. And if he was going to look into Associated Capital Equity and Hermannik, Rivera needed information, especially about other deals involving them. He needed it fast, too. But he had absolutely no idea how to go about finding this.

Then Rivera thought about a fellow student he got to know at Cal State, Tom Hartigan, who had a job in a real estate escrow office near LAX. Rivera considered him a friend, even though they didn't see each other often anymore. Rivera remembered how Hartigan once (in a bar, of course) had explained to him that escrow offices handle the paperwork and procedures after a seller and buyer agree on a contract for a piece of property like a house, but before the deal is completed.

Rivera knew Hartigan wasn't into soccer, lived nowhere near Valley Mirage and so was far less likely to ask annoying questions about Diego Diaz. He called.

"Hey man, how you doin'?" Hartigan said upon answering. "Haven't heard from you in a while."

"Hangin' in there," Rivera said. "Still running around fixing stuff for people. It's a living."

"Still with that hot chick, Dora?" Hartigan asked.

"Yeah," Rivera said. "Livin' together in Valley Mirage."

Wanting to steer the conversation away from the Diaz family, Rivera cut to the chase. "Still working for that escrow company?" he asked.

"Sure," Hartigan said. "Just promoted to junior escrow officer."

"Congrats," Rivera said. "Something's come up here. I'm looking for some information. I thought you might have some ideas."

"Shoot."

"Explain to me what escrow offices do."

"Well," said Hartigan, "after the parties agree on a deal, the buyer finds a lender willing to finance the purchase. Often with little or no down payment. That's not a very hard thing to find, especially in California.

"In most of the country the process leading up to a transfer of real estate is handled by lawyers. The final transfer is called a settlement. It usually involves everyone sitting around a table signing and swapping paper. But in the West—and particularly in California—it's called a 'closing.' Handled by escrow companies like mine. At the closing, there's nary a lawyer to be seen. Often it's just the escrow officer, with no lawyers. That usually cuts costs a bit but raises the potential for mischief. Not that every lawyer is on the straight and narrow, of course, but they usually have spent a lot more money getting their education and licensing than the typical escrow officer has spent, and they don't want to blow it lightly.

"California has thousands of escrow offices. Almost as common as dry cleaners.

"Anyway, the escrow officer makes sure the paperwork is in order. A settlement sheet is prepared, which shows what everyone in the deal owes to everyone else. That includes the escrow officer, who gets a fee.

"After a million pieces of paper are signed ahead of time and the lender funds the mortgage, the escrow officer gives the borrowed money and any down payment to the seller less fees and payoff of the old loan. Then some of that paperwork is sent to a governmental office in the county where the property sits and made a matter of public record. This is partly to stop a sleazy seller from collecting money for selling the same property over and over."

"Okay," Rivera said. "Any way of getting a list of mortgages made by a given lender around Los Angeles that have gone bad?"

"Why do you want that?" Hartigan asked. "Trying to buy distressed property? There's sure a lot more of that around now than there used to be."

"Nah, no money." Rivera thought fast. "Uh, helping a friend in trouble. Trying to make a case about unfair treatment."

"Well," Hartigan said. "There are websites you can sign up for, pay a little money, that'll list properties facing foreclosure. RealtyTrak, Foreclosure.com, others. But I don't know the databases are searchable by name of lender. You'd probably be better off making a trip yourself to Norwalk."

"Norwalk?" Rivera asked. "The town near LA?"

"Yeah," Hartigan said. "That's where Los Angeles County, in its infinite wisdom, chose to put its registrar-recorder office. The place where public records are filed about real estate. There's a records room there full of computer terminals. You can access the indexes and call up images of whatever records have been filed. Free, too."

"Uh, what's an index?"

"Okay," Hartigan said in a slightly exasperated voice. "In Los Angeles County documents 'bout real estate are indexed in a giant computer under the name of the seller, name of the buyer, name of the lender. There is this super-huge index called the grantor/grantee index. A grantor is the seller or the person taking on a loan. A grantee is the buyer or the bank making the loan. Grant makes it sound like it's free, but of course it isn't. It's just a term.

"You can search the grantor/grantee index while limiting the kinds of documents you're looking at, like deeds of trust. Also time period. The index goes back decades."

"Uh, I know what a deed is," Rivera said. "But what's a deed of trust? And what's that got to do with foreclosure?"

"Okay," Hartigan said. "It's what everyone calls a mortgage, but a little different. Unlike a lot of other states, California is a title theory state. That means you don't really own your house right away when you buy it with borrowed money. Oh, you think you do. And you're on the hook for property taxes. But instead, the property goes into its own little trust. One controlled by the lender. At the closing, the seller signs a deed conveying the property to the buyer. But then the buyer immediately signs something called a deed-of-trust. That conveys the property to the bank-appointed trustee, usually a title company or servicing firm.

"As long as you make your payments, there's no problem. You can act like the owner, be a big shot. Though you're not. But miss a few payments, and there's somethin' in the deed of trust called a power-of-sale clause. Allows the bank to request the trustee sell the property out from under you to satisfy the unpaid amount. Usually done without a foreclosure lawsuit and court order.

"It's much faster and cheaper for lenders, who really control the process. A lot of distressed owners simply sign papers that hand over the property to the lender, move out and start renting.

"Course, people walk away only if the house is worth way less than the loan. Otherwise, they would sell it through a broker and maybe even pocket something. Here in the Golden State there's a little quirk in the law. Prohibits a lender invokin' a power of sale clause on a deed of trust from then suing the defaultin' borrower who just lost his house. Lender can't seek the difference between the remainin' loan balance and the home value.

"Sort of a one-bite-of-the-apple rule. So the lender generally takes a big hit, too. No happy outcomes for anyone."

"Okay," Rivera said. "How do I figure out a lender's track record in makin' loans that go bad?"

"Like I said, go to Norwalk," Hartigan said. "There isn't a lot of public paperwork on a deed of trust repossession. But California law does require the lender to file somethin' called a notice of default. It's indexed in Norwalk by the name of the defaultin' borrower. And also by who is filing it."

Hartigan paused. "But now I think about it, the paperwork is filed by a trustee or title company, not usually by the lender," he said. "So you can't search the grantor/grantee index for notices of default filed by lender."

Rivera was distressed. "There's no way to figure this out?" he asked plaintively.

"Wait, wait, I have an idea," Hartigan said. "How big is the lender you're researchin'? Have they made a lot of loans in Los Angeles County?"

"Not sure," Rivera said. "But don't think so. Seems to be a small out-of-state lender."

"Then here's what you do," Hartigan said. "Take the name of the lender and run it through the grantee index. Then click on each entry. You'll get the name of the borrower. Write down the name, then search the name to see if a notice of default has been filed against him. You can also call up images and look at the actual documents.

"It might seem like a lot of time and work. Not really. On those terminals you can really zip through the data and the images.

"One other thing. A lot of lenders now record mortgages in the name of something called MERS. Stands for Mortgage Electronic Registration Systems. It allows banks to sell existing loans without having to pay new recording fees. MERS is like nearly half the mortgages. But it sounds like you're looking mainly for mortgages from about five years ago, when MERS wasn't nearly as common. So you should be all right."

"Okay," Rivera said. "Will I be able to figure out where the property is and what the buyer paid originally?"

"Yes, but not directly from the index," Hartigan said. "Call up the deed. Somewhere on it will be a notation reading somethin' like 'After recording, return to,' followed by a name and address. The buyer gets back the original. That's almost always the address of the home on the deed, although sometimes it's an agent.

"As for sales price, the deeds don't usually list it. But in California there's a property transfer tax. Everything gets taxed in California. The amount paid is always written somewhere on the deed. In the city of Los Angeles the tax is $5.50 per every $1,000 of sales price. But for most of the rest of Los Angeles County, including your neck of the woods in Valley Mirage, it's a lot less. A dollar ten per thou. Take the tax paid, divide it by point zero zero one one. 'Bout one-tenth of one percent. That'll be the sales price.

"So if the deed says the transfer tax in Valley Mirage was $800, the sales price was"—Rivera heard tapping on a keypad over the cell—"the grand sum of $727,272.73."

"Make sure you bring a calculator. And make sure you divide."

"Gee, this is terrific," said Rivera, who frantically was scribbling notes on what by then was his sixth Starbucks napkin. "We'll have to get together for a drink."

"Sure," said Hartigan, "but only if you bring along Dora. A real looker."

"We'll see," Rivera laughed, a little uneasily.

"Hey, still into soccer?" Hartigan asked. "The last time we talked, you were playing and coaching."

"Uh, still play, but takin' a break from coachin'." *No reason to give Hartigan the full story*, Rivera thought. "Hope to get back into it soon."

"Hey," Hartigan said, "Didn't I read something in the paper about soccer in your town? Valley Village, right?"

"News to me," Rivera replied, truthfully enough since he lived in relatively obscure Valley Mirage, which Hartigan had just confused with a Los Angeles neighborhood. Rivera was grateful for the information he'd got but wasn't prepared to reveal his reason for wanting it. "There's a lot goin' on in soccer."

"Suppose so," Hartigan said, a tad skeptically. "Everthing 'cept scoring. I admire your concentration. Me, I'd fall asleep at a soccer match."

"Not the first time I've heard that," Rivera said good naturedly. "Someday I'll go with you to a Galaxy game and show you the finer points."

"Better be a day game," Hartigan said equally pleasantly. "Otherwise, I'll be asleep by halftime."

After Hartigan hung up, Rivera looked at his watch—it was barely 10:00 a.m.—and then at his collection of annotated napkins with the distilled wisdom of Hartigan. He thought about his phone conversations with Harry Smithfield and Bill Samuels. *Not a bad use of time on a Sunday morning,* Rivera thought. *Now if only it would lead to something.*

But what? And how?

Hector drove home. He found Dora sitting in the kitchen wearing a robe, staring blankly out the window. Hector leaned over and kissed her.

"Ended up doing some research about Rick Hermannik," Hector said. "Found some interestin' stuff."

"Oh?" Dora said, turning her head to him.

"Turns out he may have signed off on appraisals for an out-of-state lender that wildly overvalued some homes from the get-go," Hector said. "People borrowed a lot more than they should have. Got into bad loans where the interest rate went way up. Homes went into foreclosure. People lost 'em. One borrower actually told me Hermannik deserved to be killed."

"Someone said that?" Dora said in astonishment, her eyes widening. "That Hermannik had it comin'? Like that song in the movie *Chicago*?"

"Yep," Hector said, diplomatically leaving out the part Samuels said about what a hothead Diego was. "For reasons having nothing to do with soccer. But that's just one person's opinion. It's not evidence. Right now it's barely a theory. Hell, even Perry Mason couldn't do much with that.

"Look, you and I both feel Diego didn't do it. The trick is to identify a suspect who did."

"How 'bout the guy who wanted him dead?" Dora asked. "Wouldn't he be a suspect?"

"Doubt it," Hector said. "It was the dad of the kid who left my soccer team when the family lost their house and had to move away. He's mad at Hermannik, but he's no killer."

"So what ya goin' to do?" Dora asked.

"Think we need a longer list of appraisals Hermannik did for this mortgage company of homes that ended up in foreclosure," Hector said. "Also like to know a little more 'bout who sold the homes that went into foreclosure. The two buyers I talked to today said they never met their sellers. Might be able to get some of this info at the county deed and mortgage recording office in Norwalk."

"That's a ways from here," Dora said. "When would you go?"

"Well, time's definitely of the essence," Hector said. "But today is Sunday and the office is closed. Maybe tomorrow. I'll just take part of the morning off from work."

"Gee, Hector, that's terrific," Dora said, putting her arms around him. "By the way, where'd ya do all this interestin' research?"

Hector looked at her. "Mostly at Starbucks," he said. "While sippin' a mocha light frappuccino."

"Boy," Dora said, "that drink must sure pack a kick!"

And so did Rivera that night, playing his weekly soccer match in an indoor adult league under the lights. He was normally an intense competitor. But the events of the week made him particularly fierce. Rivera even drew a yellow card—his first in several years—for a reckless tackle of an opponent with the ball. His teammates attributed his semi-violence to understandable personal distress over Diego's arrest.

But the real reason was Rivera's suspension as a coach, which they didn't know about. For as much as he liked to play soccer himself, Rivera liked coaching it even more. It gave him the chance to inculcate good values in a group of impressionable kids—kids that were about the same age he was when soccer helped keep him on the straight and narrow in Pacoima and afterwards in Valley Mirage. He didn't want that opportunity taken away from them, or himself.

CHAPTER 8

JEFF BERMAN WAS certainly prolific.

Sure, he cranked out plenty of newspaper stories—often four or five a day—about the daily happenings in and around Valley Mirage. Government meetings, traffic fatalities, murder of a soccer referee, stuff like that. But Berman also had to write even when there wasn't daily news. Features, they were called in the news biz.

Berman had filled part of that work obligation by writing a series of weekly essays about California history. With the availability of material in nearby libraries and on the Internet, the research wasn't all that difficult. Berman usually worked on several columns at a time, stringing out their publication. Judging from reader feedback, Berman found his articles drew a large following, especially when he wrote about topics that weren't well known or went against the grain of public understanding. To protect themselves from undue criticism, his always-nervous editors often ran them on the editorial page under the label "commentary," which was newsspeak for "don't blame us if it's not true."

For instance, there was Berman's piece on the amazing origins of the state's name:

> California came from the vivid imagination of one Garci Ordóñez de Montalvo. He was a Spanish novelist around the time the Italian Christopher Columbus was on that salary-plus-profit-sharing deal for Spain's King Ferdinand and Queen Isabella as he sailed the ocean blue in 1492. Columbus was looking for a western route across the Atlantic to India and especially to riches. "Get gold,

humanely if possible," Ferdinand had ordered. "But at all hazards, get gold." Working out of Seville, Montalvo specialized in what passed then for romance potboilers. He often picked up the narrative thread of someone else's romance potboiler (after that someone else, of course, had died and couldn't sue or duel).

Montalvo himself died in about 1504. Six years later, the novel he wrote was published with the title of *Las sergas de Esplandián* (*The Exploits of Esplandian*). *Las sergas* was a sequel to a series of books written a couple centuries earlier in Portuguese using that well-worn but still popular literary genre, the wandering knight. You know, slaying villains, getting the girl, and going where no knight has gone before. Think *Star Trek* with horses and boats.

The earlier books were about one Amadis of Gaul. Esplandián was his kid. And the son really got around, too, judging from this key passage in *Las sergas* containing the first-ever written mention of what would become a very famous place:

"For know ye that at the right hand of the Indies there is an island named California, very close to that part of the Terrestrial Paradise which was inhabited by black women, without a single man among them, and they lived in the manner of Amazons.... The island everywhere abounds with gold and precious stones.... In this island, named California, there are many griffins. In no other part of the world can they be found."

The island of California, Montalvo wrote, was named after its ruler, the take-no-prisoners Queen Califa. The details got even better: Even before the advent of plastic surgery, the women of California all had great figures ("robust in body" is how the novelist got that past Spanish censors). They mated with half-man, half-beast creatures, who were then fed to the griffins (animals possessing an eagle's head and wings affixed to a lion's body) so as to maintain a single-gender society.

So to Spanish readers, this California was some place, with vast riches, wild beasts, kinky stuff and an interesting racial angle.

Now remember that Columbus, in addition to finding no gold, had gotten nowhere near the true California. He never ever even reached the North American mainland, which in any event isn't an island. Yet fresh back from his first trip, Columbus actually wrote a report in 1493 saying he had heard about an island populated by war-like women, who occasionally allowed visits from men living elsewhere, presumably for making whoopee.

After his third voyage in 1498 (in which he again completely missed North America but skirted the coast of South America), Columbus officially reported back to Spain the exciting news that he was pretty sure he had sailed near the Terrestrial Paradise. That, Christian tradition holds, is the location of the Garden of Eden in which Adam and Eve did that thing with the apple. If nothing else, Columbus was a tremendous PR man for himself.

So with this kind of high-concept buzz, it wasn't surprising that some Spaniards actually believed *Las sergas*, and especially that stuff about gold. They evidently were not deterred by the fact that those vicious griffins were found only in mythology and Montalvo implausibly claimed he had found the manuscript in a buried chest in Constantinople, arranging for its secret shipment to Spain by a mysterious Hungarian.

One later reader was Hernán Cortés, soon to be fresh off his conquest of the Aztecs in Mexico and looting all their gold and silver. Since *Las sergas* said California was "at the right hand of the Indies," and Cortés figured that's sort of where he was, he sent a couple of his henchmen over to the west side of Mexico. They then crossed a wide body of water and landed near the southern tip of a piece of land.

Hey, boss, they reported back, looks like something's there. Maybe even an island.

They didn't note the presence of vast hordes of black Indian women—or, for that matter, gold. But clearly besotted with Queen Califa, Cortés—or someone around him—dubbed the new find California. Thus, what would become one of the world's most celebrated places—and a major center of Latino culture, to boot—was named after a fictional, bisexual, black Indian woman with a hankering for murder and an affinity for bestiality.

Cortés' men, of course, had found Baja California, the long peninsula fronting the Pacific Ocean south of the future San Diego. It would take decades more of exploration to establish that this was no mere island but an appendage of one gigantic hunk of real estate to the north.

Still, the name stuck.

Another popular essay concerned the Spanish conquest of California— the part above San Diego, originally called Alta California—and the first written record of its considerable ground movements, which would prove troublesome for the millions who eventually would follow.

After several centuries of inaction, Spain finally decided to do something decisive about our section of California. One catalyst was looming threats from Russian and British explorers. Another was the fear of Spain's paranoid leader King Carlos III that the aggressive Jesuits, who had been in Mexico since 1697 and ran their operation as much like a political machine as a religious organization, might try to unseat him. There were also rumors the Jesuits were really raking it in money-wise.

Thus, in 1768 Carlos expelled the Jesuits from all Spanish territory. This was particularly felt in Mexico, where the Jesuits were doing a lot more for the Indians— teaching them such important skills, for example, as shipbuilding—than they were doing for the Spanish. Carlos gave the civilize-the-local-Indians-but-favor-us missionary contract to the Jesuits' great and more compliant Catholic rival, the Franciscans.

So in 1769, a truly epic year in California history, Franciscans guarded by Spanish soldiers—although it seemed at times more like the other way around—marched and sailed north into Alta California. Besides an assertion of sovereignty, the Spaniards also brought along Spain's Law of the Indies. No recognition of property rights of Indians in lands they weren't actually occupying. No payments whatsoever for other land seized. Freedom to loot. Given the large number of Indian villages being passed daily—full of armed but friendly often-naked natives—this was bound to create problems.

Along the way this holy alliance of soldiers and priests was rattled beyond belief by a string of major earthquakes, an omen of things to come in California for Spain. Even Gaspar de Portolà, a seasoned and hardened military man who led the expedition, wrote in his journal on July 28, 1769, that one earthquake—"of such violence ... supplicating Mary Most Holy"—lasted "about half as long as an Ave Maria." While he didn't write this, it's a pretty good guess he invoked that famous prayer of imminent death as a measure of time because he had started uttering it as the ground beneath him trembled somewhere in the vicinity of the future Anaheim, south of the future Los Angeles.

"Hail Mary, full of grace, the Lord is with thee," the Ave Maria begins. "Pray for us sinners, now and at the hour of our death, amen," it ends.

Franciscan priest Juan Crespí, who was penning a more expansive daily journal, noted that shake, too. He didn't write down whether he prayed like de Portolà. But it is a fact he christened the nearby waterway "The River of the Sweetest Name of Jesus of the Earthquakes," as though seeking penitence. Some years later the stream was renamed the Santa Ana River.

Thanks to Crespí's writings, there is a record of what greeted the vanguard of Spanish civilization during its inaugural march across the terrain that later would give the world Disneyland and Hollywood:

July 28 (near the future Happiest Place on Earth): "We experienced here a horrifying earthquake which was repeated four times during the day. The first, which was the most violent, happened at one in the afternoon and the last one around four."

July 31 (in the vicinity of what would be the eastern Los Angeles suburb of El Monte): "At half-past eight in the morning we felt another earthquake."

August 1 (still east of Los Angeles): "At ten in the morning the earth trembled. The shock was repeated with violence at one in the afternoon, and one hour afterwards we experienced another."

August 2 (on the eastern edge of downtown Los Angeles): "We felt three consecutive earthquakes in the afternoon and the night."

August 3 (more or less right in the future downtown Los Angeles): "This afternoon we felt new earthquakes, the continuation of which astonishes us."

Berman fascinated readers in another column with his description of a largely unknown mid-19th century historical character named Abel Stearns. Despite his being fabulously rich as well as a prominent politician, Stearns later become so obscure his name adorned virtually nothing besides the odd street or public room and his own grave at Calvary Cemetery in Los Angeles.

Born in 1798 in Massachusetts, Stearns was orphaned at age 12 and went off to sea, becoming a savvy captain. In 1832, after taking Mexican citizenship, he moved to Los Angeles—then a Mexican city of fewer than a thousand residents—and became a trader. The only things then produced around in any volume around Los Angeles were cattle hides and tallow, which is cattle fat used to make candles and soap. Both were hard to get to the foreign ships that were always passing by. Stearns sent his own workers out to the ranches to bring the goods to a remote warehouse he purchased in 1834 for $150 along the coast south of Los Angeles. The location had the great, great advantage of being miles away from nosy tax collectors and other authorities who were dependent on collecting duties to fund the local government. Also, it was illegal in Mexico, which after a revolution had taken over California from Spain, to sell to foreign ships in the first place.

Stearns became a smuggler and receiver of stolen goods. Within a few years he was the richest individual in the Los Angeles area. Making good use of his sea captain skills, Stearns often arranged that ships be unloaded in places like Santa Catalina Island 25 miles out in the ocean and their goods ferried to shore in the middle of the night. Hides of Los Angeles-area cattle for which he had no official purchase receipts started appearing in his warehouse. This was the same time the famous French novelist Balzac was writing in Paris that behind every great fortune lies a crime.

As the 19th century neared and then crossed its midpoint, Stearns soared. He did mainly it with land and high interest rates—plus a convenient arrangement. In 1841 Stearns shored up his already considerable position by (1) discovering Catholicism at age 42 and (2) marrying 14-year-old Arcadia Bandini, which he couldn't do unless he was a professed Catholic. She happened to be a daughter of Don Juan Bandini, who somehow had grown wealthy while collecting taxes in San Diego—Arcadia came with a big dowry—and was a man of considerable influence in Southern California.

Because of the absence of banks and the distance from money centers like New York and even London, interest rates in California were ridiculously high—5% a month. On a compounded basis, that worked out to 80% a year.

So Stearns, who had traveled the world, was happy to lend. Thrilled, even. To facilitate his smuggling business, he always kept around large amounts of money, so why not put some of it to better use? He figured that he would get repaid or, more likely and more desirably, get the land cheaply. He charged the prevailing interest rate and even allowed distressed borrowers to forego a payment ... or two ... or three ... or whatever, tacking on the missed payments to the amount owed with the same 5%-a—mouth-compounded interest rate.

A century and a half later, this is now known as subprime lending.

In 1842, the year after he married Arcadia, Stearns lent money at the going rate—5% monthly, compounded—to Francisco Figueroa, brother of a former California governor, who owned a 26,500-acre ranch called Rancho Los Alamitos just southeast of where Long Beach is today. Figueroa couldn't keep up with the payments (a considerable irony given his family name now graces the main drag through the Los Angeles financial district). Stearns soon "bought" the ranch from Figueroa for $1,500—6 cents an acre.

Much in this way, Stearns over the next two decades amassed among the biggest private land holdings of any single person in Southern California—interests in upwards of 200,000 acres. Sometimes he bought at a public foreclosure sale; sometimes he was able to negotiate a transaction in lieu of foreclosure. With land and wealth came political clout. Ever the opportunist, he reclaimed his American citizenship after US military forces grabbed California from Mexico in 1846. Stearns eventually became a Los Angeles County supervisor and a state Assemblyman.

But what came around, went around, especially in what would prove to be the periodic Los Angeles pattern of boom, bubble and bust. In 1861 massive rains destroyed maybe a quarter of the area's taxable wealth. Then a smallpox epidemic ravaged humans. A drought destroyed what was left of the cattle industry. Finally, conjuring up a Biblical magnitude of damage, waves of locusts descended, eating what little vegetation remained.

It was as though a powerful force somewhere was demanding payback for decades of dirty dealings. Payback from people like Stearns, who had begun borrowing heavily in expectation of buying more land only to watch his own cash flow wither away. He fell behind in payment of debts and taxes and was on the verge of going bust.

But not for long. He became Southern California's first big-time subdivider, using Other People's Money. Negotiating with creditors and getting a big bank loan in what amounted to a mortgage refinancing, he started selling off his remaining 178,000 acres in parcels as small as 20 acres, at prices as low as $5 an acre and with installment-plan financing akin to a mortgage. Stearns got one-eighth of all the proceeds free and clear.

For the first time in Southern California history and certainly not the last, the region was marketed (by Stearns and his cronies) in a hard-sell across the United States and even Europe. The promotion cited great weather, great agriculture, great scenery and prospect of great riches. Paid lecturers fanned out to spread the word. At the docks in San Francisco, Stearns' agents handed gushing flyers to steamers heading south. A fair amount of the hype was malarkey. Particularly maps of towns that didn't exist on which were marked schools that didn't exist, churches that didn't exist, hotels that didn't exist, city halls that didn't exist and frequently people who didn't exist. One traveler who arrived to check out the city of Savanna, which promotional literature described as a prosperous, populated place near Santa Ana, found only a single coyote sitting on a barren hill.

But the marketing worked! Thousands of acres sold in just a few months, and soon Stearns found himself flush and riding high again.

Rivera took the paper mainly for its coverage of local high school sports. Stories about government usually put him to sleep. But he liked to read the history articles. That was why Rivera was aware of Berman's byline even before he became the main reporter on the Hermannik killing.

After returning from playing adult soccer, Rivera's cell rang. It was Scott Ambrose. He was also a soccer coach in Valley Mirage, directing a team of 10-year-old boys. Although more than a decade older, Ambrose, an accountant for a commercial real estate leasing company in Los Angeles, recognized Rivera's skill as a coach and often asked him for pointers on how to drill players. Rivera considered him a friend.

"Hey, Hector," said Ambrose. "I heard Manny Whitney suspended you for the season over Diego's arrest. It's outrageous. I'm not the only one here who thinks so. It's really goin' to hit the fan."

So much for keeping things private, Rivera thought. But he remembered that Ambrose, although not a league official, was plugged in.

"What do you know?" Rivera asked quietly.

"Manny and his executive committee didn't really want this out, at least not now," Ambrose said. "But your request for a hearing forced his hand. Made him tell the entire board and schedule a meeting. That's how word got around."

Ambrose is certainly well informed, Rivera thought.

"Some on the board ain't too happy, for different reasons," Ambrose continued. "Some resent the secrecy. Some think it isn't fair to you. 'Specially those who know your persona.

"All a bunch of 'em care about is PR and their own reps. How this will affect their own business. They're 'fraid this'll get in the paper. Since there's no good basis for suspendin' you, they'll look stupid."

"Good of the game," Rivera repeated. "That's the grounds Manny invoked in suspendin' me. Since when is the game helped by bannin' coaches who haven't done anything?"

"Agreed," Ambrose said. "I'm with ya on this. If you need a character witness at your hearing, just shout. I'll be there."

"Thanks," Rivera said, his mind racing. "But keep talking. Who's against me?"

"Well," Ambrose said, "someone on the executive committee."

"Hmm," Rivera said. "Manny told me it was a collective decision of the committee. Didn't say if it was unanimous.

"I told Manny suspendin' me would make it look like the soccer league thought I had somethin' to do with Hermannik's death."

A rare trace of bitterness crossed Rivera's voice. "Like the league had inside information or something. He didn't care."

"Manny usually looks for the path of least resistance," Ambrose said. "This wasn't his idea. Someone made a stink, and he went along with it."

"Who was that someone?" Rivera asked.

"Don't know," Ambrose said. "It could be anyone on the committee, or even someone who made a hard sell to someone on the committee. But I guarantee it was someone. I know how committees work. We got 'em at my company. Any time a committee does somethin' that looks stupid, it's usually because one person somewhere was pushing it in the first place. Others go along so he'll shut up. Often to their regret.

"And I hear they're startin' to regret it. They're getting pounded now. I know for a fact that e-mails have been flying. Most of 'em are in favor of you."

"That's great," Rivera said. "Let's have a referendum. Just like they do on everything else in California."

"Don't let these bastards get to you," Ambrose said. "My point is that you've got some stuff goin' for you. You're in a lot better shape than Diego."

Rivera alerted. "What do you mean by that?" he asked.

"Um, ah, well, not much," Ambrose stammered. "I mean, you're not charged with anything."

Ambrose paused. "Hey, you're my friend," he said. "I don't know Diego very well. But I know he's prone to, shall we say, loud outbursts against referees. Looks like the cops have some kinda case against him.

"They can't convict him just on talk. Even if it's talk that ended up for the whole world to see on YouTube."

"Well, they're tryin'," Rivera said. "They're tryin'. And I'm tryin' to do something 'bout it."

"Like what?" Ambrose asked.

"Like tryin' to figure out if there's anyone out there with a really good reason for wantin' Rick Hermannik dead. Diego didn't have a really good reason.

"He was a real estate appraiser," Rivera continued, remembering that Ambrose was somewhere in that field of work. "Know anything about his career?"

"Nope," Ambrose said. "But if he's like every other appraiser I know, he worked for himself. Was paid for each appraisal.

"Look, the only reason real estate appraisers even exist as a profession is because every single piece of property is different. Unique. Even if it's a subdivision of identically built homes. Maybe one house gets a little more light or has a slightly better mountain view than the next one. It's not like stock in a big company, like IBM. Shares are identical. Anyone can look in the paper to see what they're worth.

"Yeah, sure, appraisers put a value on the home. Lenders aren't supposed to lend more money than a house is worth after subtractin' the buyer's down payment. But they do it all the time. 'Specially here in California where prices are pumped up more than our Governator.

"Woe to the appraiser who won't certify a house is worth more than the loan. Pretty soon the appraiser won't be getting repeat business."

"Who hires the appraiser for a given deal?" Rivera asked.

"In principle again, whoever is making the initial loan," Ambrose said. "Countrywide. IndyMac. Or AmeriQuest, the guys who invented loans without proof of income. Whoever. But a lot of the time the real estate agent representing the buyer 'suggests' a friendly appraiser, especially if the lender is from far away. As I said, the important thing is that the paperwork look good, not that it *is* good."

Rivera thought about this. "Sounds like the appraisal business is pretty loose," he said.

"Tis," Ambrose admitted. "Appraisers have to have a license. But that's not very hard to get. There are a lot of appraisers out there."

CHAPTER 9

EARLY THE NEXT MORNING, Rivera sat in his truck crawling along The Legendary 5 during The Legendary Rush Hour—part of why the average Southern California commuter spent the equivalent of four days a year in stationary vehicles. Eventually, he reached his destination in Norwalk, a suburb two towns southeast of Los Angeles.

Thanks to Berman's historical articles, Rivera knew all about Norwalk and its environs. They had pretty much the same old sad heritage as most of the other towns adorning Southern California. From time immemorial the area had been populated by Indians living in huts, scratching out an existence and causing trouble to no one.

That 1769 Spanish takeover—the march of soldiers and priests went right through the future Norwalk—changed everything. Although the Indians of California—all 130,000 of them—didn't realize it, their days became seriously numbered. Within three generations all but a couple thousand were gone—dead, mostly. This was from a combination of things: (1) illnesses brought by the foreigners, (2) oppressive tactics supervised by corrupt Catholic priests running a system they set up of religious outposts like the San Fernando Mission near Los Angeles that also doubled as prison farms—and which later were turned into pleasant tourist attractions that ignored the death stuff, and (3) greedy land practices that featured the murderous use of force as an eviction tool.

Goodbye Indians.

The area around Norwalk was part of one of several huge cattle leasing deals that ex-Spanish soldiers got for nothing in the 1780s as part of an unsuccessful effort by Spain to put Spanish boots on the ground. Heirs managed to turn those cattle leases into clear title. But after Mexico ousted the Spaniards in 1821 and became the law in California, the heirs squabbled. The Latino culture was not especially cut out at the time for world commerce. "The Californians are an idle, thriftless people, and can make nothing for themselves," Harvard dropout Richard Henry Dana Jr., who worked as a seaman, wrote memorably in an 1840 book. "The country abounds in grapes, yet they buy, at a great price, bad wine made in Boston."

Then came the largely bogus Mexican War, provoked by the United States in the 1840s as part of President James K. Polk's doctrine of Manifest Destiny, which basically meant gringos from sea to shining sea. Polk sent to California military man John C. Frémont, who distinguished himself by ordering massacres of Indians and Latinos. History being written by the victors, war criminal Frémont later became the first senator of the new state of California and, in 1856, the new Republican Party's first presidential candidate. Meanwhile, he made a fortune through shady practices, balked at paying his property taxes, was convicted in France of fraud and ultimately died flat broke—but very famous.

The Treaty of Guadalupe Hidalgo, the dictated-by-the-Yankees pact that ended the Mexican War, plus a later law passed by Congress requiring all land titles to be proven in court, had the effect of swindling Mexicans out of millions of acres of their land.

Goodbye, Latinos.

But the first wave of gringos into the expanded United States, and especially southern California, ran into those old bugaboos of flooding and drought, causing them to default on their high-interest loans. This allowed a second wave of gringos to buy at bargain prices.

All this eventually put the newly emptied land around Norwalk in the ownership of Yankee adventurers Atwood and Gilbert Sproul. Like many of the gringos, they were from New England—Maine to be exact—and had come to Northern California in the 1850s to prospect for gold. Enjoying only mixed success—it seemed half the world was in Northern California doing what they were doing—they wisely decamped for sparsely populated Oregon, where they pursued mining and timbering. In the late 1860s, drawn by yet another building land boom in Southern California, they paid $5,100 for 463 well-located acres.

The Sprouls gave the railroad a right of way across "North walk," later shortened to "Norwalk," on condition a station regularly served by passenger trains be built on their property.

But aside from a small migration of Dutch dairy farmers, a brief oil boom and the construction by the State Lunacy Commission of a large hospital for the dangerously deranged, pretty much nothing happened in Norwalk for the next eight decades until after World War II. That's when home builders discovered the town and started putting in cheaper subdivisions. The population exploded. Homes in Norwalk were priced less than surrounding towns, which meant the buyers were individuals of lesser means.

Hello again, Latinos.

They soon triumphantly achieved the local population dominance their ancestors had gained running off the natives ("The Indian tribes suffered the loss of much of their culture, and were unable to successfully cope," an official City of Norwalk history declared in a masterful whitewashing of ethnic culpability) but lost to the gringos a century earlier.

And on this particular day, Rivera was among the Latinos in Norwalk. He was at the grandly named Harry L. Hufford Registrar-Recorder Building on the grandly named Imperial Highway just off The 5. The Huff, which honors a county employee who rose through the ranks for 40 years, was a large six-story structure with a glass facade.

As Rivera pulled into the parking lot, he had a feeling of dread. Why wouldn't he? Big government buildings were not the most hospitable of places to most folks. And certainly not to Latinos in Southern California. They often found themselves a lot worse off when they left.

If they were lucky, they were simply shorn of money they paid out and couldn't afford for permissions, penalties or paperwork they didn't understand. If they weren't so lucky, they found themselves in front of a judge being lectured about unpaid child support—at least there were no handcuffs—or told they couldn't get bail—usually wearing handcuffs. Now that only happened at a courthouse, which the Huff wasn't. But Los Angeles County had more than 40 state courthouses—far more than every other one of the 3,000 counties in the United States, which usually had just one state courthouse. So there was a lot of unpleasant chattering by judges in government buildings around Los Angeles.

Like most government buildings, the Huff was a very busy place. And like most government buildings, part of that action stemmed from people working their own angles.

For Rivera, the bustle—or hustle—began in the large parking lot between Imperial Highway and the Huff. "Sir, are you here to register a business?" a tall man asked just after Rivera got out of his truck. The man held a clipboard and wore a large badge on his sports jacket that said, "Not a county employee."

"Uh, no," Rivera said. "I'm here for something else." He glanced around. Maybe a dozen other people—all wearing a "not a county employee" badge—were badgering other people who had just parked their vehicles. And there were signs on all the light poles in the parking lot: "Solicitors Are Not County Employees." The word "Not" was in red.

Who are these people? Rivera wondered. *What's going on?* He learned later from one of his Cal State buddies turned law student. The solicitors were there taking advantage of an old California law that required anybody starting a business whose name didn't consist of their own name to register with the county the name of the business and its real owner. This was called a fictitious business name registration, and it was a pretty easy thing to file, not much harder than registering to vote. The law also required the fledgling owner to run a small classified ad announcing the business and his ownership in some newspaper in the county once a week for four consecutive weeks. That's where the hustle came in. The guys with the badges offered to arrange for the fictitious business name registration and the required publication—for a lot more money than would be charged by the county or the newspaper. Of course, a lot of people registering new businesses didn't know that.

From time to time, county officials tried to rid the Huff's parking lot of these solicitors. But they claimed a hallowed freedom of speech right on public property to ply their trade—such that it was—and help their less knowledgeable fellow citizens navigate the perils of government. They also threatened to sue. The badges were the compromise.

Like all public buildings in the Golden State, the Huff was full of dire warnings. They caught Rivera's eye, partly because he was curious by nature, and partly because he wasn't in such locations all that often. DO NOT PLACE MORE THAN ONE CHILD AT A TIME ON

CHANGING TABLE, read a sign in the men's room where Rivera stopped to take a leak. CAUTION: DOOR OPENS OUTWARD, said a sign above an automated portal he passed through. Thanks to passage of Proposition 65 in 1986, there were the usual California-only warnings that cancer-causing material was everywhere.

The Huff was a county building where people went to do things and file stuff. Besides listing a business, one could register to vote, request a birth certificate, obtain a marriage license and, for $25, even get married. Walking through the lobby, Rivera saw off to one side a door marked WEDDING CHAPEL with a removable sign that said, CEREMONY IN PROGRESS. The door was closed. Nearby, waiting to use the room were a number of couples. Rivera noticed that the men all seemed to be very nervous, and the women all seemed to be very pregnant.

Another warning, Rivera thought with a grin.

But the most important function within the Huff was its role as the repository of all Los Angeles County real estate records going back centuries. Even though the Spanish Law of the Indies had made it possible to take land used by Indians without permission or payment, there still had to be a written record signed by someone. And again, when the stolen land was resold. And subdivided. And resold. And mortgaged. And resold. And remortgaged. And foreclosed upon. And, until courts finally outlawed their legal force, tagged with restrictions prohibiting non-whites from living in the wrong parts of the county, which was most of it. Again and again. Since the county had more land than Rhode Island and Delaware combined, and more people than any other county, that made for a lot of paper—millions and millions of pages—pouring each year into the Huff.

Moreover, land records in the United States were largely public, unlike many other countries in which they were secret or available for examination only by licensed individuals. In America, anybody could come in and poke around for any reason. Rivera was one of those anybodies, determined to somehow find his way through the tons of paper and clear the good name of Diaz.

After consulting the building directory, he took the steps to the second floor and headed to Room 2207. That's where the real estate records could be researched. Rivera opened the door expecting to see an ominous place filled to the gills with a mass of files and paper. Instead, he found a largely empty big room.

In the old days photocopies of deeds and mortgages were numbered sequentially, then bound into big heavy books that sat on rows and rows of shelving almost as high as the room. Each document was then indexed in separate sets of books by the last name of the individuals involved and their relationship to the transaction.

But in a place like Los Angeles County, the big heavy books with the sequentially numbered deeds and mortgages eventually took up too much space. They were phased out in favor of plastic cassettes holding microfilm rolls containing the images of those sequentially numbered deeds and mortgages. The cassettes could be viewed on banks of microfilm readers. Eventually, this, too, was phased out in favor of a computer-based system. Images were scanned into a giant mainframe computer and the grantor and grantee indexes put in a giant searchable database.

This was why Rivera found Room 2207 largely empty. The space consisted mainly of a cluster of tables holding several dozen computer terminals on which real estate records—the indexes and the actual documents—could be researched and viewed. With windows from a southern exposure running its entire length, overhead lights and a white linoleum floor, Room 2207 was a surprisingly bright place.

The problem was the mood, which was not helped by signs posted everywhere that said, NO FOOD, NO EATING, NO DRINKS ALLOWED IN THIS WORK AREA. Huddled around several of the terminals were what looked like Latino families—a man, a woman, couple fidgety young kids. Rivera overheard one worried couple talking in Spanish about the *ejecución de hipoteca*—foreclosure.

Rivera sat himself down in front of one of the terminals. *Now what do I do?* he thought. Then he remembered his goal was to see what he could learn about bad loans in Valley Mirage involving Associated Capital Equity and Rick Hermannik.

From the drop-down menu on the computer screen, he selected "grantor," typed in "Associated Capital Equity," and hit the enter button.

Nothing came up.

How can that be? Rivera thought. Then he remembered that Hartigan, his real estate buddy, had told him lenders were listed as grantees, not grantors.

My bad, Rivera said to himself.

So he redid his search and hit the enter button. This time about 40 hits came up listing Associated Capital Equity as a lender in Los Angeles County.

That's a manageable number, Rivera thought. *Not like the tens of thousands from Countrywide or Wells Fargo or that MERS system to cheat the county of fees.*

By scanning the index, Rivera saw the deals stretched back about six years to 2000. He couldn't tell from the index itself where the properties were. But by clicking on each entry, he could see the name of the buyer, the person or couple who had given the deed of trust, or mortgage. Rivera quickly came across the listing for the house that was bought by the Samuels family, who lost it (costing Rivera a player), and also that of the Smithfields, who also lost theirs. But he couldn't tell from the index itself where the other homes were located.

Looking at the notes he had taken on that wad of Starbucks napkins, Rivera found what Hartigan had told him about how to research this. On his pad of yellow paper he wrote down names of everyone who had bought with an Associated Capital Equity loan. Then he punched them one by one into the grantee index. For each name he got a listing to the deed—and, almost every time, a listing to more recent notice of default. That, he knew, meant the property was going into foreclosure because the mortgage hadn't been paid.

Boy, ACE really has a lousy track record, Rivera thought. *Their loans all went into the tank.*

By clicking on each deed citation and then calling up the image of the deed itself, Rivera saw the name of each seller, the person who unloaded the house that the hapless buyer (a group that included the Samuels and Smithfield families) was losing in foreclosure. He also saw the location of the home. Wading through weary boilerplate language, Rivera was struck by several things.

First, the addresses were all clustered in Valley Mirage or in adjoining towns. Secondly, they generally weren't the most expensive homes.

Thirdly, the names of all the sellers were equally common, almost generic, and just one person, a male. He saw the deed from Larry Murphy, the named seller of the home that the Samuels family bought and lost, and the deed from Richard Stevens, the named seller of the home that the Smithfield family bought and lost. Rivera also saw other deeds on ACE loans bearing bland names like Albert Bailey, Charles Douglas, James Smith and Edward Thomas.

The only missing name is John Doe, Rivera thought—before coming across a seller named John Jones, which was pretty close.

Rivera wasn't sure where he was going with any of this. Then he had an idea. *If Richard Stevens sold the house to the Smithfields, then somebody sold the house to Richard Stevens,* Rivera thought. *So who was that?*

He looked again at the Stevens-to-Smithfield deed. Hartigan had said the price could be figured out by dividing the listed property transfer tax by point zero zero one one. Rivera whipped out the calculator he used in figuring the sales tax on parts for WeFixItRightNow repairs. The price worked out to be $925,000.

Then Rivera started looking for Richard Stevens through the computer's grantee index. It took a little time—after all, Richard Stevens was a very common name—but Rivera finally found the deed. It was in the name of Gary Frank—another common name. The deed was dated just three months before the $925,000 Stevens-to-Smithfield deed. The price, Rivera figured, was $900,000.

Who owns a house for just three months? he asked himself.

Wondering who had sold the house to Gary Frank, Rivera ran Frank's name through the grantee index. The answer was a couple, Scott and Lacey Koenigsburg.

Finally, names that sound like real people, Rivera thought. But then he looked at the rest of the deed and worked his calculator. The Koenigsburg-to-Frank deed was dated just eight days before the $900,000 Frank-to-Stevens deed. And the price was a lot less—$600,000.

What house goes up 50% in one week, even in California? Rivera asked himself.

It occurred to Rivera to check from whom the mysterious Gary Frank and Richard Stevens had gotten their loans. *Maybe ACE,* he thought, although that would only add to the mystery. So Rivera ran both their names through the grantor index looking for a deed of trust, which would indicate the identity of the lender.

Nothing came up.

What am I doing wrong? Rivera thought to himself. He checked the spelling he had entered for both men, and also looked to make sure he didn't have their names reversed. *Got that right.* Rivera looked again at his napkin notes to make sure it was the grantor index he should be searching through. *Yep, the person taking the mortgage is givin' his okay, just like the seller does in sellin' the home.* He made sure he actually was searching the grantor index and not the grantee index. *Check.*

Rivera hit the enter button again.

Nothing came up.

He was flummoxed. *Still must be doin' somethin' wrong,* Rivera thought. *But what?*

So he tried the search several more times on both names, with the same result. Rivera gave up. *Okay,* he thought. *They were both cash deals. But who buys a house for cash in California?*

Rivera decided to work his way back from the house the Samuels family lost. He had seen the deed into the Samuels' from the seller they had never met, Larry Murphy. The price was $900,000. Having climbed the learning curve a bit, Rivera quickly found the deed that conveyed the property to Murphy.

And it proved to be just like the scenario that led to the Smithfields. Someone named Harry Wilson—another common name—had sold the house to Murphy for $875,000 two-and-a-half months before the $900,000 Murphy-to-Samuels transaction. But just a week earlier, Wilson had bought the house from what seemed like real sellers—a couple by the name of Annette and Brad Reisenoff—for a mere $583,000.

Another 50% gain! Rivera thought. *What's goin' on?*

He started running title and taking notes on a sampling of the other deals in the Valley Mirage area among the 40 he had identified in which a loan from Associated Capital Equity ended up in default. As Rivera found to his surprise, almost all had the same three-deed pattern. A seemingly real owner, usually a couple, selling to a single common-name buyer, who quickly resold at a huge profit to another single common-name buyer—neither of whom took out a loan—who resold soon to a family that obtained a mortgage from ACE and lost it all in foreclosure.

How can this all be a coincidence? Rivera thought as he looked at his notes. *But what does it mean?*

One thing Rivera couldn't tell from the land records in the county office was whether Hermannik was the appraiser on any of the other ACE-funded deals that went south. Rivera knew of just two—the properties lost by the Smithfields and the Samuels. But now he had a bunch of names and could start looking for people. He might even get some answers.

But of course there was no guarantee this would lead anywhere concerning the matter at hand—helping Diego Diaz and, perhaps, himself. *Suppose Hermannik was the appraiser in many or even all of these deals*, Rivera pondered. *What would that prove? That he was a lousy appraiser? So what?*

Rivera glanced at his watch. 11 a.m. He had been at the Huff since it opened at 8:00 a.m. Covered a lot of ground, too. But he hadn't phoned in sick to WeFixThingsRightNow or otherwise taken the day off. So Rivera headed downstairs back to his truck for a full day of repair activities to make expensive toys safe for Southern California. *I'll hit the phone tonight when I get home*, he thought.

He headed down The 605 toward his first call, fixing a high-end $3,000 Jura-Capressa Impressa cappuccino machine in a house in decidedly middle-end Lakewood. The suburb just north of Long Beach had been an instant city poster child for the wild boom after World War II: 17,500 homes built rat-tat-tat—more than 100 a week—on empty farmland during a three-year period. The town, however, also gave the lie to that persistent California myth of rugged individualism free of government help: A full 100% of the financing came from federal loans. At the same time Lakewood re-enforced the area's persistent segregation: the three white developers condoned a process in which housing applications were not accepted from blacks.

Even though it was mid-day, traffic was still a mess. Rivera was going maybe nine miles per hour.

He turned on the radio. Usually, Rivera tuned into one of the stations with traffic reports every few minutes. One thing about most Southern California drivers was that no matter how bad the traffic, they almost never abandoned freeways for parallel surface streets that could move them along better. The familiar over the faster. Hell, a sinkhole could open up ahead across two lanes next to an overturned truck spilling 20 tons of lye amid reports of both a road-rage gunman and a police pursuit, and Los Angeles motorists still would take that freeway. So the radio traffic reports generally were totally meaningless to the average motorist, whose DNA mandated a straight-ahead trajectory.

But like the way he coached soccer, Rivera drove strategically. If the cause of the slow traffic was the general crush of simply too many cars—as opposed to a single obstacle like a one-off wreck or that remarkably frequent Los Angeles happening, a ladder in lane two that had fallen off a pick-up truck to which it was secured inadequately—he was happy to bail. However, Rivera needed to know the extent and cause of the backed-up traffic, and for that he relied on the radio.

But Rivera hit the wrong button and found himself listening to one of the half-dozen or so NPR stations in the Los Angeles area. These reliably liberal outlets generally eschewed incessant traffic reports and actually provided news, sometimes even individual items of length and substance.

Rivera heard a long account about a burial. But not just any burial (otherwise, it wouldn't have been on an NPR station). The burial of an 11-year-old soccer player in Arizona.

Aven Darby was on his way home with his family from a soccer tournament in suburban Phoenix in which he had scored the only goal in a 1 to 0 victory. The family car in which he was riding blew a tire and the car skidded, smashing into a wall. Aven's parents and siblings escaped serious harm, but not Aven. Paramedics rushing to the scene got him out of the mangled vehicle. As he lay on the side of the road, they started cutting off his soccer jersey and shorts to administer aid.

"No, no, don't cut them," the injured boy murmured. "Got a match next week. Team needs all its players." He then lapsed into unconsciousness.

His father pulled the jersey off over his head. But 10 minutes later, Aven died of his injuries in the ambulance rushing him to the hospital.

Aven was the team captain and a leader. His selfless final words thinking of the team, first reported on the league's website, then by bloggers and finally in the traditional local media, electrified the area soccer community. His church funeral a week later was attended by hundreds, most of whom had never met him but were struck by his tragedy. Aven lay in the coffin clad in the very soccer jersey his father had retrieved. He later was buried in the church cemetery. After the casket was lowered into the ground, but before the grave was filled, his teammates stepped forward and one-by-one threw their own jerseys into the hole.

"He brought us together in soccer," one crying player told the NPR reporter. "So we'll stay together in soccer."

By the end of the radio report, Rivera was crying, too—not a very safe thing to be doing on The 5 even if traffic was slower than a dial-up Internet connection. He was crying because the story was poignant and sad, of course. Identifying with Aven's selflessness, Rivera was also crying because he, too, had been pushed away in soccer. Forcibly separated from the sport he loved. Torn from the players he cared about. Upset that his Latino heritage probably played a role.

CHAPTER 10

FOR THE REST of that Monday, Rivera rushed through the motions. In the appliance-and-gadget fix-it biz, that wasn't always possible. But he wanted to get home to follow up leads about the puzzling real estate pattern he had found in Valley Mirage.

Fortunately, the gods of American consumer ineptitude shined brightly upon him.

After Lakewood, Rivera slid up The 710 to a call in old-money Pasadena, a town founded in the 1870s by folks from Indianapolis who thought the air quality would be better than in the Hoosier State. He was in a nice upscale home on one of those residential streets that got choked with traffic when anything big was at the Rose Bowl. Another high-end coffee machine call. As was so often the case, the problem was a clog in the tubing channeling the water. It was a common malfunction whose simple fix was described in the easy-to-read owner's manual the stay-at-home woman of the house—"Call me Ginny," she told Rivera at the door—couldn't find or didn't read. Rivera took care of the blockage with what amounted to a straightened paper clip.

Although in a hurry, Rivera pretended to fiddle with the gizmo for a couple more minutes so Ginny wouldn't feel too silly. It was part of his natural compassion, although it didn't hurt—Dora notwithstanding —that she was a stereotypical non-Latina California female, which is to say, blond and trim. Her kids were at school—private school. The public schools in world-famous Pasadena, home of brainy world-class institutions like the California Institute of Technology, ranked among the very worst in California. That was due to their abandonment by such well-to-do families who cared much more about supporting the Rose Parade on New Year's Day.

"My husband works downtown at Arthur Mutual Funds," she said to make conversation and perhaps brag a bit. "Has a big job there."

Rivera nodded. He knew about Arthur from one of his college friends. It was a big mutual fund operator that brought in big money by paying big commissions to financial advisors—commissions, of course, ultimately paid by their clients whose money was being steered in the form of lesser returns.

He also remembered one other thing he had been told. Advisors who sold Arthur products often downplayed the fact to their clients that equally good investments were available elsewhere with less risk and no commissions—meaning a better return for the client and less income for the advisor.

At least this household can afford its fancy cappuccino machine, Rivera thought. Of course, it wouldn't be prudent to bring up the reason.

"Bet he needs a good strong cup when he gets home," Hector said as he removed the paper clip. "Must be a tough job."

"It's more for me, really," Ginny replied quietly. "Clark prefers, uh, harder stuff."

"Oh, I see," Rivera said, sheepish at his ignorance of worldly upper-class ways. He quickly wrote up the bill, which Ginny paid in cash.

For his next call, Rivera scooted up The 210 and then The 5, through the San Fernando and Santa Clarita Valleys, and then west on Highway 128 along the dry-as-a-bone Santa Clara River toward the farm town of Fillmore, named not for a US president but for a railroad employee. Rivera passed by yet another key venue in the myth-making that courses through the fabric of Southern California. It was Rancho Camulos, the supposed inspiration for one of the most famous and influential novels ever written about California. Famous and influential, that is, for all the wrong reasons. Rivera remembered a Berman column about that, too.

The book, *Ramona*, was written in 1884 by Helen Hunt Jackson. She was a widowed Massachusetts native and prominent magazine writer who had become an Indian rights activist. In an effort to generate interest she invented some characters, drew on real-life events and crafted a tale of searing, naked racism set in the wild days after the Mexican War when gringos poured into Southern California.

The daughter of an Indian mother and a Scottish sea-captain father who disappears, Ramona is raised on Rancho Moreno (clearly modeled after Rancho Camulos, which Jackson had visited) in an aristocratic family that loses much of its wealth. She marries an Indian, Alessandro, whose family is killed by rampaging American settlers seeking land. Ramona and Alessandro are constantly forced to flee ahead of the killer Americans. The US government is depicted as highly unsympathetic to Indians. The infant child of Ramona and Alessandro dies when an American doctor refuses treatment. Alessandro accidentally takes a wrong horse and is killed by its angry gringo owner, who is acquitted of murder. Fearful of the Yankees, Ramona finally moves to Mexico City, remarries, has more children and lives happily ever after.

Ramona became an immediate best-seller and has remained in print ever since. But it didn't stir up the ruckus its author hoped for with its profound message of profound injustice. "A dead failure," Jackson wrote before her own death just 18 months later. Instead, readers focused on its sentimental depiction of life on the Spanish/Mexican ranchos of Southern California. Pretty soon, tourists—and eventually immigrants—started arriving in large numbers enchanted by the described environment looking for Ramona landmarks.

Of course, since *Ramona* was a novel, there really weren't any. But enterprising locals were quite happy to oblige. Thus was born a house in the San Gabriel Valley touted as Ramona's birthplace, a villa in San Diego touted as the site of Ramona's first marriage, and a grave on an Indian reservation touted as Ramona's final resting place (even though at the novel's end Ramona still was very much alive in another country). The Southern Pacific even built a rail spur to the very Rancho Camulos that Rivera was passing.

The City of Fillmore was hardly a posh area like Pasadena. Yet Rivera found himself pulling up in front of a tiny, run-down bungalow to fix a $55,000 indoor golf course simulator.

Luis met him at the door. "Damn thing sparked out," he told Rivera in Spanish, hooking a thumb over his shoulder toward a set-up that took up the entire living room. The simulator consisted of a giant cage of netting, a fake-grass area in the middle for the tee, and, outside the netting, a giant screen on which a computer projected views of famous golf holes like, say, the 12th at Augusta. A gazillion computer sensors measured Luis's "shot" and put the imagined trajectory up on the screen.

Rivera quickly identified the easy-to-fix problem: a loose wire from the computer. Meanwhile, Luis, who resembled Diego Diaz in physique—fat—garrulously chatted about his life. He was a truck driver for an area tortilla factory. He happened to love golf but had little time, especially during daylight hours, to get out on actual links. Ergo the simulator.

Wonder how a truck driver managed to swing this? Rivera thought.

Luis read his mind. "Took out a second mortgage," he said. "This ain't Beverly Hills, but prices have gone up a lot here, too. Doubled since 2001 when I bought. Some people borrow to put in a hot tub. Me, I just went for golf.

"My extra payments are still cheaper than greens fees and memberships."

It was a song Rivera had been hearing a lot lately, and he sung the refrain.

"But what if the prices go down just as fast?" he asked quietly. "Or you lose your job? You're still stuck with that extra debt."

Luis laughed. "Prices can't go down that far," he said. "So I get another job."

Rivera was in a hurry, and Luis was not nearly as easy on the eyes as Ginny. So Rivera cut short the chitchat, wrote up the bill, took his check and headed to the door.

"Hope you get a hole in one," he said.

"Me, too."

As Rivera got into his truck, he heard a lusty roar from the house— "FORE!"—followed by a loud thwack. *Another satisfied customer even if he can't afford it,* Rivera smiled to himself.

Driving away, he thought again about that gossip-filled phone call from Scott Ambrose. *I wonder what people are sayin' 'bout me,* Rivera wondered to himself.

A few minutes later, Rivera's cell phone rang. "VM Daily Post," the caller ID read. Rivera figured it was Berman, and that little good could come at this point from answering and speaking with him. So Rivera let the call go into his voicemail, then retrieved the message.

"Hi, Hector. Jeff Berman here. *Valley Mirage Daily Post.* Reason I'm calling, I heard the soccer league suspended you as a coach. Don't know the exact reason. But I'm assuming it has something to do with

Diego Diaz's, ah, situation. I may write a story. But I first wanted to get your side. Please call me back." Berman gave a number.

Rivera grimaced. *Word really is getting around,* he thought. Rivera was no student of the media, but he pondered whether or not to call back. He really didn't want to draw attention to himself—it certainly wouldn't help Diego—but it looked like someone else had done that for him.

Time to play some offense, Rivera concluded. He dialed a number.

"Manny? Hector Rivera here. The reporter on the local paper covering the Hermannik case just left me a message sayin' I had been suspended as a coach and he was writin' a story. You said this wouldn't get out. Two days, and it's everywhere."

Whitney sighed. "So sorry," he said. "Mr. Berman called me, too. I answered thinking it was the paper's ad department handling one of my death notices. So I had to talk with him."

"Whadya tell him?" Rivera asked.

"Not much," Whitney said. "He knew about your status. Guess that's not surprising, judging from all the calls and e-mails I've been getting. He didn't have a lot of detail. Wanted to know why. I told him it was a temporary thing until things died down. So that players and parents wouldn't be distracted. And that it was no reflection upon you.

"I thought saying no comment would sound a lot worse. And that *was* the reason."

"Did you tell him I'm appealin'?"

"Uh, no, because he didn't ask. I wasn't about to volunteer information."

Then Rivera had a lawyer moment.

"Not very fair to me," he said. "You promised confidentiality. Now here you are confirmin' secret stuff to the paper.

"I should be reinstated 'til the hearing. Not suspended 'til the hearing."

"Well," Whitney said, "remember you're the one who requested the hearing. After finding that you had a right to one, of course. It's in a couple days. I think we'll just wait until then."

"So should I call back Berman?" Rivera asked.

"It's up to you," Whitney said, a little nervously. "I can't tell you not to speak. But watch your words."

After the call ended, Rivera pulled over to the side of the road and thought for a minute or two. The last thing he wanted at this point was a back-and-forth with Berman. But he didn't want it to look like he was hiding something. So Rivera tapped out a short e-mail to him from his cell.

The rest of the day went by in a blur.

Dora called twice. The first time, she wanted to know if he had learned anything at the deed room.

"*¿Qué pasa?*" she asked.

"Not sure," Hector told her. "Gotta lotta names. Don't know what they mean yet."

She called a couple hours later in something of a panic because she had gotten cut off in the middle of a jailhouse telephone conversation with Diego. Hector calmed her down.

"Plenty o' calls between get dropped, too," he said.

"Yeah, but he's in a place where he could get assaulted!" Dora shouted.

"Like that couldn't happen to you or me?" Hector replied. "Remember, we live in Southern California."

Dora emitted a tight giggle. "Maybe so," she said. "But I just worry about him."

"Me, too," Hector said.

He had one more stop, unclogging the intake on a $2,000 robotic vacuum cleaner that its owner had nicknamed Anteater. That was on 25th Street in beachside Santa Monica. It was a block from a home once rented during World War II by refugee German poet and playwright Bertolt Brecht, whose *Threepenny Opera* had posed the question, "Which is the greater crime: to rob a bank or to own one?" While living in that house, Brecht wrote a short poem entitled "On Thinking About Hell," which ended, "It must be still more like Los Angeles."

On his way home, Rivera finally called Charles Gramm, Diaz's defense lawyer.

Rivera started to tell him what he had found. Hermannik's authorship of some questionable appraisals blessing sharp value increases in astonishingly short periods of time. Missing mortgages followed by ACE mortgages. An angry ex-homeowner. Hermannik's involvement in strange three-deed deals.

But Rivera wasn't very good when it came to explaining things on the fly, particularly when they were complicated, unless it was about soccer. Rivera could put together a PowerPoint presentation in a snap, having learned how to run Microsoft's ubiquitous visual presentation program in a Cal State course. But without that as a backup, he got nervous and tongue-tied.

Like many lawyers, Gramm was a reasonably good listener, and he asked obvious, straightforward questions. And as Rivera hemmed and hawed, he took notes. "Okay, Hector," Gramm said. "Not sure I get all this stuff 'bout what you're sayin'. But if I'm understandin', you see a pattern. I think it goes somethin' like this. Grantor-grantee-no-mortgage; grantor-grantee-big-price-jump-no-mortgage; grantor-grantee-bigger-price-jump-bigger-mortgage with Rick Hermannik appraisal and default.

"Yeah, that's it!" Rivera said excitedly. "That's it exactly!"

"Okay," Gramm said. "Then let me ask you. How does this prove Diego's innocent?"

End of excitement for Rivera. "Well, it doesn't," he acknowledged dejectedly, realizing that he had told himself pretty much the same. "At least not yet. But it might show others had a motive to kill him."

"Okay," Gramm said. He paused a beat. "Who?"

It was Rivera's turn to pause. "Don't know," he said finally. "Still working on that."

Gramm laughed. "A theory is nice," he said, "but a theory with some facts behind it is even nicer."

He turned serious. "Look, I told Dora the state in some ways has a weak case," he said. "But Diego right now has an alibi that can't be proven. What I really need is another suspect. One with a name. One with a better motive for killin' Hermannik than the one breakin' all the viewing records on YouTube.

"I suppose it's possible to check out a bunch of Hermannik's deals. Strikes me as a long shot. But I'd have to hire a private detective. And I can't do that 'til I get some more money from Diego or his family.

"So for the time bein', you're my private detective. Keep pokin' around. Don't lie. Don't threaten anyone. Don't put words in people's mouths. Write stuff down. Keep talking to me."

"Okay," Rivera said, deflated by the lawyer's assessment of the case. But he was relieved Gramm didn't order him to end his efforts as an amateur Paul Drake, Perry Mason's detective.

Rivera finally arrived at his apartment. Once again, Dora wasn't there; she had texted she was going to visit Diego. Normally, he looked forward to seeing her when he got home. But he had a lot of stuff to do, and when that was the case, she sometimes got in the way.

Sitting down at his computer, Rivera took out his pad of notes scribbled in the Norwalk deed room. He was trying to find people—people whose names were on deeds to property around Valley Mirage that had some connection to Rick Hermannik.

There were all those strange three-deed sequences. He decided to start with the ones he knew the most about.

The Samuels' had bought their house for $900,000 from one Larry Murphy, no address listed. Rivera went to an Internet site that searched other Internet sites for addresses and phone numbers, and entered the name of Larry Murphy and Lawrence Murphy.

Up came about 500 hits just in Southern California alone.

Don't think I'm going to find Larry Murphy tonight, Rivera thought.

Murphy—whoever he was—had owned the house for just two-and-a-half months. He had bought it from Harry Wilson, no address listed, for $875,000. With a slightly sickening feeling, Rivera put in Wilson's name.

Four hundred hits around Los Angeles.

Not going there, either, Rivera thought.

The hard-to-locate Wilson had bought the house just a week earlier for a whole lot less from Brad and Annette Reisenoff. *Now, how many Reisenoffs can there be?* Rivera wondered. He punched in the man's name.

A hit!

Up came an address and phone number near San Diego.

With excitement but also trepidation, Rivera dialed the number.

A woman answered. Annette?

"Hi, uh, my name is Hector Rivera. I'm—"

"We're on the do-not-call list," the woman said, cutting him off. "Please don't call again."

"But I —"

Click.

Rivera looked at his phone. *What would Paul Drake do?* he thought. *Try someone else.*

So he looked at the Smithfield sequence. They had bought their house for $925,000 from Richard Stevens. *Good luck there,* Rivera thought. Stevens had acquired it three months earlier for a little less from Gary Frank. *Plenty of them out around,* Rivera thought.

But like Wilson, Frank had made a killing; he had paid $600,000 for the property just eight days earlier from Scott and Lacey Koenigsburg.

Bingo again!

Rivera found a listing in Laguna Hills. It was one of the many Lagunas (Spanish for lagoon) that made Orange County such a confusing place to outsiders: Laguna Hills, Laguna Beach, Laguna Niguel, Laguna Woods. Rivera had fixed contraptions in all four and still got them mixed up. But now he had a phone number.

Rivera dialed.

The phone rang.

And then a man's voice came on: "Hello."

"Hi, my name is Hector Rivera. Trying to reach the Scott Koenigsburg who used to live on"—Rivera looked at his notes—"Vivendi Avenue in Valley Mirage."

"You got him."

"Wow," Rivera exclaimed, betraying his inexperience in poking around. "Uh, actually, I'm trying to find Gary Frank, the person you sold your house to. Hope you can help me."

"Why do you want him?" Koenigsburg asked.

"It's"—Diaz's lawyer had warned against lying—"a legal matter," which was true enough.

"Can't help you," Koenigsburg said. "No idea where he is. Don't even know what he looks like. Never met him."

"Never met him?" Rivera repeated. *The Samuels and Smithfields never met their sellers, either,* he thought.

"We decided to move. Listed our house for sale. His real estate agent contacted our real estate agent. Stevens looked at the house when we weren't here. Next thing we know, we had a contract at our asking price. Cash deal. No new mortgage.

"Check cleared. All we cared about. Paid off our mortgage and moved."

"Gee, that was terrific," Rivera said, zero conviction in his voice. *This is going nowhere,* he thought.

Suddenly, Rivera had an idea.

"Are you aware," he asked, "Frank resold your house a week later for 50% more?"

"What?!" Koenigsburg shouted. "How much more?"

"Uh, $300,000 more," Rivera said. "He resold it for $900,000. He paid you $600,000."

"You're kidding!" Koenigsburg shouted again.

"That's what the deed shows," Rivera said. But Koenigsburg, who had pulled the phone from his head, didn't hear him.

"Hey, Lacey," Rivera heard over a muffled phone. "Someone on the phone says the guy who bought our Valley Mirage house resold it right away for $300,000 more! Unbelievable!" Rivera couldn't hear Lacey's response.

Koenigsburg returned to the line. "No, we didn't know that at all," he said. "But if Frank could get a better price, more power to him. Guess we left a lot of money on the table."

He paused. "Now that I think about it, we did know that Frank never moved in. One of our old neighbors said a family named Smith-something bought it. Heard they just lost it in a foreclosure, too."

"I think that's correct," Rivera said. "But Frank didn't sell the house to the Smithfields. He sold it to someone named Richard Stevens. Stevens sold it to the Smithfields."

"Richard Stevens?" Koenigsburg said. "Never heard that name before. Who's he?"

"Don't know," Rivera said, truthfully. "I'd like to find him, too."

"No idea," Koenigsburg said.

"Say," said Rivera, who after all, was exploring Hermannik's role, "do you happen to remember the name of the appraiser on your sale?"

"Sure," Koenigsburg said. "There wasn't one. It was an all-cash deal. No mortgage, so no appraisal."

"I see," Rivera said. "How about the name of the agent for Stevens?"

"Can't remember."

"Name of your agent?"

"Can't remember that, either. It was a while ago. Sorry."

"No problem," Rivera said. That was a lie; it was a big problem.

"Why did you say you were calling?" Koenigsburg said. "Are you a debt collector?"

"No, no, not at all," Rivera said quickly. "It's possible Stevens knows something about, uh, a matter in litigation." *There, no lie again,* Rivera thought. *A murder prosecution's definitely a matter in litigation.*

Rivera ended the call, more puzzled than before. Each answer just led to more questions.

He looked at his notes. Another three-deed sequence started with ownership by Mark and Lucille Masterello. He found them living near San Francisco.

Mark answered his call. Rivera started his pitch. But unlike Scott Koenigsburg, Masterello was unfriendly and hostile. Especially when Rivera tried to smoke him out by playing what he thought was his trump card—that Masterello's buyer had resold the house nine days later for a whopping 53% more.

"So what?" Masterello snapped.

"Well," said Rivera, who couldn't tell if Masterello had known that or not, "it, it seems like a pretty big jump."

"So what?" Masterello said.

Rivera, who figured there was no appraiser because the public records showed it was a cash transaction, asked Masterello if he remembered the names of the real estate agents.

"None of your business," Masterello said curtly. "This was a private deal. Why are you asking these questions again?"

"Trying to locate people who might have knowledge about another matter in litigation," Rivera said, a little more smoothly than when Koenigsburg asked. "I'm not at liberty to say much more."

"Well, neither am I," Masterello said. "Goodbye."

Click.

Nothing to show for that call, thought Rivera, who didn't know what to make of Masterello and his demeanor. *But if someone called me asking such questions, I probably wouldn't say much, either.*

Rivera continued to work his way down the three-deed list, trying to locate the original sellers. Some he couldn't find. Several calls were greeted by answering machines. Rivera didn't leave a message, figuring it wouldn't make much sense and that he might lose whatever small element of surprise he had.

Despite some more hang-ups, He managed to connect with several of the sellers. It was clear to Rivera that all were unaware their homes had been resold immediately for so much more, then quickly resold again. But the gleanings beyond that were lean. Since their own buyers paid cash, there were no mortgage appraisals. So Hermannik's name never came up. And no one could identify any of the real estate agents who might help him work his way up the chain of title and through the featureless thicket of ordinary names and extraordinary transactions.

Rivera tried looking for some of the other people who had lost their homes on ACE mortgages like the Smithfields and the Samuels—the end of the three-deed deals. The few phone numbers that came up were disconnected with no forwarding number. Rivera didn't find this surprising. *Guess people who lost their homes don't want to be found*, Rivera thought.

Hector was midway down the list when Dora walked in.

"Hector, you gotta find out something fast because jail is killin' Daddy," she said. "He doesn't like being confined."

"Who does?" Hector said. "How's his treatment?"

"All things considered, not that bad, I guess," Dora said. "In fact, he's even sort of a hero. He's accused of killin' a soccer referee. A lot of the others in there behind bars played soccer. But a referee's an authority figure. Like a cop. Inmates don't have the greatest opinion of authority figures.

"Daddy tells them he didn't do it. And everyone tells him to stop bein' so modest."

Hector laughed. "Diego loves an audience," he said.

"Find out anything?" Dora asked.

"Yes and no, but mainly no," Hector replied. "The run up to the two deals that I know Hermannik did appraisal work for were sort of strange. And the mortgage company that was involved, ACE? Wrote a lot of bad mortgages here in Valley Mirage. People lost their home in almost every one.

"But I couldn't find a lot of people who might know somethin'. Hermannik's name didn't even come up. So I don't know if he had anything to do with the others. Even if he did, don't know how that'd lead to his murder."

"Somebody killed Hermannik," Dora said, "And it wasn't Daddy."

"Well," Hector said, "As Charlie Gramm told me today, theories are nice, but facts are even better."

"You talked to Gramm?" Dora said excitedly. "What did he say?"

"Keep looking around, don't threaten anyone," Hector said, a tad sarcastically. "Not a whole lot, actually."

"So what are you going to do?" Dora asked.

"Keep looking around, not threaten anyone," Hector said, a tad sarcastically. "But first I'm going to bed. I'm beat."

Even with all these things on his mind, Hector slept well. He always did, if for no other reason than the rest of his days were always so active.

But he got up on Tuesday a little earlier than normal. It wasn't because of insomnia. Putting on a robe, he went outside to fetch his thrown copy of the *Daily Post*. Coming back in, Hector read Berman's front-page coverage of himself.

Soccer League Suspends Coach Who Dates Daughter of Accused Referee Killer

Official says presence of Hector Rivera might be distracting

By Jeff Berman

The Valley Mirage Soccer League confirmed Monday it has put on a leave of absence a coach who dates the daughter of the man accused of killing a referee after a rant that was posted on YouTube and now seen worldwide by millions.

The volunteer coach, Hector Rivera, who managed a team of 11- and 12-year old boys known as the Artful Dodgers, was temporarily relieved of his duties, according to Manuel H. Whitney Jr., the league commissioner. He is also proprietor of the M.H. Whitney Funeral Home Mortuary and Crematorium.

Whitney said the only reason for the leave was that the presence of Rivera on the soccer fields might prove to be a distraction for players, parents and league personnel. "This is no reflection whatsoever upon Mr. Rivera," Whitney said. "We have no knowledge he was involved in the tragic event. But we want everyone to focus on the matches."

Asked about the authority for taking such a dramatic action in the absence of any evidence of personal culpability,

Whitney said, "It was for the good of the game. That's a long-standing rule in soccer." He declined to say which league officials were involved in the suspension decision or whether it was unanimous.

Rivera, who is in his mid-20s and works as an appliance repairman, did not return a phone call seeking comment. But in an e-mail message to the *Daily Post*, he wrote, "Not much I can say right now. I hope to be back on the field very soon."

Rivera was a member of the 2000 Valley Mirage High School soccer team that won the state championship.

His girlfriend, Dora Diaz, is the daughter of Diego Diaz, 49, who is charged with the violent murder of...

At least he quoted my e-mail correctly, Hector thought. It was the first time he had been mentioned in the paper since that championship. There was no further reference to him in the story, which rehashed well-known background. There also was no mention of Hector's upcoming hearing on his suspension, an omission he considered to be a good thing.

The less attention the hearing gets, the better, Hector thought.

He looked at the story again, trying to figure out whether a casual reader would try to read between the lines and think that somebody — Whitney, the paper, the cops, all of organized soccer — somehow thought he was involved. Hector wasn't sure.

Going into the bedroom, he gently shook the shoulder of the sleeping Dora. "Wake up," he said softly. "We're in the paper today."

"Huh?" a groggy Dora muttered. Then she was suddenly alert. "What do you mean, we?" she said, grabbing the paper out of Hector's hands and reading the story.

"Damn reporter!" she spat. "There's no story here. Just tryin' to make Daddy look bad by stirrin' up things."

"Well," Hector said. "It probably is a story. People will read it. I'd rather it not be written. Easier for me if I'm not too well known.

"But it's fair enough. Doesn't even say we live together. Just that we" — Hector again made air quotes with his fingers — "date. Guess that's all a family newspaper is allowed to say."

"At least it's just the local rag," Dora said.

"Yeah," Hector said. "But these things get picked up. Remember, it was the *Post* that broke the story about that YouTube video of Diego. Then everybody latched onto it."

"So whatcha goin' to do today?"

"Paper says I fix appliances. So I'm goin' to go fix appliances and try to think of something. Maybe I'll get some inspiration from soccer...."

Hector was interrupted by the doorbell and, almost simultaneously, several rather sharp raps on the door.

CHAPTER 11

THE POUNDING AT the door continued. Leaving Dora in the bedroom, Hector went and opened the front door.

It was Valley Mirage Police Department Detective Reynolds Wolfington, flanked by his ever-faithful silent companion, Sergeant Mark Kelly.

Wolfie was mad.

"You're in big trouble, Rivera," he said menacingly. "Big trouble."

Rivera shuddered. No Young Latino Male in Valley Mirage likes to hear that from any policeman, even if, like Rivera, they weren't gang members. And especially from Wolfie. But Rivera, knowing he hadn't done anything wrong, managed to put on his soccer cool.

"What's the problem, officer?" he asked.

"You know what the problem is," Wolfie said.

"Not sure what you mean," Rivera said. "I'm sure you saw the story in the paper today. I've been suspended as a soccer coach. That problem?"

"Don't get smart-ass with me," Wolfie said. "I'm talkin' 'bout the calls."

"The calls?" Rivera repeated.

"Yeah," Wolfie said, "The calls. You've been callin' folks involved in real estate deals here and suggestin' Rick Hermannik was killed for something he did in real estate. I should run you in for intimidating witnesses, obstruction of justice."

"Oh, those calls," Rivera said, genuinely surprised but inadvertently sounding a little more flip than he intended. "Just trying to get information. Don't think Hermannik's name came up at all, by me or anyone I called."

"Aha!" Wolfie said, as if he had just broken California's famously long-unsolved Zodiac serial killer case. "You admit you made calls!"

"Sure I made calls," Rivera said. "You know I think Diego didn't do this. He's entitled to a defense. It seemed like a good idea to look for others who might have a motive."

"That's the job of his lawyer, or his private investigator," Wolfie said. "Are you licensed as a PI?"

"Course not," Rivera said. "But I'm not getting paid. And Diego's lawyer gave me the go-ahead to do this. If you want, I'll call him now and you two can chat."

The last thing Wolfie wanted was to get on the phone with a lawyer who might tell him he was depriving a client of a fair trial. Still, he kept up a front.

"So maybe I should run both of you in," Wolfie snarled. "Look, you are this close to being arrested." He leaned closer to Rivera and held the thumb and forefinger of his right hand about a quarter-inch apart.

"Don't see how an honest effort to find facts is so bad," Rivera said. "Exactly what did any of the people I called say I said to make them feel intimidated? From your comments, you obviously talked to them."

"I heard they felt like they were being targeted," Wolfie said.

"You heard?" Rivera said, sensing an opening. "You didn't speak to them yourself?"

Wolfie realized he had given away too much. "Actually, no," he confessed. "I heard about this from your soccer board. There was a complaint to someone on the board."

"I'm no lawyer," Rivera said, "but that sorta sounds to me like hearsay."

"Sounds to me like you're trying to stir the pot," Wolfie said, trying to direct the interview away from the holes in his own evidence.

"What is it you understand I was asking about?" Rivera asked.

"Trying to find people," Wolfie said.

"What's wrong with that?" Rivera asked.

"They know you used to be a gang member. Like Diaz."

Rivera looked at him. "I was never a gang member," he said. "You know that, too. So why would anyone else think that?"

"They do," Wolfie insisted.

"Don't think anyone I called had any idea who I was," Rivera said. "If they did, they didn't let on. They all had left Valley Mirage long before the Hermannik killing. And I didn't recognize any of the names as ex-soccer parents."

"Really?" Wolfie asked, smirking a bit. "How do you think the soccer board found out?"

"I don't imagine you'd tell me who on the soccer board got that complaint," Rivera said.

"You imagine correctly," Wolfie said.

"Well," Rivera said, "it's a little hard to defend myself on the basis of anonymous accusations. But I'm 'specially concerned your source is someone on the soccer board."

"How so?" Wolfie asked, a little intrigued.

"The board is holding a hearing on Thursday night 'bout my suspension," Rivera said. "At my request. If someone on that board thinks I am going around intimidatin' witnesses or somethin', I might not get a fair hearin'.

"Sorta like in a court case. You don't want people on the jury who've already made up their minds against your side."

"Can't help you on that one," Wolfie said.

But he paused.

"Why *were* you calling around?" he asked.

Rivera looked at him. "Hermannik may have been involved in appraisin' a lot of property that later went into foreclosure even though we're still havin' good times," he said. "Might have created hard feelings. Maybe real hard feelings."

"So didja find anythin'?" Wolfie asked.

"Found a lot of people who lost overpriced homes bought from sellers they never met," Rivera said. "And a lot of people who didn't know if Hermannik had been involved in their deal." *No reason to tell Wolfie yet about Samuels saying Hermannik had it coming*, Rivera thought.

"Frankly, found a lot more questions than answers."

"So you don't have another suspect?" Wolfie said, a tad too eagerly, or even relieved.

"Not yet," Rivera said. "Still working on that."

He looked at Wolfie. "When I find someone, you'll be among the first to know," he said. Rivera even managed a wan smile.

"Well, you're not out of the woods yet on this, Rivera," Wolfie said, but his tone indicated otherwise. "Better watch what you do."

"Okay, Detective," Rivera said. "Is there anything else?"

"Guess not," Wolfie said. He and sidekick Kelly, who once again had remained silent, turned and went down the steps from the apartment to the ground where their cruiser was parked. As they got into the car, he overheard Wolfie tell Kelly, "This doesn't add up...."

Hector turned and saw Dora—still clad in a nightgown and wearing a robe—standing in the bedroom door. She ran forward and hugged him.

"Oh, Hector," she said. "You really stood up to him. Such an evil man."

"Well, he certainly has his views," Hector said. "But I guess he's actin' on information he was given."

Suddenly Hector stiffened.

"Somethin' wrong?" asked Dora, who was still clutching him.

"I didn't call anyone who had a soccer connection or who knew me," Hector said slowly. "No one. And I didn't mention soccer at all. Or Hermannik's name. Not once.

"Yet Wolfie said someone on the soccer board got a complaint from someone I called.

"That doesn't make any sense."

Hector paused.

"Wolfie could be bluffin', makin' it up. But he can't be that lucky. I *was* making calls."

Hector paused again.

"Unless ..."

"Unless what?" Dora asked in a whisper.

"Unless," Hector said slowly, "someone on the soccer board got a call for a reason having nothin' to do with soccer."

"Who?" Dora said softly.

"Someone who doesn't want me to be asking questions of the people I'm asking questions of," Hector said.

He grimaced. "But it could be anybody. Everyone on that board is wired. Banker, lawyer, agent, financial types, politician. And of course" — Hector glanced at the newspaper story again—"his Imperial Excellency himself, Manuel H. Whitney Junior. Funeral director to all of humanity.

"It's a big board. They all know everyone. But they're volunteers, so they have all kinds of other interests.

"I called a bunch of people who haven't lived here for a while askin' 'bout long-ago real estate deals. For some reason, someone decided to call someone on the soccer board. No idea why. But that someone on the board made it sound to Wolfie like I was threatening a hit or somethin'.

"Someone was makin' it up, f'sure."

"Gee, Hector," Dora said. "Is there someone you could call who might know somethin'?"

"Maybe," Hector said, "but I have to be careful. Don't know who my friends are anymore. And Wolfie would love to run me in for any little thing."

Rivera's cell phone signaled. Unlike the call from the newspaper reporter, this was one Rivera had to take. From the caller ID he could see it was from Seth Upland, his boss at WeFixThingsRightNow, calling from the World Headquarters in fancy Santa Monica.

Rivera shared the common view among WeFixThingsRightNow workers that, like many bosses, Upland was a total asshole, demanding far too much while blaming others for problems often of his own making. But Rivera's unassuming personality and general competence had kept him out of Upland's crosshairs.

"Hi, Seth," Rivera said. "What's up?"

"At this end, not much," Upland said. "At your end, seems like a lot."

This doesn't sound good, Rivera thought.

"What do you mean?" he asked.

"Didn't realize until I saw a story on the Internet today. You're connected to that soccer coach accused of killing that soccer ref," Upland said.

"Oh," Rivera said. "Not all that much of a connection. Just date his daughter. Don't even rise to the level of son-in-law."

"Story I read said you were suspended as a soccer coach in the same league," Upland said.

"True," Rivera said, trying to control a growing sense of dread. "But not for anything I did. League just thought my presence would be a distraction. I don't agree. In fact, I'm appealin' it. There's a hearing 'bout it Thursday night."

"Story I saw said you worked as an appliance repairman," Upland said.

"True again," Rivera said, thinking quickly. "But it didn't say for whom or where. Hell, we compete with a half-dozen similar outfits."

"That's not good for business," Upland said.

"What's not good for business?"

"Your connection to a killer. And your goin' into people's homes as our employee to fix things."

"So what?" Rivera said, figuring it would do no good to point out that Diaz was just an accused killer. "I'm not charged with anything. All I do is go around Southern California and fix fancy popcorn machines."

"What if something happened?" Upland said.

"What if what happened?" Rivera repeated, astonished. "Like, if I killed someone?"

"Well, yes," Upland blurted out.

"What makes you think I am a killer?" Rivera demanded in a once rare but, thanks to Wolfie, increasingly common display of personal defense. "And since when is it wrong to know someone accused of a crime?"

Upland ignored the reply. "What does your soccer league know?" he said.

"As far as I can tell, nothing," Rivera said. "The league commissioner himself told me it was nothing I did."

"This could make us look bad," Upland said. "Very bad."

"Still don't get it," Rivera said. "I go out on assignments. Fix things. Get paid. Leave. Go to the next job. All day long. I'm polite. Most customers don't remember my name. The things I fix stay fixed. You don't get calls 'bout my work."

"Correct," Upland agreed. "But I have to look out for the business."

"What does that mean?"

"WeFixThingsRightNow thinks that it might be a good idea for you to lay low for a little while as one of our workers. You know, until this thing plays out and gets resolved."

"You mean," said a stunned Rivera, "you're suspendin' me like the soccer league did? Even though I've done nothin' wrong? You're suspending me for what someone else did?"

"I wouldn't put it that way," Upland said. "It's for the good of the company. For the good of WeFixThingsRightNow."

Yeah, good of the company, Rivera thought. *Just like Manny Whitney's good of the game. And just as bogus.* Rivera didn't speak his mind.

"So you want me to cancel all my appointments starting right now?" he said.

"Well, not exactly," Upland said. "That wouldn't be for the good of the company, either."

"What?" Rivera asked, confused.

"Uh," Upland said, clearing his throat. "We're a little short-handed this week. You carry a heavy load. Today is Tuesday. Finish the rest of the week, then take a little time off."

That was too much even for the mild-mannered Rivera. "Oh I see," he said, with more than a trace of bitterness in his voice. "I'm suspended once you figure out a way to replace the income I generate for the company."

Upland was a bully, but like many bullies backed off when challenged. "Guess that's one way of lookin' at it," he said.

Rivera's head was spinning. But then he had a realization. *I'm going to need more time to work on Diego's defense—and my own at the soccer board on Thursday night,* Rivera thought. *Won't be able to do that if I'm fixing broken gizmos all week in Beverly Hills.*

So Rivera took a stand.

"If that's how you and the company feel, fine. I'm not going to work the rest of the week, Seth," he said. "I'm booked solid today. About to go out when you called. I'll keep those jobs. Not fair to those customers if I don't. But I haven't been given any assignments yet after today. So starting tomorrow, Wednesday, I'm off."

Upland wasn't used to seeing his orders rejected by underlings, but there wasn't much he could do except, maybe, apply a little leverage. WeFixThingsRightNow let its help take vehicles home at night. It was one of the very few benefits WeFixThingsRightNow threw its workers, but that wasn't really the reason. The company figured the gaudy markings sitting in neighborhoods across the Los Angeles area were terrific advertising, while getting around laws prohibiting commercial signs in residential areas. So many of its workers didn't have their own cars, a group that included Rivera.

"Uh, okay," Upland said. "Course, we're going to have to get the van back. We'll send someone for it tomorrow."

"No problem," Rivera said. *I'll use Diego's car,* he thought. *It's not like he needs it these days.* "When I get home tonight, I'll get my personal stuff out of it."

Ending the call, Hector turned—to see a wide-eyed Dora staring at him. "Oh Hector," she said, barely holding back tears. "You need this job."

"I need a job, all right," he said, "Maybe not this job. But I got to do the right thing, too. Somehow I have to figure all this out."

And with that, Hector set out on his last journey to make Southern California safe for people with $10,000 toys that weren't working right.

Like so many of his days, the calls carried him past notable landmarks of the region. The house on North Bundy Drive in LA's swank Brentwood section that, in 1961, a between-jobs Richard Nixon saved from yet another local wildfire by using his water hose, declaring, "I have seen trouble all over the world, but nothing like this." The Hollywood Freeway through Cahuenga Pass, site of inconclusive 19th-century battles for the same political-instability reason that Mexico had to appoint 22 governors of California in its 26 years of control. The main campus of the University of Southern California, whose second president, Joseph Pomeroy Widney, later wrote an outrageously racist—and best-selling—book entitled *Race Life of the Aryan Peoples*, which predicted Los Angeles would become the center of white supremacy. The USC library contained more copies of that book than, say, *The Autobiography of Malcolm X*.

When he returned that night, Rivera pulled the truck close to his apartment so he could unload all the non-WeFixThingsRightNow stuff in the back. It was amazing how much had accumulated. Some of it was trash. But there was a fair amount connected with soccer. Balls. Corner flags. Clipboards with soccer field diagrams etched on their backside. Empty water bottles and Juicy-Juice containers. Spikes for holding down goal posts. A first-aid kit. Somebody's shoe.

Rivera also came across the several boxes of refresher soccer laws tests that he had cleared out of the soccer league office as part of that fall housecleaning. He had been told to toss the boxes, but hadn't gotten around to it yet.

Guess it's time to pitch this stuff, Rivera thought. As he removed the boxes, Rivera casually leafed through their contents. One exam he saw brought him to a full stop.

Hermannik's.

At first glance there was nothing really special about his test. Nothing except that Hermannik was killed weeks later. So it almost was like a voice from beyond, at least to Rivera, who gingerly held the exam like it was some kind of ancient relic. More out of morbid curiosity than anything else, he carefully flipped through the pages. For some reason he looked at which questions Hermannik got right and which questions he got wrong.

Something clicked.

Loudly.

How can this be? Rivera wondered. *It makes no sense at all.*

But then with a racing pulse he realized something. *It makes perfect sense.*

Rivera also realized he had a lot of work to do, and not a lot of time in which to do it.

He quickly brought all of the stuff he took out of the truck into the apartment, including the boxes of soccer exams with Hermannik's on top. Hector piled everything on the floor next to the table in the living room corner where he kept his laptop computer. He started going through all the paperwork, page by page.

Then he pulled out his pad of handwritten notes from the deed room in Norwalk, got on the Internet and started googling.

Everyone and everything.

Hermannik's name, of course. The names of everyone and everything that had popped up in all of those strange deeds and mortgages he had looked up in Norwalk. The names of every person he knew in Valley Mirage, especially the soccer crowd: parents, board members, coaches and other referees. Their spouses and any relatives they had mentioned or bragged about. Businesses they owned or served. Hector even googled Diego—lots of recent hits there—Dora—none aside from the *Daily Post* story—and for good measure, himself—mostly a smattering of references to his high school championship soccer days.

Of course, he googled Wolfie and his sidekick.

Rivera googled street addresses, post office box numbers, e-mail addresses, phone numbers, account numbers.

Then he started googling combinations of names, places and things.

At Cal State, Hector had taken a course in research methods. He knew that the ability to troll the Internet provided by search engines like Google could turn anyone into Sherlock Holmes. He also knew that not even Google could find everything on the Internet, and much that was there was of dubious veracity. So he repeated all his searches on Alta Vista, another search engine.

Hector also reread some of Berman's California history pieces in the *Daily Post*.

And he couldn't believe what he was finding.

"Oh my God!" he exclaimed over and over as he took notes and made screenshots of pages to store on his laptop. "Unbelievable!"

Dora was dying to know what he was finding, but was afraid of breaking his chain of concentration. So she pulled up a chair and sat next to him trying to make out what was popping up on the screen. She didn't learn very much.

Hector stayed up until nearly 1:00 a.m. googling, screenshot-saving, note taking and occasionally looking through the boxes of soccer records strewn around his feet. Finally, he stopped.

"Gotta catch some sleep," he told Dora. "I have places to go tomorrow. Didya get Diego's car?"

"Yes," Dora said. "It's parked around the corner in a visitor's spot. Keys are on the kitchen table. Where ya going?"

"Back to the Norwalk deed room, and then to a college library." Hector said, laughing. "Haven't been in a library of any kind since I left Cal State. So you know it's important. Trying to tie up some loose ends."

Hector paused.

Dora cocked her head. "What kind of loose ends?" she asked.

"Stuff that might do some good."

"Hey," Dora said. "Are you defending Daddy or yourself?"

Hector looked at her.

"Both of us, I guess," he said. "We're sort of in this together."

He went over and kissed Dora on her forehead. "Together," he whispered. "All of us."

On Wednesday, Rivera weathered the onslaught of public-spirited citizens in the Norwalk parking lot trying to help him register a business and went directly to the deed room. Thanks to his previous visit he was a little more knowledgeable about how the place operated. Rivera even helped another Latino family that for some reason wanted to look up the deed for the house they were about to lose to foreclosure.

A lot more focused on his objectives, he covered a lot more ground and took more notes. His efforts were fruitful. He even ordered photocopies of a few of the more interesting items at a painful $3 a page—clearly a profit center for the county. Then it was over to a college library to look up on microfilm a research paper he had seen mentioned on the Internet. He also made copies of a few pages—this time at a more reasonable 10 cents a page.

Getting home, Rivera powered up his laptop and sat down. He had a lot more work to do, including hitting the phones, research on the Internet and organizing his efforts. With Dora keeping her distance, he spent a long Wednesday night that morphed into what would be one of the longest days of his life.

CHAPTER 12

AFTER CATCHING some sleep, Rivera spent the day Thursday refining and thinking through his presentation. Then he headed over to his hearing. Like all soccer board meetings, it was held in the boardroom just off the banking floor of the Valley Mirage National Bank, whose president, Sidney Keating, a member of the soccer board, would be among those passing judgment on him. *Too bad I don't bank here*, Rivera thought. Like a lot of young adults, he didn't have a checking account, or even a savings account. What good were they if one had no money?

Rivera arrived about 10 minutes early, entered the boardroom from a separate entrance off the parking lot and found all the board members present and milling around. Rivera knew most of them by sight and occasionally even their voices, since many liked to brag about their terrific lives while standing on the sidelines. But other than Commissioner Whitney, Rivera had spoken to few of them. When he walked into the room, it fell silent as everyone stared at him.

"Uh, hi, everyone," Rivera said. He saw Whitney standing in the corner and moved toward him.

"Should I wait outside?" he asked.

"No, just sit along the wall," Whitney said. "You're the first order of business." He paused. "You're the only order of business."

Rivera sat down. So, around the big mahogany table, did all the board members.

"We're here to hear the appeal of Hector Rivera to the decision of the executive committee that for the good of the game suspended him as a coach for the rest of the season," Whitney said. "As you all know, he exercised his right of appeal under our bylaws in a timely fashion. Mr. Rivera is here to present his case. I ask that you all listen carefully to what he has to say. Hector, please proceed."

In effect acting as his own lawyer, Rivera stood up.

"Thank you, Commissioner," he said. "I do have some things to say. But I'd like your okay to use a PowerPoint presentation I put together to help make my points. I'm not too good at thinkin' on my feet. I brought my laptop and a projector. I see the room has a drop-down screen."

"Well, it's the bank's screen," Whitney said. "Sid, do you mind?"

"Not at all," Keating said.

Rivera put all those years of repairing computers and doodads for WeFixThingsRightNow to good use. Within two minutes he had his deck running, and turned to the board.

"I was suspended for reasons I consider unfair," he said. "I hope to show you why."

Rivera hit his clicker. Up came a picture that appeared in the *Daily Post*. The room grew silent.

"This is Rick Hermannik," Rivera said. "A good referee. Reffed some of my matches. I had no complaint with him. He's relevant to this matter only 'cause the commissioner says his death formed part of the basis for my suspension.

"I'm sure you've all seen the tape of Diego Diaz screamin' at Hermannik. Not so well known is the video of the play that led to the shouting. But it was recorded, too. Here it is."

As the tape played, Rivera narrated. "Two players on a breakaway. Player with the ball is trailing. Nearing the goal. Player in front veers away to the left maybe five yards. Teammate kicks the ball right past the keeper into the goal."

Rivera stopped the tape. "Remember, as the Laws of the Game state clearly, it is not an offense to be in an offside position," he said. "The player in front never touched the ball. There was no pass to her. The only way she would be offside is if the referee decided she was interferin' with the keeper. Maybe by blocking her view. None of that here."

He turned the tape back on. "Hermannik correctly indicated a goal," Rivera said. He froze the image of Hermannik pointing to the halfway line, the signal for a goal under soccer's signaling system of indicating the place where play resumes.

Rivera showed the Hermannik mug again. "We know from the affidavit for the search warrant issued to get into Diego's apartment what was on the computer screen where Hermannik was found," he said. Rivera clicked to a highlighted passage and read it out loud. "Diaz continued to complain bitterly about the no-offside call I made near the end of Saturday's match. I told Mr. Diaz the offside offense requires the offside player to physically play the ball. He profanely disagreed and threatened...."

Rivera looked at the board members around the table. "An incorrect statement of the Laws of the Game," he said. "It's unusual. But it's certainly possible to be guilty of offside without touching the ball. For instance, if an attacker in an offside position challenges an opponent going for the ball.

"Hermannik was a ref for several years. Could he have been so ignorant?"

Brennan, the assistant commissioner, laughed loudly. "We'll never know now," he cracked. Several board members eyed him disapprovingly, and Brennan turned off his smile.

Rivera looked at him.

"Maybe," he said, "and maybe not.

"Remember the mandatory annual laws test that everyone—all of you—took back in August? 'Bout a month before Hermannik's death? Not graded 'cause they're more of a refresher. Not sure how seriously non-referees took the test. I was told to throw them out but just didn't get around to it.

"So I have them all. Including Hermannik's."

Somebody in the room gasped. Voices of the dead will do that.

"Remember this question?" Rivera asked, displaying it on the screen and reading: "Under the Laws of the Game, can a player be guilty of the offense of offside without physically touching or playing the ball?"

Rivera paused briefly. "Let me show you Hermannik's answer in his own hand," he said, displaying the next slide. "He wrote in 'Yes.' "And that indeed is the correct answer."

"Wait a second," Keating interjected. "What does this have to do with anything?"

"Well," Rivera said, "just a few weeks later, Hermannik was killed while supposedly writing a note indicatin' his belief this was not the correct answer."

Now that caused a stir in the room. With more than one board member contributing to it.

"And that note implicated the hell out of Diego Diaz," Rivera continued. "But to me, this test suggests the words on the screen weren't written by Hermannik, but by someone else.

"Like the killer.

"And that would rule out Diego for a bunch o' reasons."

Bullet points appeared on the screen.

"One, Diego obviously would have no reason to implicate himself.

"Two, he's a klutz with a computer. All technology, for that matter. I know that from personal knowledge. He has trouble using cell phones.

"Three, he can't spell. But this is spelled perfectly.

"And four, about the location of the whistle. Diego has trouble putting on a bandage."

Rivera kept the four reasons on the screen. "The police said there was no sign of forced entry," he said. "That suggests Hermannik let in the killer and probably knew him.

"I can go with that. But what are the chances Hermannik would have let in a hoppin' mad Diego Diaz and bring him all the way upstairs to his office knowing he had a nasty note about him waiting on his computer screen?"

Rivera stopped to let that sink in.

"As it turned out, Diego took the same laws test, too," Rivera said. "Here was his answer to the same question."

Projection.

"'Yes,'" Rivera read off the screen. "Also correct. So Diego was objecting not because he didn't know the rules, but probably because he had a bad angle on the play. Or just as likely, 'cause he objects to every call goin' against him."

"Look," said Janis Johnson, the stay-at-home mom. "This is all very interesting. But what does it have to do with your suspension?"

"Well," Rivera answered slowly, "the commissioner has indicated the executive committee suspended me due to my connection with a man accused of murdering a referee. Even though I haven't been implicated in that crime.

"Of course, I don't think there're any grounds for suspension. Not a one. But if I can show you Diego isn't the killer, then maybe you'll all really agree with me."

"It's true Hector's connection with Diego was a factor in our decision," Whitney said. "So he's entitled to make his case.

"Go ahead."

Back up on the screen: that newspaper mug of Hermannik.

"A real estate appraiser by profession," Rivera told the rapt board. "His job was to put a value on a house for a loan. To protect the lender. Borrower, too. 'Cause real estate here has been zoomin' up for a long time. More and more people are borrowin' the increase in their value to fund their lifestyles. Even buyin' the kind of fancy gizmos I repair for a livin'."

Rivera flashed a quick grin. Then he turned serious again.

"When it comes to housing, the market is still frothy," Rivera said. "But the storm clouds have been gatherin'." He displayed a page from the *Congressional Record* for October 7, 2004, only two years earlier. "This was testimony by Chris Swecker, assistant director of the FBI. He was speakin' to a House subcommittee about real estate crime." Rivera highlighted several passages of Swecker's testimony and read aloud his words:

"Based on various industry reports and FBI analysis, mortgage fraud is pervasive and growing.... 80% of all reported fraud losses involve collaboration or collusion by industry insiders.... The FBI defines industry insiders as appraisers, accountants, attorneys, real estate brokers, mortgage underwriters and processors, settlement/title company employees, mortgage brokers, loan originators and other mortgage professionals.... Some of the current rising mortgage fraud trends include: equity skimming, property flipping and mortgage identity related theft.... Property flipping is nothing new; Once again law enforcement is faced with an educated criminal element that is using identity theft, straw borrowers and shell companies, along with industry insiders to conceal their methods and override lender controls."

Rivera then put up a news article from the *The Washington Post* dated December 15, 2005—just nine months earlier. He read the headline: "'FBI Vows to Crack Down on Mortgage Fraud; Hot Real Estate Market Drives Report of Suspicious Activity, Agency Says'.

"The story was about an FBI press conference," Rivera said. "With the same star of the show." Rivera had a circle appear around a paragraph that he read:

" 'It's a pervasive problem, and it's on the rise,' said Chris Swecker, assistant director of the FBI, as officials described investors and consumers drawn to the hot real estate market only to find themselves the prey of savvy criminals who use loopholes in lending practices to strip borrowers of their savings, in most cases also ruining their credit. Lenders are becoming victims as well, induced to make bad loans that will go into foreclosure.' "

Rivera turned to face his audience. "Unfortunately, Hermannik was the appraiser of many homes that went into foreclosure. People lost their homes.

"And many of them followed a strange pattern.

"Here's an example."

More images, this time of deeds and mortgages.

"On March 6, 2002, Scott and Lacey Koenigsburg sold their house in Valley Mirage for $600,000 to someone named Gary Frank. That probably was a fair price. But just eight days later, Frank sold the house to someone named Richard Stevens for $900,000.

"That's remarkable: a 50% increase in barely a week. California real estate has been a good investment. But that good?

"Three months later, Stevens sold the property to Harry and Lita Smithfield for $925,000. This last transaction involved an appraisal from Hermannik certifying to the value.

"He had no problem signin' off on a valuation 50% more than the price just three months earlier. I got this appraisal from the Smithfields. They lost their house after the interest rate on their mortgage reset to a much higher rate, real estate stopped going up 20% a year and their employment was cut way back.

"I think the appraisal was a little out there. But that's not the only funny part. There was no mortgage on the first sale, from the Koenigsburgs to Frank. Nor the second one, eight days later. The one from Frank to Stevens.

"But the sale from Stevens to the Smithfields, now that had a mortgage. It was from Assurance Capital Equity of Pittsburgh, Pennsylvania. Let's call it ACE. ACE made an $873,000 loan. Ninety-seven percent of the purchase price, which didn't leave a lot of downside if values didn't keep going up."

"ACE made so many bad loans that the authorities closed it for reckless lending. Here's a story about it." Rivera displayed a month-old newspaper clipping from the *Pittsburgh Post-Gazette*.

He looked at the board.

"There are several dozen of these three-deed deals in Valley Mirage. When the rate on the last buyer's adjustable mortgage tripled after the introductory teaser period ended, the loans all went into foreclosure.

"In every single one of 'em that I can document, Rick Hermannik had signed off on a value that had zoomed in weeks. Defyin' gravity.

"As an appraiser, he had to cite the price of other recent deals. So what did he use? His other pumped-up appraisals! It was sort of like writing anonymous letters praising yourself. A self-fulfilling prophecy. Over and over."

Newspaper mug of Hermannik again.

"Who is Rick Hermannik?" Rivera asked. "You all knew him as a soccer referee. Perhaps a bit of a loner. We all have a past. Rick Hermannik had a past, too."

On the screen: the beginning of the image of a 1983 article from the *Dallas Times Herald*. Rivera started reading.

"Real estate appraiser Richard A. Hermannik was sentenced to two years in the Texas Department of Corrections yesterday after pleading guilty to charges he helped an organized ring extract millions of dollars from mortgage companies and savings-and-loans with fraudulent violations. Hermannik, 25, of suburban Garland, admitted he plotted with three other men, who also have pleaded guilty, to create the appearance of high values on suburban real estate used as collateral for loans from innocent lenders. Prosecutors said Hermannik was part of a group that flipped properties by manufacturing phony sales transactions listing ever increasing prices. That created a false paper record used to justify the basis of high loans."

Someone on the board gasped.

"Okay," said lawyer Brennan, interested but skeptical. "How do we know this was our Rick Hermannik?"

"Fair question," Rivera said. "His name is a little unusual. The age is about right." On the screen faded in the cover sheet of Hermannik's laws test, with a highlight on the name he had written in. "Our Rick Hermannik's middle initial, as you can see, was A."

"That doesn't prove anything," Brennan said.

"True again," Rivera said. "But there was a mug shot picture of the long-ago swindler Hermannik with the Dallas story. Take a look."

On the screen the rest of the story was revealed showing the picture of Hermannik. Allowing for a nearly quarter-century time lag, the pictures were a match.

This time, several people on the board gasped.

"We all know that referees can change the color of their jerseys," Rivera said. "But can they change the stripes of their personality? At some point after his release from prison, Hermannik moved to Southern California. He somehow ended up in Valley Mirage. He resumed his appraisal activities. And became a soccer referee on the weekends."

"Look," said Brennan, "this is all fascinating. But it's irrelevant to what we're here to do, which is to consider your suspension."

"Okay," Rivera said. "Gettin' to the point. Just hear me out for a few more minutes."

Brennan backed down.

"Let's go back to those three-deed deals," Rivera said. "I haven't been able to locate any of the people listed as the buyers on deed one or deed two. I 'specially wanted to ask the deed one buyers, who were also the deed two sellers, how they could make so much money in such a short period of time.

"The names of these people are pretty bland. Richard Stevens. Gary Frank. There are thousands of people by those names."

Rivera projected that Dallas newspaper story again, zoomed into a different passage, which he highlighted and read.

"As part of his plea bargain, Hermannik admitted that he was aware that some of the sellers and buyers on the deeds were nonexistent persons with common, hard-to-trace names. They were used deliberately, Hermannik acknowledged, because they were common and difficult to locate."

Some board members were now bug-eyed.

"I can't ask Rick Hermannik 'bout this anymore," Rivera resumed. "But his whole history seemed to be aiding and abetting and helping others up to mischief. It's what he seemed to know how to do best.

"Someone else was calling the shots. Who was that someone? I might not be the only person who wants to know."

More of that Pittsburgh newspaper story on the screen.

"'Authorities have begun a criminal investigation into the collapse of ACE,'" Rivera read, then turned to the board. "The stated hunch is that it gave loans on the basis of inflated appraisals and fake documents generated by those seeking loans, especially in far-away venues. The story seems to suggest ACE was a victim."

Zooming image.

"This story appeared about three and a half weeks before Hermannik was killed. He sounds like the kind of person the authorities in Pittsburgh might have been interested in talking with.

"And he sounds like the kind of person that someone else might have wanted to shut up."

Total silence in the darkened room except for some extremely heavy breathing.

"Let's take a look at one of those three-deed deals," Rivera said, putting up the first pages of each instrument. "I want to talk a little bit about the role of notaries."

"Notaries?" blurted Whitney. "What do notaries have to do with soccer?"

"Maybe nothing and maybe everything," Rivera said. "I guess everyone in this room has bought or sold a house. Everybody 'cept me, anyway. Notaries are clerks appointed by the government. But they often are just secretaries and employees of real estate professionals and lawyers. They certify the person signin' documents that will be recorded in the county deed office is actually the person the document says he is. You're supposed to show ID like a driver's license and sign in front of the notary. Then the notary signs and adds his stamp. Sometimes the notary even takes a thumbprint and puts it in his own log. The idea is to fight fraud.

"The county deed room won't record a document that doesn't have a notary seal. But the government doesn't check to see if the notary is real. They sort of take it on faith."

Back to the screen.

"On a deed, only the seller signs. Here's that three-deed deal again. The first deed had a real seller, in the sense that it was a couple that actually existed," Rivera said. "And there's a real notary. Her name is Barbara S. Clarkson.

"The last two deeds have different sellers but carry the same notary signature. It says R.P. Lopez. He was a busy guy. His name is on the last two deeds of *all* these three-deed deals ending with a second Rick Hermannik appraisal.

"Now, I can't find a notary by that name. There's an online list of all the notaries from Sacramento you can download. I did. There's no R.P. Lopez.

"If he exists, Mr. Lopez could probably tell us something. But I can't find Mr. R.P. Lopez."

"Soccer," Brennan interjected. "We're here to talk about soccer."

"Gettin' to that," Rivera said, continuing.

"All documents sent to the county clerk are recorded and then returned to someone. Deeds go to the buyer. The document always lists an address."

The screen again.

"Look at these first two deeds. They bear the inscription, 'Return to buyer, PO Box 2040, Valley Mirage.' That PO box is on the first two deeds of all these sequences. Sort of suggests they're all connected. All these homes that people lost to foreclosure.

"I can't talk to Rick Hermannik. Dead men don't speak. But it occurred to me that the owner of PO Box 2040 might know something.

"I was able to figure out the owner of that box. By sheer luck."

Rivera projected a document showing only that PO box.

"And quite a coincidence, too. PO Box 2040 is an address that appears on the list of contacts for the leaders of this very soccer organization. It was on a page in those soccer records I was supposed to throw out."

Rivera widened the screen to show that.

"In fact, it's someone sittin' in this very room."

A little wider.

"It's a PO box belonging to Mark Rigas. A member of the board and a big real estate man."

Gasps sucked all the air out of the room. The face of Rigas turned beet red.

"Then it dawned on me," Rivera continued. "I had been calling around running down names on these deeds. Couple days ago, Wolfie—ah, Detective Reynolds Wolfington of the esteemed Valley Mirage Police Department—came by to ask me some questions. He wanted to know why I was calling around. Said someone on the soccer board had told him. Wouldn't tell me who. No one I called had a soccer connection I knew of. So I had no idea how anyone on this board would know I was calling around.

"But after discoverin' Mr. Rigas owned that PO box, I called back some of those first-deed sellers and third-deed buyers. The ones who talked to me all confirmed Mr. Rigas was involved in their deals.

"I realized what must have happened. One or more of the people I had called earlier at some point had called Mr. Rigas. Not 'cause of soccer but because he was their real estate broker. Maybe they were the sellers on deed one who wanted to know why the home they sold through him was resold so quickly for so much more."

"Outrageous!" shouted Rigas. "Sure, those were my deals. And sure, I called the detective. But I operated in good faith. Hermannik must have been pullin' a scam on me."

"Maybe so," Rivera said coolly. "But you simply made it up when you told Detective Wolfington I had mentioned Hermannik to people I called and they got scared. That doesn't sound like good faith to me.

"Once I got onto you, I called back some end buyers. The ones who lost everything. I specifically asked 'bout you. They told me you helped them fill out mortgage applications listing net worth and incomes far above what they really had. They said you said it was normal and the mortgage company never checked anything. Don't think Hermannik was actin' alone."

Back up on the screen: the Pittsburgh story about the criminal investigation of ACE. "Were you aware of this?" Rivera said, looking directly at Rigas.

"Heard somethin' 'bout it, I suppose," Rigas said slowly. "Wasn't worried. Nothing to hide."

"Did Hermannik know 'bout the investigation?" Rivera asked

"Didn't say anything to me," Rigas said. "Probably not."

"Okay," Rivera said. "Do you know the whereabouts of the elusive Gary Frank and Richard Stevens?"

"No, but why would I?" Rigas said. "Don't keep track of ex-customers who move away."

"Okay," Rivera said. "Where can we find notary R.P. Lopez? You sure did a lot of business with him. Surely *he* didn't move away."

"Uh, he's somewhere around here," Rigas said. "Don't have his contact info right handy. He's just a notary."

"It seems your clients did a lot of business with ACE," Rivera said.

"Sure," Rigas said. "They offered good rates. Easy closings. Didn't require a lot of documentation."

"Several of the end buyers I chatted up said they came to you respondin' to ads you put on Craigslist. Ads that are offerin' help to people who wanted to buy and had good credit but didn't have enough of a down payment. They said you suggested ACE."

"So what?" Rigas said. "A good broker should help find financing for clients."

"All right," Rivera said. "But I think a good broker should also disclose he is the real seller."

"Oh my God," muttered Brennan, who figured what was coming next.

"Is it possible, Mr. Rigas," Rivera said, "that Gary Frank and Richard Stevens do not exist? That you were the real owner before the Smithfields bought that house? That by briefly payin' cash with no mortgage you made that house seem a lot more valuable than it really was? Without having to qualify for mortgages that would have revealed the true ownership and required honest appraisals? That you sold it to a really stupid client, who borrowed nearly the entire price from ACE? That you did this with all these other deals?"

"Not going to dignify that with a comment," Rigas said defiantly— and defensively.

"Okay," Rivera said. "Maybe you can comment on this. I once heard you tell someone along the touchlines that real estate's in your blood 'cause your great-great-great-something grandfather was Abel Stearns. In his day a long time ago, he was a big-time Southern California land guy. The *Daily Post* ran a profile of him. As it turns out, written by the same reporter now coverin' the Hermannik case."

"Damn right and damn proud," Rigas shouted.

Rivera projected on the screen a yellowing image of a page from a California newspaper. It contained an 1871 obituary of Stearns from a San Francisco newspaper. Rivera had fished it up on the Google News archives of old newspapers. He zoomed in on the second paragraph, and started reading:

"Don Abel leaves behind his gracious wife, Arcadia Bandini de Stearns. Together, they had no children."

Rivera looked directly at Rigas. "If Don Abel had no children in California," he asked, "how could you be a direct descendant?"

"Um, Um," Rigas stammered, "That's what my late mother always told me. That's all I know."

"Hmm," Rivera said. "Have any relatives named Stearns?"

"Uh, no."

"Now, Mr. Rigas, you went back to school and eventually earned an MBA in 1995, correct?"

"Yes."

"For that degree, did you write a master's thesis?"

"Sure. It was required."

"Do you remember your topic?"

"Something about real estate, but I don't remember exactly. More than a decade ago."

Rivera looked at him again. "I found a reference to it online and went yesterday to the campus to look it up."

First page up on the screen.

"You titled it 'Capitol Gains: How Federal Government policy concerning credit may create opportunities for astute investors in real estate,' " Rivera said. "Using the spelling for the home of Congress in Washington rather than the tax spelling. Because your paper was about government action.

"Or inaction."

Second page up on the screen.

"You wrote a summary of your paper. It's called an abstract. Here it is. Let me read it out loud:

"'Ruling national politicians from both parties in the executive and legislative branches have strong self-interested motives to keep interest rates low and to facilitate lax credit and regulatory policies so that significant year-to-year increases in real estate values will be created for the foreseeable future. Democrats seek to help their generally poorer supporters buy homes, while Republicans seek to help more affluent home builders, who are among their biggest financial backers.

"'In addition, Federal Reserve Chairman Alan Greenspan, whose agency oversees interest rates and lending, has a longstanding philosophical aversion grounded in libertarian theory to strong regulation of any kind, including actions that would prevent financial bubbles in which prices of assets such as real estate rise too quickly. He is on record as saying the marketplace will discipline itself such that aggressive protection of individual citizens by regulators is not necessary.

"'The evolving system of real estate finance blessed by these politicians and regulators, in which intermediaries bundle real estate loans and sell them to financial institutions for resale as complex mortgage-backed securities, will lessen individual accountability. In an effort to stimulate business, there will be a correspondingly increasing disincentive to review the paperwork submitted by borrowers for accuracy, because any ultimate losses will be borne by others.

"'Properly positioned real estate professionals should be able to take advantage of these trends.'"

Rivera looked across the room. "Mr. Rigas, are you one of those 'properly positioned real estate professionals?' "

"I'm proud of what I do."

"That's a lot of fancy language there," Rivera said. "But it sort of looks to me like what later went on with all those deals involving you and Hermannik and leading to foreclosures."

"Think what you want," Rigas snarled.

"Like a lot of youth soccer leagues, we have an online sign-up system for referees here," Rivera said. "Refs can self-assign themselves to games, subject to the right of the referee supervisors to move them around."

Image of the signup screen.

"In each of a couple weeks prior to his death, Hermannik had refereed a match of Diego Diaz. Diego is a very volatile fellow. We all know that. Not many refs sign up voluntarily to do his matches. Frankly, they're not paid enough. Hermannik complained that somehow he kept getting switched at the last minute to Diaz. A quiet guy, he went along.

"It was like pouring gasoline onto a flame. It's almost like someone was trying to arrange things so Diaz would blow up at Hermannik in a big way. Providing cover for something very bad to happen to Hermannik."

"I can tell where you're going with this," Rigas said. "I have nothing to do with scheduling referees."

"There's no computer security here," Rivera said. "Everyone knows that. The password for each referee is their last name and the word ref. It would be pretty easy for someone else to log in and change an assignment."

"Absurd!" Rigas shouted. "That video of Hermannik identified his killer. So did the stuff he was writing on his computer when he was killed. And that whistle, too!"

"The video certainly is interesting for identification," Rivera said, putting it back up on the screen. "But look who else is in it."

Rivera zoomed in on a corner of the scene. Along the sideline was Rigas, intently watching the action.

"None of your children was in that match," Rivera said. "Why were you even there?"

"Well, I'm on this board," Rigas said, "and we're supposed to watch things. I watch a lot of matches."

"Really?" Rivera said. "I usually only see you around at times when your son is playing, or about to."

Rigas said nothing.

"Mr. Rigas," Rivera said. "As a board member, did you take that laws test?"

"Well, yes," Rigas said.

"Do you remember how you answered that question about offside?"

"Uh, not really."

New image on the screen.

"Remember, I have all the tests. Including yours. You wrote your name on the first page."

Another image.

"You got the offside answer wrong," Rivera said. "Just like whoever wrote those words on Hermannik's computer screen after killing him.

"Mr. Rigas, where were you when Hermannik was killed after someone lured Diego Diaz out of his house on a bogus pretext?"

"Getting gas on the north side of town."

"Was anyone with you?"

"No."

"Perhaps you have a time-stamped credit-card receipt?"

"Nope. Paid cash."

"Cash?" Rivera said. "Maybe money you got under false names from ACE at the expense of people like the Smithfield family?"

Rigas stood up. "I don't have to take any more of this slander!" he said. "I'm leaving!"

"Afraid not, Mr. Rigas. Stay right there."

The speaker standing in the doorway was Detective Wolfington. He was flanked by Sergeant Kelly and another cop. "Been in the next room watching and listening," Wolfie said. "Mr. Whitney invited us to come. Thought it might help our investigation. Right about that!

"Mr. Rigas, you're under arrest for the murder of Rick Hermannik. We're going to have to take you to police headquarters. But I'm afraid we're first going to have to frisk you now for weapons."

Kelly started patting down Rigas. "What's this?" Kelly said, pulling out of the inside of Rigas' sports jacket pocket a very fat and fancy pen.

"I think that might be Hermannik's very expensive fountain pen," Rivera said quietly. "The one he bragged about. Filled out soccer game cards with. I imagine it went missing 'bout the time of his murder.

"It's possible the pen also might have been used by Hermannik at Rigas' direction. To sign the names of those phony buyers and sellers. The nub and ink are pretty distinctive. And some of those signatures really resembled Hermannik's handwritin' on game cards. I have those cards, too.

"Mr. Rigas had every reason to get that pen away from Hermannik. It's very incriminatin'. I suspect it was taken immediately after the killing. But I guess Rigas couldn't bring himself to throw out something worth $24,000.

"For him, a pity. But terrific for Diego. And for me."

Wolfie turned to his underlings. "Take him away, boys," he said, nodding toward Rigas, whose hands had been cuffed behind his back. "I'll be along in a bit."

Then Wolfie looked at Rivera. "You remember when I came to your apartment on Tuesday?" he asked.

"Every encounter with you is memorable," said Rivera, a little more bolder than usual. "Sure I do."

Wolfie for once looked startled, but continued. "You said that in all your callin' around, you had never mentioned Hermannik's name," he said. "Didn't know at the time if that was true. But it got me to thinkin' sorta like it got you to thinkin'.

"We started looking into Rigas' background. Just found he had been in the Army during Vietnam. In one of those special ops units that did some get-rid-of-the-enemy commando stuff. Quick and dirty. And deliberately left some nasty calling cards.

"Like maybe what happened to Hermannik with the whistle. We're getting Rigas' complete service record now."

Rivera was astonished—both because of Rigas' background and because Wolfie actually acted constructively on something that a

Young Latino Male had told him. "Well, I hope you keep him locked up," he said. "I imagine he's thinking dark things about me now."

"We'll do our best," Wolfie said. "He's in a lot of trouble."

The detective looked at his feet, then looked up. "I have a confession," he said. "We initially ran Hermannik's name through a standard criminal database. Came up clean. Turns out his name was misspelled, with one N plus a C before the K. Just realized it watching your PowerPoint. Could have speeded this up. Something we run into a lot. It's a tricky spelling. Somewhere along the way, Hermannik got lucky. Probably how he passed a background check to be an appraiser again. Maybe a ref, too.

"As you said, it looks like Rigas was waiting for a way to ice Hermannik. Throw the blame elsewhere. Rigas must have thought his ship had come in when Diaz blew up big time at Hermannik talking 'bout whistle positioning.

"Another thing we figured out today. That YouTube video was shot by a parent with no connection to this. It threw us off"—Wolfie looked at Rivera—"but I guess not you.

"Going to need the originals of those soccer tests and all the other paperwork you mentioned. A copy of that PowerPoint, too."

"Okay," Rivera said. "When is Diego going to get out of jail?"

"As soon as I can get in touch with the prosecutor to get the charge dismissed," Wolfie said. "Probably tomorrow."

"That'd be nice," Rivera said. "An innocent man locked up for way too long."

Rivera wasn't usually one to lecture anyone, but now he had a soapbox. "Detective," he said, looking at Wolfie, "perhaps this will prompt you to rethink your general attitude about Young Latino Males. And older ones, too."

"Already has," Wolfie said, pursing his lips. "Already has."

"Any chance you can get Diego on the phone right now?"

"Maybe," Wolfie said. He called the jail, had Diaz brought to a guard station, then handed his phone to Rivera.

"Diego, Hector here. You're going to be freed soon. Cops just arrested someone else for killin' Hermannik."

"What?" Diaz shouted. "Who?"

"Mark Rigas."

"The real estate guy on the soccer board?"

"Yeah. He and Hermannik had a long-runnin' mortgage fraud. Rigas killed him to cover it up, then made it look like you did the murder."

"Hermannik was involved in the scam?"

"Yeah."

"See? I told you he was no good."

"Diego, you say that 'bout every ref. Killin' had nothing to do with soccer. Even though that's what almost everyone in the world thought, thanks in part to your big mouth. Gotta go."

Wolfie took back his phone and left the room through the bank floor to catch up with Rigas at headquarters.

After using his own cell to call Dora and Diaz's lawyer with the good news, Rivera looked around the room. The remaining board members were still sitting in stunned silence at the denouncement they had just witnessed. "Manny," Rivera said, looking directly at the league commissioner. "Was Rigas a force behind my suspension? Did he put the bug in your ear?"

Whitney looked at the floor, then looked up. "Guess so," he said. "Not proud of that now."

"Okay," Rivera said, snapping back into lawyer mode. "You've heard my case. In light of these developments, I'm wonderin' if you would kindly vacate my suspension so I can coach my team on Saturday. Diego's suspension, too."

Whitney sprang into action.

"Somovedallthoseinfavorsayaye," he said in one long word, like he wanted to put behind him as soon as possible his role in Rivera's questionable suspension.

"Ayeshaveitallsuspensionsareliftedmeetingadjourned."

"Ah," said Brennan, ever the lawyer. "The record should reflect that Mark Rigas did not vote, having left the room."

"Yeah," cracked Keating. "Probably never to return." This time, there were no disapproving looks.

In the post-meeting clamor, Rivera became the center of attention. Board members offered apologies and platitudes. "Finish college and go to law school!" said Janis Johnson. "Why, you were like … like Perry Mason up there!"

Rivera beamed. *Maybe that's something to think about,* he thought.

Suddenly, there was a commotion just outside the boardroom. The door from the parking lot swung opened, and a young man recognizable from TV interviews stepped through.

"Jeff Berman, *Daily Post,*" he said to no one and everyone. "Heard you were having a hearing 'bout Hector Rivera's suspension. Decided to drop by and wait outside. Then I see cops come out takin' away someone in handcuffs. Who got arrested?"

"The real killer of Richard Hermannik," Rivera said stepping forward.

"What?" Berman shouted, both confused and excited.

"The police who were just here said they are charging Mark Rigas with the murder," Rivera said. "The cops think he killed Hermannik to cover up a real estate fraud, then framed Diego Diaz. Diaz will be released. You might get another of your scoops once you verify the arrest with the police."

"Wow!" Berman said. "Who are you?"

"Hector Rivera. Don't think we've met. But since you wrote about it, my suspension as a soccer coach was just canceled here by the board."

"It was?" Berman exclaimed. He looked around the room. Most everyone nodded their head.

"Hector will be coaching again on Saturday," Whitney said.

"Okay," Berman said. ""I better get over to the PD." He literally ran out the door, thinking, *My second graf will say the* Daily Post *was present when Rigas was taken away by police.*

In the boardroom, things got a little quieter. "Good thing scum like Rigas are few and far between," Johnson said.

Rivera cocked his head. "When it comes to murder, sure," he said. "But in researchin', I came across an awful lot of other news stories on the Internet 'bout real estate and mortgage fraud. More and more cases each week. Everywhere in the country. Especially as prices keep goin' up so much. Year after year.

"It's just like Rigas wrote in his paper. Interest rates bein' held too low. Easy money. Then springing up too high to catch folks unawares. Nobody's watchin' the paperwork. Losses are being handed off to suckers. ACE isn't the only mortgage outfit to go under. A couple have already in California. Fraud at many levels.

"Course, in California there's nothing new about funny land stuff. Read a lot 'bout that, too, when I checked out Rigas' bogus claim to be kin of Abel Stearns. Goes way back. Remember, all of California once belonged to Indians. They lost it all. Think any of 'em got paid? That is, before they got run off and killed?

"Then California belonged to the Spanish. They lost it all. Then to the Mexicans. They lost it all. Think any of 'em got paid much? That is, before they lost the land in the gringo courts to gringos?

"So here we are in '06. Hard to tell where things are headed. But not a good trend. Look at all the folks losin' their homes already." Rivera shook his head. "This is not goin' to end well."

Whitney looked at him. "Hector, you're so pessimistic," he said. "Do you feel this way about soccer?"

"Nah," Rivera said. "I love the game of soccer. You know that. Everyone in this room knows that. Soccer is a pure sport on the pitch. The game is great. The kids we coach here are great.

"It's the stuff off the pitch that's so troublin'. Not just in this place called Valley Mirage. All across soccer. The politics. The posturing." Rivera looked directly at Whitney. "The people in charge."

Whitney winced, but said nothing.

"Hermannik was killed by someone on your own soccer board of directors," Rivera said. "A soccer parent. But not for a soccer reason.

"But think about this in soccer terms. Offside is an offense in soccer. But it's okay to be in an offside position. So long as play isn't affected. It's all about personal responsibility. Not taking that wrong final action. Not going over that line.

"A lot of folks would still be in their homes—Hermannik would still be alive—if certain people hadn't taken that last move. People who should have paid more attention to the consequences of what they were doin', or maybe not doin'.

"Sure, Rigas did the killin'. Offside in a big way. But he wasn't alone. He just tried to take advantage of his offside position. But someone else had to play it to him, give him the opportunity. And not just Hermannik.

"He needed someone with a stronger kick. Y'know, someone like Alan Greenspan."

END

A CODA FROM THE AUTHOR

AS ITS VERY name suggests, Valley Mirage simply doesn't exist, in the suburbs of Los Angeles, the rest of California or anywhere else on the planet. As an allegorical symbol, the largely upscale town is an absolute figment of my imagination. So, too, are the inhabitants of Valley Mirage—the referees, coaches, players, parents, athletic officials, city officials, politicians, cops, lawyers, financial service professionals, business owners, gang members, spouses, boyfriends, girlfriends, companies, organizations, journalists. Everyone. Like their fictional hometown, the folks and fixtures of Valley Mirage are fictional originals all.

However, this book has elements of historical fact, meaning the made-up plot is set in 2006 against a larger backdrop of events that really happened—or would happen—involving people who really lived and institutions that really existed. There was a kick-a-ball sport in ancient China, a 16th-century Spanish novel first mentioning California, prudently run mortgage companies. There was a Pelé, an Abel Stearns, an Alan Greenspan (whose name is the book's final words). There were soccer laws without referees, troubled California police agencies, wild uses of Other People's Money. There would be fresh soccer controversies, more fires in Southern California, and a withering national economic bust caused in no small part by years of housing fraud and regulatory neglect at so many levels.

Manifestly, no documentary backup can be offered for anything written about the mythical Valley Mirage. But sources abound for the recurring interacting topics that form the book's Historical Holy Trinity—soccer, Southern California and money. Citation to sources can be found online at www.offside-a-mystery.com, where I invite comment from readers.

However, please be advised. I offer up my own interpretations as to significance and meaning, as well as cause and effect. My spin is informed by personal experience and perception. This may put me at sharp variance with some readers. To all I can offer only my belief that, in the circular nature of the human existence, things are not always as they first appear.

BIOGRAPHY

CHRONICLING A WIDE cross-section of the human condition, William P. Barrett has worked as an award-winning journalist across the country and abroad on prominent newspapers and national magazines for more than four decades. At various times he's been a police reporter, court reporter, local government reporter, feature writer, foreign correspondent, war correspondent, national correspondent writing about very small places with very big problems, investigative reporter and business reporter. Barrett's longest stretch was at *Forbes*, where his writings illuminated dark sections of the financial world and sent miscreants to prison. A native of New Jersey, Barrett holds two degrees from Rutgers, one in law, and is a Chartered Financial Analyst charterholder. On weekends he has refereed youth soccer matches in the West, including Southern California, for 17 years. Barrett now lives in Seattle. This is his first book.

MORE GREAT READS
FROM BOOKTROPE

Revontuli by **Andrew Eddy** (Historical Fiction) Inspired by true events, Revontuli depicts one of the last untold stories of World War II: the burning of the Finnmark. Marit, a strong-willed Sami, comes of age and shares a forbidden romance with the German soldier occupying her home.

The Old Cape House by **Barbara Eppich Struna** (Historical Fiction) A Cape Cod secret is discovered after being hidden for 300 years. Two women, centuries apart, weave this historical tale of mystery, love and adventure.

Dead on Her Feet: A Tango Mystery by **Lisa Fernow** (Mystery) For those who dedicate their lives to finding that perfect connection on the dance floor, tango is a drug that proves fatal. But tango instructor Antonia Blakely doesn't want the police to solve the crime.

The Duel for Conseulo by **Claudia Long** (Historical Fiction) The second novel of the Castillo family, a gripping, passionate story of a woman struggling to balance love, family, and faith in early 1700's Mexico—a world still darkened by the Inquisition.

The Secrets of Casanova by **Greg Michaels** (Historical Fiction) Loosely inspired by Casanova's life, this novel thrusts the reader into an adventure overflowing with intrigue, peril, and passion.

Discover more books and learn about our
new approach to publishing at **booktrope.com**.